PETER
SORRY YOU'V   ⌐⌐⌐⌐D

REGINALD Evelyn Peter Southouse Cheyney (1896-1951) was
born in Whitechapel in the East End of London. After serving
as a lieutenant during the First World War, he worked as
a police reporter and freelance investigator until he found
success with his first Lemmy Caution novel. In his lifetime
Cheyney was a prolific and wildly successful author, selling, in
1946 alone, over 1.5 million copies of his books. His work was
also enormously popular in France, and inspired Jean-Luc
Godard's character of the same name in his dystopian sci-fi
film *Alphaville*. The master of British noir, in Lemmy Caution
Peter Cheyney created the blueprint for the tough-talking,
hard-drinking pulp fiction detective.

PETER CHEYNEY

SORRY YOU'VE BEEN TROUBLED

DEAN STREET PRESS

Published by Dean Street Press 2022

All Rights Reserved

First published in 1942

Cover by DSP

ISBN 978 1 915014 13 9

www.deanstreetpress.co.uk

Chapter One
So Long, Admiral

EFFIE Thompson was asleep. She was wearing an *eau-de-nil* satin nightgown. Her red hair, draped over one shoulder, tied with a ribbon, made an effective contrast.

She was dreaming in a rather agitated manner. She dreamed that she was dreaming about Callaghan. When the telephone at her bedside jangled she woke up and spent ten seconds considering if she were awake or asleep. She decided she was awake, took up the telephone, shot a quick glance at the clock on the table. It was two o'clock. The call, she thought, would be from Callaghan.

She was right. He said:

'Hallo, is that you, Effie? I suppose you weren't asleep by any chance?'

'Yes, Mr. Callaghan, I was asleep, strangely enough. But *please* don't worry about that. You wouldn't think I was annoyed, would you?' Her tone was slightly acid.

Callaghan said: 'That's big of you, Effie. . . .'

Under her breath she called him a rude name. Always, she thought, she left herself open for a wisecrack from Callaghan. Always, half an hour afterwards, she thought of some terrific come-back that would have slain him. She sighed.

He said briskly: 'You remember that Starata case – the people who put in a big claim for fire damage on the Sphere & International? Well, I've just run into Jack Starata. He doesn't know I'm me. He and one or two friends of his are going to play poker. They're all pretty high. I think they might talk.'

She said quickly: 'You know, Mr. Callaghan, Starata is supposed to be dangerous.' She heard him laugh.

'You don't say?' he said. 'Listen . . . get on to Nikolls. Tell him that if I don't call through to him by four o'clock this morning and say I'm back in Berkeley Square, he's to come along to 22 Chapel Street – that's off Knightsbridge – and find where I am.'

Effie said: 'You're expecting trouble?' She felt scared.

Callaghan said: 'I've been expecting trouble all my life, Effie, and I usually get it. Sleep well . . . Oh, by the way, what colour nightgown are you wearing?'

She gasped a little. She said:

'Well, if you *must* know, Mr. Callaghan, its *eau-de-nil* satin.'

He said: 'Charming! That must look pretty well with those green eyes and that red hair of yours. I always like to feel that my staff look well turned out. Good-night.'

She hung up. She called Callaghan another rude name. Then she picked up the receiver, dialled Nikolls's number. She hoped that nothing would happen to Callaghan – in the same breath asking herself why she bothered.

When the telephone rang Nikolls wakened quickly. He looked like nothing on earth. His tongue tasted like a yellow plush sofa. He sat, his hands folded across his plump stomach, regarding the instrument malevolently. He wished he had not drunk that half-bottle of Bacardi on top of the whisky. He took off the receiver.

Effie Thompson said: 'Listen, Mr. Nikolls . . . Mr. Callaghan's just been through. Apparently he's still working on that Starata case. He's met Starata and some friends of his. He's going to play poker with them. As far as I can understand Starata and his friends are drunk, and Mr. Callaghan thinks they might talk.'

Nikolls said: 'Like hell they will! That bunch are too clever, and if they *do* talk, and find out who he is, that he's a sleuth for the Sphere & International, they'll pull him into little pieces. There's over a quarter of a million in that claim.'

'Quite,' said Effie. 'That's the point. Mr. Callaghan says if he doesn't ring you by four o'clock this morning, you're to go to 22 Chapel Street, Knightsbridge, and find out what's happening. Do you understand that? He sounded as if he thought there *might* be some trouble.'

'Yeah,' said Nikolls. 'Ain't life just too sweet? I have to stick around here till four o'clock waiting for the telephone bell to ring. If it don't ring, I have to go and find if somebody's killed Slim. Me . . . I wonder why I ever left Canada . . .'

'That's easy,' she said. 'A woman, I expect.'

'Look,' said Nikolls. 'You got a wrong impression, Effie. Any dames I knew in Canada was all shot to pieces when I left . . .'

'I can believe that too,' she said. 'But don't worry, Canada's a long way away, and they can't get at you while the war's on.'

The apartment telephone on the other side of Nikolls's bedroom began to ring. He said: 'Hang on, Effie, my other phone's goin'. It might be something.'

'All right,' said Effie.

Nikolls got out of bed. He was wearing pale-blue pyjamas with white spots on them. He looked like an apparition. The cord of his pyjamas was tied very tightly round his middle; he bulged both above and below it.

On his way to the telephone he picked up the water carafe and took a copious draught.

It was Wilkie, the night porter at Berkeley Square, calling. He said: 'That you, Mr. Nikolls? Look, I'm sorry to trouble you, but there's too much going on around here for my liking.'

'Yeah?' said Nikolls. 'There's too much going on around here too. Any time I wanta sleep somethin' happens. What's the matter, Wilkie? What's cookin' around there?'

The night porter said: 'About an hour after you left the offices to-night an Admiral Gardell came through. He wanted to speak to Mr. Callaghan. He said it was important. He asked where Mr. Callaghan was. I told him there was nobody in the offices, and I told him that I'd been through to Mr. Callaghan's flat on the floor above and couldn't get a reply. I said I didn't know where Mr. Callaghan was and he had better get through to-morrow morning. He said all right. Half an hour later he came through again. He said he'd got to see Mr. Callaghan. It was a matter of life and death. He said he was certain Mr. Callaghan would see him. I told him what I said before – if I knew where Callaghan was I'd get in touch with him, but I didn't.'

Nikolls sighed.

'Ain't this guy persistent?' he said. 'What's the matter with him? Has somebody run off with his wife?'

Wilkie said: 'I don't know, Mr. Nikolls. But half an hour ago he came round here. He looks awfully bad. I don't like the look of him at all. He said he'd got to see Mr. Callaghan somehow. He said he was going to stay here until he turned up.'

Nikolls yawned.

'So what?' he said. 'Is he there now?'

'No,' said Wilkie. 'He's gone off to get a cup of coffee at a coffee stall. He's coming back in twenty minutes' time.' His voice changed. 'He looks in a bad way, Mr. Nikolls,' he said. 'I didn't know what to do. I thought I'd better tell you.'

Nikolls said: 'Thanks, Wilkie. But what do I do? We can't start talking to people in the middle of the night. Besides, how do we know it's urgent? Everybody thinks their business is urgent. Doesn't this guy know that even private detectives have to go to sleep sometimes? Or maybe he thinks we're the "Eye That Never Sleeps" . . . ?'

Wilkie said: 'What shall I tell him when he comes back?'

Nikolls said: 'You tell him to come around or call through to the office to-morrow morning at eleven o'clock. You tell him that Mr. Windemere Nikolls, Mr. Callaghan's principal assistant, will be at his desk punctually with a first-class hangover at that time. You got that, Wilkie?'

'I've got it,' said Wilkie.

Nikolls hung up. He went back to the other telephone.

He said: 'Hey, Effie . . . there's more excitement poppin'. Some guy called Admiral Gardell is rushin' around town tryin' to find Slim – one of those urgent cases.'

She said: 'I see. Well, it can wait till to-morrow morning. Perhaps it's as well that we can't get in touch with Mr. Callaghan – otherwise he might want to start something now. I'd love to go and open up the office at three o'clock in the morning.'

'We don't do that for Admirals, do we, Effie?' he said. 'We only do that for beautiful dames like Miss Vendayne . . . you remember that case?'

Effie said: 'I remember. It's a funny thing, but the only time we do any night work is when our clients are women.'

Nikolls said: 'Listen, baby, if I had a client like Audrey Vendayne, I'd do a bit of night work myself.'

She said nothing.

Nikolls went on: 'Too bad you being woke up like this. I bet you're lookin' swell. I bet you got that red hair of yours tied up with a ribbon. You know,' he went on, 'I don't know whether I ever told you, Effie, you got something . . .'

She said acidly: 'You've been telling me that ever since you've been with the firm, Mr. Nikolls. Anything I've got I'm going to keep.'

'O.K.,' said Nikolls. 'But there's no need to get tough. Just because you know I go for that hip-line of yours, you get snorty. Did I ever tell you about that dame in Chattanooga . . . ?'

'Not once but sixty times,' interrupted Effie. 'Do you *mind* if I go to sleep?'

'No,' said Nikolls. 'If you feel that way, O.K. Me – I'm goin' to stay awake. I'm sorta reminiscent to-night.'

Effie said: 'I hope it keeps fine for you.'

She hung up the receiver with a jerk.

Callaghan stood in front of the fireplace. He was slightly glass-eyed, but was wearing well otherwise. He wondered vaguely how much whisky he had drank since seven o'clock. He thought it must be a lot. He concluded that it didn't matter anyhow.

Starata was mixing drinks at the sideboard. The short fat man, Lingley, was putting up the card-table, and the other one – Preem – was sitting on the settee looking at the electric light and blinking. Preem was almost in the last stages. He needed about four more drinks to go right out.

Lingley was having a lot of trouble with the collapsible table. His language was ornate.

Callaghan thought that Starata was all right. He carried his liquor well. But then he did most things well. He was good-looking too, and well dressed. Everything about Nicky Starata was rather high-class, and even if it was a little *too* high-class it got by. The women liked him. He had money. He had brains. He ought to have been in the Army and wasn't. He ought to have been in prison and wasn't.

Nicky was a pip. He had seventeen suits, a cottage in the country, one or two bank accounts, a safe deposit, and a very well-filled stocking. Every one – except, apparently, the proper authorities – knew all about Nicky.

He came over to Callaghan, handed a whisky and soda. He stood in front of Callaghan, smiling. He said:

'Well . . . here's luck, Pelham.'

Callaghan said: 'And to you. And my name's not Pelham.'

Nicky grinned. When he grinned you thought he was the most charming fellow in the world. He said:

'What does it matter. I don't give a damn what a man's name is. If I like a man, I like him.' He drank some whisky. 'I like you,' he concluded.

Callaghan smiled.

'That's fine,' he said. 'I like you, too.'

They stood smiling at each other. Starata looked at his glass and twiddled it round in his fingers.

'I don't know how you got in on this party,' he said. 'But I'm glad you're here. You're a friend of Preem's, aren't you?'

Callaghan took a quick look at Preem. He concluded it was safe. He said:

'Yes . . . I've known him for a hell of a long time. He'll improve in a little while. How d'you find things?'

Callaghan shrugged his shoulders.

'Not so good and not so bad,' he said. 'You know how it is?'

Starata said he knew. He smiled again.

'What d'you do, if it isn't a rude question?' he asked.

Callaghan smiled back.

'It isn't rude,' he said. 'I do more or less the same as you do. I fiddle around a little . . .'

Starata laughed.

'You'll do,' he said. 'You and I must get together some time and have a talk. We might be able to do something together.'

'That would be nice,' said Callaghan. 'Let's do that.'

They sat down. Starata began to shuffle the cards. Then he put the pack down, lit a cigarette and looked at them.

'Straight poker,' he said. 'Five pound rises, no limit to betting, and a pound to play. O.K.?'

Everyone said O.K. They picked cards for deal. Starata drew an ace and dealt. Callaghan was on his left.

They all played. Callaghan put in his pound-note before he even looked at his cards. When he looked he was mildly surprised. He held a full house with Queens.

He bet five pounds. Preem and Lingley checked the first time round. Starata raised it to ten. Callaghan put it up to twenty. Preem and Lingley threw in their cards. Starata raised Callaghan to thirty. Callaghan made it forty. Starata saw him at forty. He had two pairs. Callaghan picked up the money.

'Nice work – if you can get it,' he said.

Preem's head was nodding a little. He said thickly:

'That damned whisky we had to-night wasn't so good. I believe they make the stuff themselves up in the bathroom at that cursed Anchor Club. I feel like hell.'

Starata smiled amiably. He said:

'You look like hell, Preem. But then you always do. You want to get wise to yourself. You've started slipping.'

Preem looked at Starata with narrowed eyes. He said:

'Oh yes? Well, look . . . you better have a look at *yourself* too. Let me tell *you* something . . . Willie Lagos is walking around talking a bit too much. He's not very happy. You want to know why?'

Starata folded his hands on the table before him. He was still smiling.

'You tell me why,' he said.

'O.K.,' said Preem. 'I'll tell you why. He's been sore at you ever since you took that girl off him. You know – the strawberry number. And why shouldn't he? Willie's got an idea you're too goddam fond of pinching other people's women.'

Starata said, quite pleasantly: 'Yes? Go on. You interest me, Johnnie.

Preem said: 'Don't worry, I'm going on. I got a bit of news for you. The Sphere & International don't like that claim of yours on the warehouse fire. They think it stinks.'

Starata said: 'This is getting *very* interesting. Tell me some more, Johnnie.'

Preem hiccoughed. He said:

'Willie Lagos and Callaghan were drinking highballs in the Silver Bar in Mayfair the day before yesterday.'

He stopped speaking as the door opened.

A man came in. He was short, thin, too well dressed. His black hair was sleeked down with some shiny hair compound, a cigarette was hanging from one corner of his mouth, a black soft hat was perched precariously over one eye. He stood in the doorway looking at the quartet. Callaghan put his hands on the table and tilted his chair back a little.

Starata said: 'Hallo, Leon, I'm glad to see you.'

The newcomer leaned up against the doorpost. He put his hands in his pockets. He looked at Starata with a peculiar smile playing about his lips. He said:

'Well, may I be sugared and iced, but I never expected to see Nick Starata playing cards with Mister Callaghan of Callaghan Investigations.'

There was a silence. It was broken by the noise of Starata gently drawing his breath through his teeth. Callaghan grinned at him.

'Too bad, isn't it, Nicky?' he said. 'Anyway, I told you my name wasn't Pelham.'

Starata said to Preem: 'Listen . . . did you bring him in on this party?'

Preem said: 'What the hell! I never saw him before to-night. I thought he was a pal of Lingley's.'

Callaghan said to Starata: 'The trouble with your friend Preem is he talks too much and thinks too little. That bit of information he gave me about Willie Lagos was just too sweet. I'll be able to go to work now.'

Starata smiled. He said: 'Will you . . . ?'

Callaghan pushed back his chair, and in almost one movement kicked over the table; threw his chair at the electric standard. As the light went out, he swung round, hit Starata in the mouth with his left elbow. Leon's quiet voice came from the door. It said:

'All right, Nicky. I'm looking after the door. The bastard won't get out of here.'

Callaghan put his hand out. It found something soft. It was Preem's face. Callaghan hit it hard. Lingley's voice said:

'Where is that son of a bitch?'

Leon said casually from the doorway: 'Well, he's still here.'

Starata said coolly: 'Somebody strike a match.'

Behind Callaghan was the mantelpiece. He ran his hand along it until it met the clock. Callaghan took a careful aim at the doorway; he threw the clock. It was a lucky shot. It hit Leon in the stomach. He yelped, subsided on the floor.

Callaghan, moving round the left-hand side of the room along by the wall, got round to the doorway. He put his foot on Leon. As he did so someone charged at him. Callaghan thought that would be Lingley. Starata wouldn't be so excited. Callaghan went with the charge; he allowed himself to be forced backwards against the wall by the weight of Lingley's body. Then he brought his left knee up with a jerk into Lingley's abdomen. As Lingley went back, Callaghan hit him in the face.

He slipped quietly through the doorway. As he was closing the door Starata called out:

'Listen, Callaghan . . . don't get this wrong. We can square this, hey? And there'll be a nice piece of change in it for you. I . . .'

Callaghan closed the door. He felt for the key, turned it in the lock. He began to walk down the stairs.

At the end of Chapel Street, Callaghan turned into the telephone-box; called through to Nikolls. He told Nikolls not to worry about going to Chapel Street at four o'clock. Then he hung up. He came out of the box and began to walk in the direction of Berkeley Square.

II

The Chinese clock on the bedroom mantelpiece struck four. Callaghan woke up, yawned, looked at the ceiling. His mouth was dry; his head ached. Through the window a gleam of cold March afternoon sunlight made a pattern on the carpet. He got up, sat on the edge of the bed running his hands through his thick black hair. He was thinking about Starata.

It looked as if the Starata case was in the bag. Callaghan thought that in the normal course of events Nicky Starata would clear out his safe deposit and make a getaway, but in these days of war there was no place to make a getaway to. It would be easy. A nice job, thought Callaghan. He made a mental note to ask the Sphere & International Insurance to increase his retainer.

He got up, began to walk towards the bathroom. On the way he stopped suddenly, turned off into the sitting-room, went to the corner cupboard, took out a bottle of Canadian Club, put the neck of the bottle into his mouth and took a long swig. He shuddered. He wondered if the man who invented the proverb of 'the hair of the dog that bit you' really knew what he was talking about.

The inter-communication telephone from the office downstairs rang. He took off the receiver. It was Effie Thompson. She said:

'Good-afternoon, Mr. Callaghan.'

He said: Is that all?'

'No,' said Effie, 'it isn't. I hope you didn't mind my saying "Good-afternoon." I rang through to tell you that Mr. Gringall's down there. He's just arrived. He says he'd like to see you personally.'

Callaghan said: 'I wonder why. Where is Mr. Gringall?'

'He's in the outer office,' said Effie. 'I'm talking from your office. Do you think it might have something to do with last night, Mr. Callaghan?'

Callaghan said: 'Why should he be concerned with last night?'

She said: 'I don't mean about the Starata business, Mr. Callaghan. Didn't Mr. Nikolls tell you about the other thing?'

Callaghan said: 'He hadn't a chance. I didn't see him. I rang him up and told him not to worry. What happened last night?'

'An Admiral Gardell came here last night. He spoke to Wilkie. He wanted to see you urgently; said it was a matter of life or death. Wilkie stalled him, but when the Admiral bothered some more he rang up Nikolls and told him.'

Callaghan said: 'I see.'

'Also,' Effie went on, 'this morning Wilkie brought me an envelope containing a note that the Admiral had left for you. Shall I send it up?'

'No,' said Callaghan, 'don't bother. Bring Mr. Gringall up and send up some tea.'

'Very good,' said Effie.

Callaghan hung up; went into the bathroom. He came out five minutes later wearing a pastel-grey crêpe-de-chine dressing-gown with black fleurs-de-lis.

Gringall was sitting in the big chair by the fire. He said:

'Hallo, Slim. How are you? That's a pretty good dressing-gown. Must have cost a lot of money. I suppose one of your women clients gave you that.'

Callaghan said: 'How did you know? But then you know everything, don't you?'

Gringall smiled.

'Just a little bit,' he said, 'not very much.'

Callaghan stood in front of the fire looking at Gringall. His hair was black and tousled; his face thin and long. His jaw was obvious but not too obvious. His shoulders were wide, tapering down to narrow flanks. He was five feet ten inches – compact – impatient-looking.

He said: 'Tell me why I am honoured by a visit from Chief Detective-Inspector Gringall, and would it be in order for me to tell you that your waistband's down by about four inches?'

'Whose waistband isn't?' said Gringall. 'This war will take more than four inches off me by the time it's through.' He smiled suddenly. 'You haven't been doing too badly for yourself lately, have you, Slim?'

Callaghan said: 'I don't know what you mean.'

'No?' said Gringall. 'What about those three or four nice little jobs you had from the Home Security Department?'

Callaghan raised his eyebrows.

'I see, so you were behind that, were you? Well, that's all right. Look at the good turn I did you over that Haragos case. But for me you'd still be scrubbing around in the undergrowth looking for somebody you'd never find.'

Gringall sighed. He said:

'I think you private detectives are just too wonderful.'

Callaghan grinned. He said:

'For once I agree with you.'

The door opened. Effie Thompson came in carrying the tea-tray. There was a chocolate cake on the tray.

Callaghan said: 'You see how we look after you. Even with rationing in the condition it is, Miss Thompson remembers you like chocolate cake, or maybe she's trying to get on the right side of you.'

Effie went out. She closed the door quietly behind her.

Gringall said: 'That's a pretty girl. She doesn't look too pleased about something, does she?'

'Right again,' said Callaghan, 'she isn't. She's annoyed with me. She gets that way occasionally.'

Gringall said: 'I don't wonder.' He scratched his nose. 'It must be tough working for you,' he said, 'especially for a girl like that who's crazy about you . . .'

'Nonsense,' said Callaghan. 'Where'd you get that idea?'

Gringall smiled.

'That Canadian bloodhound of yours,' he said. 'He told me. He said she had to be crazy about you, otherwise she wouldn't work here.'

Callaghan said: 'Effie's a very efficient secretary. She just happens to dislike me some of the time.'

Gringall said: 'You mean to tell me that women don't like you *all* the time?'

Callaghan went to the sideboard, helped himself to a cigarette. He said:

'Have you considered how boring life would be if women liked you *all* the time?' He grinned. 'But maybe you haven't been troubled a lot?' he said.

Gringall poured out the tea. He poured out a cup for Callaghan. He cut himself a large piece of chocolate cake. After a minute he said:

'I suppose you wouldn't have heard of an Admiral Gardell?'

Callaghan thought for a moment. Then he said:

'No, why should I?'

Gringall shrugged.

'He was murdered last night,' he said. 'Or rather early this morning. It must have been early this morning because he was here about two o'clock.'

'You don't say?' said Callaghan.

'Yes,' said Gringall. 'He was looking for you. Apparently he saw the night porter downstairs, who got in touch with Nikolls, your assistant. Perhaps they didn't tell you about it?'

Callaghan said: 'I was on a job last night. What did the Admiral want to see me about?'

'I don't know,' said Gringall. 'I hoped you'd be able to tell me that. I thought it might give us a lead.'

Callaghan said: 'What's it all about?'

The Chief Detective-Inspector finished his chocolate cake. He said:

'They found the Admiral in a coppice near his house, nearly forty miles from London, at ten o'clock this morning. The local police surgeon thinks he was killed somewhere between four and five. He was shot at fairly close range. He must have died immediately.'

Callaghan nodded.

'Have they found the gun?' he asked.

Gringall shook his head. 'No!' He felt in his overcoat and produced a short briar pipe. He began to fill it. 'The County police came through to us this morning. The local force is depleted because of the war, and they thought we might get on to it right away. I made some inquiries on the telephone, and I found that Gardell came up here late last night by car. I discovered that he'd been here. I thought I'd come and ask you if you knew anything about it.'

Callaghan said: 'I'm sorry, Gringall, I don't know a thing. If I did I'd tell you.'

Gringall got up. He was smiling pleasantly. He said:

'You mean you'd tell me if it suited your book to tell me.'

'All right,' said Callaghan, 'you have it that way.'

Gringall picked up his bowler hat. He said:

'Well, I'll be seeing you, Slim.'

Callaghan said: 'So long!'

Gringall went out.

Callaghan looked at his untasted cup of tea on the tea-tray. It was nearly cold. The surface of the tea was discoloured with tannin. He thought it looked awful. He went over to the cupboard in the corner, extracted the bottle, took another long pull. He put the bottle back and went to the window. Outside, crossing Berkeley Square, was the sturdy figure of the Detective-Inspector. He was walking briskly along, his hands in his raincoat pockets, his bowler hat almost at a jaunty angle. Callaghan grinned. There were very few police officers like George Henry Porteous Gringall, he thought – very few.

Callaghan went to the telephone. He called through to Effie Thompson.

'Effie,' he asked, 'is Nikolls in the office?'

'Yes, Mr. Callaghan,' she said. 'I'll put him on.'

Nikolls came on the phone. He said:

'Hallo, Slim. How're you feelin', or aren't you?'

Callaghan said brusquely: 'I'm not. Listen – I discovered last night that it *was* Willie Lagos who started that warehouse fire for Starata. Lagos is frightened and is prepared to talk. Starata may try to get at him, but I don't think he will. I think he'll lay off because if anything happens to Lagos, Starata will be suspect. He'll probably try to disappear for a bit.'

Nikolls said: 'I see. What do we do?'

Callaghan said: 'We don't do anything. If the Sphere & International want Starata pulled in that's a police job.' He drew some cigarette smoke down into his lungs. 'You get on to the Sphere & International,' he said. 'Tell 'em to hold up that claim over the Starata Factory. Tell 'em it was a fire-bug case. Then get out and find Willie Lagos. Put the screw on him and make him talk. Get a signed statement from him. Try and do that to-night. You got that?'

Nikolls said: 'I got it. It's goddam funny, but every time I make a date with a dame to take her to the movies I have to start being a detective.'

Callaghan said: 'Why worry? There'll be another night, and – I should imagine – another woman.'

'I *hope*!' said Nikolls.

Callaghan said: 'Give me Effie.' He said to her: 'Effie, you can bring that letter up from the late Admiral – now.'

Somewhere in the vicinity a clock struck nine. Callaghan came out of the Albemarle Lounge in Dover Street and began to walk towards Hay Hill. When he arrived at the top of the street he turned down towards Berkeley Square, stopped to light a cigarette.

He went into the telephone-box on the corner of the Square. He dialled the office number. Effie Thompson came on the line. Callaghan said:

'Has Nikolls been through yet?'

'He came in the office half an hour ago,' she said. 'He's seen Lagos. Lagos has made a statement. I've locked it in the drawer in your desk.'

'All right,' said Callaghan. 'I'll deal with it to-morrow. And, Effie, remind me to write a line to the Managing Director of the Sphere & International, to suggest that, owing to war conditions, etc., Callaghan Investigations would like its retainer doubled.'

'Very well, Mr. Callaghan,' said Effie. 'Of course you remember they doubled your retainer four months ago.'

Callaghan said shortly: 'I remember.'

'Sorry,' she said. 'I thought you might like to be reminded.'

'So I gathered,' said Callaghan.

The sound of a long-suffering sigh came to Callaghan's ears. He grinned and said:

'I think you might go home now, Effie. Go to a movie. Get your mind off your work. Why don't you buy yourself some new stockings or something – it makes a change.'

She said tartly: 'Stockings need coupons. Anyway, you can't buy them at nine o'clock at night, and I don't *want* to go to a movie.'

'All right,' said Callaghan. 'Don't go. Just go home, relax, and get some sleep.'

'I'd like to,' she said. 'And in order that I *do* get some sleep, I'd better tell you that a Miss Gardell has been on the telephone asking for you. She wants to see you. She was speaking from the Regency . . . she sounded urgent.'

'Did she?' said Callaghan. 'What did she sound like – besides sounding urgent . . . ?'

'If you mean her voice,' said Effie, 'she had a soft, cultured voice.' There was a pause. 'I think she had the sort of voice you'd like,' she went on.

Callaghan asked: 'What sort of voice do I like?'

Effie said primly: 'I imagine it would be a composite sort of voice. A mixture of some of the clients in your more successful cases. Something like Miss Vendayne's or Mrs. Riverton's or Mrs. Thurlston's or Miss . . .'

'I've got it,' said Callaghan. 'Just one of those voices . . .'

'Quite,' said Effie. 'You see, I've had ample opportunity of studying them in the small hours when I've been trying to get to sleep and you've been wanted on a case. I was thinking . . .'

'What were you thinking?' said Callaghan. He stubbed his cigarette out against the telephone-box.

'I was thinking that it would be a nice change if some of our *male* clients telephone in the middle of the night.' He heard her yawn delicately.

Callaghan said: 'Well . . . have patience, Effie. It *might* happen . . .'

'Is that all?' she asked.

'That's all,' said Callaghan. 'Good-night, Effie.'

'*Good*-night, Mr. Callaghan,' she said.

He hung up. He went out of the telephone-box, and began to walk towards Freddy's Bar in Conduit Street.

In the Berkeley Square Office, Effie Thompson put the cover on her typewriter. She exuded rage. Her green eyes flashed.

She banged the catch on the typewriter, slipped into her fur coat, adjusted her hat. She stood with her hand on the outer office door.

'Good-night, Mr. Callaghan,' she said. 'And *damn* Miss Gardell's voice . . .'

III

Freddy's Bar was deserted. It was a well-furnished fourth floor, reached by a passenger lift, and most of Freddy's rather peculiar clients were elsewhere. The bartender, wearing a white jacket and a bored expression, polished the chromium top of the bar, sang wearily under his breath. In the far corner, opposite the solitary pin-table, a lady in a very well-fitting black suit, cut so as to show the lines of her well-developed figure to the best advantage, drank a glass of crème-de-menthe, and dreamily considered bygone days.

Callaghan ordered a double whisky and soda. He took it to the table farthest from the bar. He sat down. He took an envelope from his pocket, opened it, and read the note from Admiral Gardell:

Chipley Grange,
Chipley,
Sussex.
17th March, 1941.

Dear Mr. Callaghan,

I proposed to see you to-night to discuss with you a rather urgent matter which I feel requires your attention. I had hopes, as I have elicited the fact that your flat is above your office in Berkeley Square, that I should be able to contact you through the night porter. He informs me, however, that you are out, and that he may have difficulty in getting in touch with you. I am therefore leaving this note, which I hope he will get into your hands as quickly as possible, so that when I return in an hour's time I may be sure of seeing you.

I have heard that you are an extremely busy person and I have no doubt that you will not care to be troubled in the middle of the night, but this is the only time at my disposal.

The reason that this sudden appointment with you is the only time at my disposal is because I am afraid (and I cannot even say I regret it) that I shall have no further opportunity of seeing you, as I propose to commit suicide some time in the early hours of to-morrow morning.

I hope therefore that I may claim your indulgence, as you will note that the matter is one which you might consider sufficiently urgent to merit your immediate attention.

Yours truly,
Hubert Gardell.

Callaghan replaced the letter in the envelope, put it back into his pocket. He drank the whisky and soda, carried the glass to the bar, ordered another one. He leaned up against the bar. The bartender said:

'I've not seen you for a long time, Mr. Callaghan.'

Callaghan nodded.

'I've been busy,' he said, 'and it doesn't look as if *you* are.'

The bartender shrugged.

'Everybody's away,' he said. 'The sort of people who used to come here and spend a little money don't do it in London any more. All the fun's just on the outside of London – twenty or thirty miles around.'

Callaghan said: 'Yes? I wonder Freddy doesn't get some places open in these spots.'

The bartender grinned.

'He's opened about six in the last five months,' he said.

'I see,' said Callaghan. 'But he still keeps this place going.' He grinned. 'I suppose a headquarters is necessary,' he said. 'You've got to have some place for the suckers to come into *first* – a sort of ante-room.'

The smile disappeared from the bartender's face. He said nothing.

Callaghan emptied his glass. He put on his hat and went out. He walked down the four flights of stairs to the street. He stopped in Bond Street to light a cigarette. It was a dark, gusty night. Callaghan thought there was some rain about. He wondered why he should spend time considering the weather. He wandered slowly down Bond Street, along Grafton Street, and down Hay Hill. He went into the telephone-box. Inside he stood leaning up against the wall, drawing the smoke from his cigarette down into his lungs, thinking of some interesting conversation he had had from this same box. He remembered the night when he telephoned Gringall about Eustace Riverton in the Riverton case. He began to grin.

He took out a small pocket torch, flipped through the pages of the telephone directory. He found and dialled the number of the Regency Hotel. He asked to be put through to Miss Gardell. After a moment a feminine voice came on the telephone. Callaghan listened carefully. He was thinking of Effie's description of the voice. He concluded after hearing one word that she was right. He said:

'Good-evening, Miss Gardell. My name's Callaghan, of Callaghan Investigations. I believe you telephoned through to my office. You wanted to talk to me about something.'

'I did want to talk to you, Mr. Callaghan,' said the voice, 'rather urgently.'

Callaghan said: 'Perhaps you'd like to indicate what you wanted to talk to me about.'

She said: 'I wouldn't like to do that now on the telephone.'

Callaghan said: 'I see. Just how urgent do you think the matter is, Miss Gardell?'

She said: 'I don't know. You might even consider that it isn't very urgent, but I think it is.'

Callaghan said: 'I gather you want me to do something for you. Is that right?'

'I don't know,' she said. 'That again is a matter for you to decide. At the moment I want to talk to you.'

'All right,' said Callaghan. 'Where do we talk – and when?'

She said: 'I hadn't thought about that. When I telephoned your office I had a vague idea that I should be in touch with you earlier than this.

I've been busy and I haven't had any dinner. I was thinking of getting supper somewhere. Perhaps you'd like to see me to-morrow morning.'

Callaghan said: 'No, I wouldn't. I'm not awfully keen on seeing people in the mornings. If you haven't dined, perhaps you'd like to have supper with me. Then we can talk.'

She said: 'That's very nice of you. It should be an experience. I've never had supper with a private detective before.'

Callaghan said: 'Well, I don't want to disappoint you, and I can't promise any *special* excitement because I happen to be a private detective.'

She said: 'Oh!' Then went on: 'I didn't mean *that*, Mr. Callaghan.'

'No?' said Callaghan. 'Exactly what did you mean?'

There was no reply. Callaghan waited a moment. Then he went on: 'Anyway, that's something we might discuss at supper. I suggest that I call for you in ten minutes' time.'

She said: 'Very well, Mr. Callaghan. I'll be ready. Oh, by the way, I suppose I ought to ask you about your fees.'

Callaghan said: 'I wouldn't worry about that at the moment. I never charge anything for having supper with clients – well, not often – but we can discuss that too. *Au revoir*, Miss Gardell.'

He hung up. He came out of the telephone-box and began to walk towards the taxi rank in Berkeley Square.

CHAPTER TWO
MANON

I

CALLAGHAN parked the Jaguar in a narrow street opposite the Regency. He got out, locked the car doors, lit a cigarette, began to walk up and down the dark pavement. He was thinking about Admiral Gardell.

Gringall hadn't wasted much time about the late Admiral, thought Callaghan, and the County Police hadn't wasted any time in asking the Yard for assistance. Every one, including Miss Gardell, seemed urgent about the business. And Gringall had, in the few hours at his disposal, discovered *something* of the Admiral's movements of the night before; had elicited the fact that Gardell had come to town for the purpose of seeing Callaghan – a process that he must, being ordinarily intelligent, associate with the murder. If it *was* murder.

Gringall would think, ruminated Callaghan, that the Admiral was in fear of something or someone; had decided to tell Callaghan about it. Whatever it was, Gringall would think, must of necessity be something too odd to see the police about. People who are in fear of their lives usually go to the police. But the Admiral had preferred Callaghan. Gringall would not know that Gardell had decided to commit suicide; was definite in his idea that he had been murdered.

Did Gringall know, or surmise, anything else? The private detective wondered just how much, or how little, the police officer knew.

He threw his cigarette away, crossed the street, pushed open the blacked-out swing doors of the Regency. He went inside. The large hall was deserted except for an elderly night porter in the desk in the far corner, but in the little smoking-room on the right of the hallway Callaghan could see a woman. She was lighting a cigarette. He looked at her with interest.

She was tall, slim, superbly curved. The action of the arm which held the lighter to the cigarette in her mouth had opened her black Persian lamb coat. Beneath she wore a black wool frock, relieved at the neck and wrists with neat collar and cuffs of lavender blue. Her hair was fair, her face delicately carved. As she lit the cigarette, turned and saw him, he could see that she had large dark eyes, a very neat nose and chin and a delightful mouth. Callaghan smiled appreciatively. This one was beautiful, and if Callaghan Investigations had to do business with women, they preferred them to be good-looking.

She began to walk towards him. As she came out of the smoke-room he noticed her slow, deliberate and graceful movements. She knew how to stand, how to walk.

He took off his hat. She said:

'Good-evening, I expect you're Mr. Callaghan. I'm Manon Gardell. I'm very glad to meet you. I think it was very kind of you to want to take me to supper.'

Callaghan said: 'It was nice of you to consent to come. I'd much rather talk business *outside* my office.'

She raised her eyebrows.

'How did you know I wanted to talk business?' she asked.

Callaghan said: 'I imagine that you weren't keen on seeing me just to see what I looked like.'

'No?' she said 'Why not? As a matter of fact, Mr. Callaghan, I *was* rather curious to see what you looked like.'

Callaghan grinned.

'I hope you are satisfied,' he said.

She nodded.

'Up to the moment, yes!'

He took out his cigarette-case. The lighter which she had used was still in her right hand. She snapped it on, lit his cigarette. He noticed that her hands were shaped as beautifully as the rest of her. There were two or three valuable rings on her fingers.

He asked: 'Where would you like to go to supper?'

'I don't mind,' she said. 'I suppose we ought to go somewhere fairly near. It's not easy to move at night in these days and cabs are sometimes difficult.'

Callaghan said: 'Don't let that bother you. I've a car outside.'

She considered for a moment. Then:

'Do you mind driving in the dark?'

Callaghan smiled. He said:

'I don't mind anything. Where do we go?'

She laughed.

'I've heard stories of you, Mr. Callaghan,' she said. 'I've heard that you are rather amazing and amusing person. I believe that if I suggested that we drive to Edinburgh you'd be quite happy . . . Would you?'

Callaghan: 'Why not? I'll try anything once.'

'That's what I thought,' she said. She regarded the glowing end of her cigarette. 'I don't want to go to Edinburgh – not quite so far. And I don't want you to think that I'm making a convenience of you. But if you wouldn't mind driving to a place I know – a rather attractive inn where we could get supper, in Surrey – we could not only eat as well as one can in present-day circumstances, but I could also pick up my car which I left in the garage there two or three days ago. That would save me a lot of trouble.'

'Why not?' said Callaghan, 'Shall we go?'

'I'll be ready in one minute,' she said.

She moved away from Callaghan, went to the mirror on the wall at the side of the entrance. She produced a crêpe-de-chine scarf from the inside pocket of her coat, put it on, turban fashion. Callaghan watched her appreciatively. She was sure of herself, he thought. Her movements were deliberate and easy. She came back. She said:

'I am ready, sir . . . !'

He pushed open the swing doors of the hotel for her, followed her out into the dark street. A minute later, he let in the clutch and the car moved quietly in the direction of Bond Street. He drove slowly, keeping to the regulation twenty miles an hour. There was a long silence; then she said:

'I expect, Mr. Callaghan, you are intrigued at my wanting to see you?'

Callaghan said: 'Not particularly. I never get intrigued – well, not easily. I gathered that what you might have to say to me *might* be interesting if not urgent. But having met you' – Callaghan grinned in the darkness – 'I've come to the conclusion that it that it will only be interesting.'

'I see,' she said. 'You're awfully clever, aren't you, Mr. Callaghan? You've already discovered that it is not *urgent.*'

'If it is, you're an extraordinary woman.'

She laughed softly.

'Am I now? Do you know, Mr. Callaghan, I think you're definitely exciting. Perhaps you can tell me some more things about myself.' Her voice was mildly sarcastic.

Callaghan said: 'I don't know that I can. You see, I don't know very much about you. I know you're very attractive – at least you'd be attractive to most men. You have a definite sense of clothes, and as my Canadian assistant, Nikolls, would say, "When they handed out sex-appeal someone put you right up in the front line." '

She laughed again.

'You are exciting, Mr. Callaghan. And I suppose you meant when you said that I'd be attractive to most men that I'm not particularly attractive to you.'

'On the contrary,' said Callaghan. 'I think if I wanted to be attracted I could be.'

'You just don't want to be?' she asked.

Callaghan grinned at her sideways.

'Not at the moment.'

She lowered the window, threw out her cigarette end. Then:

'How did you know that my business with you was not urgent?' she said.

Callaghan said: 'I doubt if anything would be really urgent as far as you are concerned. I think you're a casual sort of person. I imagine that you're either the daughter or the niece of the late Admiral Gardell. Presumably you know that he was murdered in the very early hours of this morning?'

She said: 'I don't know anything of the sort.' He voice was matter-of-fact.

Callaghan grinned.

'So I was right about you. It's going to be interesting but not urgent. So the Admiral wasn't murdered?'

She said: 'No definitely not. Are you surprised?'

'Nothing could surprise me,' Callaghan replied. 'I'm interested because I have an idea that the Sussex police think he was. They're so certain of the fact that they've already asked assistance from Scotland Yard.' He drove with one hand, felt in his overcoat pocket for his cigarette-case. 'The police don't often make a mistake of that sort,' he said.

She said: 'I'm not suggesting that the police are stupid, Mr. Callaghan. But you know as well as I do that my uncle committed suicide.'

Callaghan extracted the cigarette with one hand; then he lit it. They were in the Fulham Road. He accelerated slightly.

'Do I?' said Callaghan. 'How do I know that?'

She said: 'Are you trying to tell me, Mr. Callaghan, that my uncle didn't see you last night; that he didn't explain to you the circumstances under which he intended to commit suicide?'

Callaghan did not reply. After a moment he asked:

'Miss Gardell, do you know exactly how your uncle died?'

She said: 'Yes. I understand he was shot through the head.'

Callaghan said: 'How could the police make a mistake, fail to differentiate between a case of murder and suicide?' There was another pause.

She said: 'I don't know. I don't know what the police think. The point that I'm concerned with is the circumstances under which my uncle committed suicide.'

'All right,' said Callaghan. '*You're* concerned with the circumstances under which your uncle committed suicide. Well . . . what am I supposed to do?'

She said softly: 'Do you *like* being rude?'

'Sometimes,' said Callaghan. He looked at her sideways. 'Do you?' he asked.

She laughed.

'You're rather impossible,' she said. 'But also a trifle unique. I like unique people.'

'That's fine,' said Callaghan. 'I'm sorry I'm not sufficiently unique for you to carry out your original idea.'

She looked at him quickly.

'Really!' she said. 'What original idea?'

'Ever since I met you this evening you've been stalling for time, or playing for the right opening,' said Callaghan. 'Evidently you thought my reactions to your ideas would give you an opportunity to say what you wanted to say. Apparently you've been disappointed. You're doing quite a lot of talking, but you aren't saying anything. If you've something to say, why not get it off your chest?'

She sighed: 'You are difficult, aren't you?' she said. 'Perhaps I haven't talked to you as intelligently as I might have done.'

Callaghan said: 'You haven't talked at all yet – about anything that matters.'

She smiled in the darkness.

'Perhaps I'm a little nervous about you.' she said. 'Not quite sure of myself . . .'

He laughed.

'Now *I'll* tell one . . .' he said.

There was a silence. Then she said, suddenly:

'Let's not talk. I'm rather enjoying this. I feel out of humour with talking. Perhaps I'll feel more conversational at supper, or . . .'

'Or more certain?' asked Callaghan.

'What do you mean by that?' she asked. He saw the glowing end of her cigarette as she turned towards him.

He shrugged. 'I've an idea you had it all rehearsed,' he said. 'You knew exactly what you wanted to see me about, exactly what you wanted to say. But having seen me and discovered that I'm not quite what you expected, you're considering a new angle on the business. If you find it you'll talk, and if you don't you won't.'

'Not bad! You *are* clever, aren't you?'

'Like hell . . . !' said Callaghan. He flipped his cigarette end out of the window.

She sighed.

'This *is* nice,' she murmured. 'I'm going to relax now. I love driving in the dark. Can we go a little faster, please?'

Callaghan grinned.

They turned on to the Kingston by-pass. He put his foot on the accelerator. The car shot forward. Steering with one hand, he extracted a cigarette from his case, lit it.

He was beginning to wish that he *had* seen the Admiral. It might have been worth while.

II

Callaghan parked the car in the garage – originally a row of stables – behind the Blue Cloud Inn. He sniffed the air appreciatively. The place was quiet. It was a fine night.

He took a small flashlight from his pocket and walked the length of the garage. There were only two other cars – one an old Fiat and, at the end, a long, rather smart Buick roadster. This, he thought, would be Manon's car. He switched off the torch and walked round to the entrance of the inn.

She was waiting in the hall. The place was attractive. The ceiling was low and supported by oak beams. On the left, at the far end of the hall, two folding doors led into a room which combined the furniture of a past generation with the modern lay-out of a dancing club. The lighting around the walls was adequately concealed.

They sat down. Callaghan ordered cocktails; asked the waiter to do the best he could about supper.

When the cocktails were brought, Manon Gardell produced a cigarette-case. She offered it to Callaghan, took one herself. As he lit their cigarettes, she said:

'It must be exciting being a private detective, Mr. Callaghan.' She smiled. 'I suppose a lot of people have told you that?'

Callaghan said: 'Excitement's a matter of comparison. I don't suppose it's any more exciting being a detective than anything else. One gets used to it.'

'Does one?' she said. 'Does even the parade of the weaknesses and sins of humanity become boring?'

Callaghan said: 'Private detectives aren't interested in the weaknesses and sins of humanity. They're concerned to get a case finished.' He grinned. 'The part they like best is sending the bill in.'

She did not reply. After a minute Callaghan said:

'Miss Gardell, exactly what was it you wanted to talk to me about? I gather that there are circumstances in connection with your uncle's death that don't please you very much. Is that it? Not only that, but for some reason best known to yourself, you're convinced your uncle committed suicide in spite of what the police think.'

She waited while the waiter served them; then she said:

'I'll deal with the first part of your question first. The point about whether my uncle committed suicide or was murdered is not at the moment fearfully important.'

Callaghan raised his eyebrows.

'Well, that's good news,' he said. 'That ought to please somebody – even if it's only the murderer. All right, Miss Gardell, you tell me what is important.'

She said hesitantly: 'I'm not sure.' She smiled suddenly. 'I expect I sound rather odd about this,' she went on. 'But I do assure you I'm not trying to annoy you. The thing is this: I'm certain my uncle committed suicide because I know he *intended* to commit suicide.'

'How did you know that?' Callaghan asked.

'How does one know anything?' she replied. 'I was told. Desirée told me.'

'Excellent!' said Callaghan. 'And who is Desirée?'

'Oh,' she said, 'don't you know about Desirée? She's my cousin. *You'd* be awfully interested in Desirée.'

Callaghan grinned.

'More excitement,' he said. 'So I'd be awfully interested in Desirée. Why?'

'Because she is, I think, the loveliest woman I've ever seen in my life. She's quite delightful. Everything about her is right.'

Callaghan said smoothly: 'If you think she's lovely she must be. You're not so bad yourself, are you?'

'Do you think so, Mr. Callaghan,' she said. 'That's good news. But in any event, I can't hold a candle to Desirée.'

Callaghan nodded.

'All right,' he said. 'Desirée's lovely and I'd be interested in her, and Desirée – your cousin and, I gather, the Admiral's daughter – told you that he was going to commit suicide, and that's how you know that he did commit suicide?'

She nodded.

'That's right. It's logical enough, isn't it?'

Callaghan shrugged his shoulders.

'The fact that Desirée told you the old boy was going to kill himself doesn't make it a fact that he did so.'

'Agreed,' she said. 'But there's corroborative evidence. The whole attitude of my uncle indicated that he was entirely fed up with life. He wasn't at all fit. He wasn't expected to live more than another nine or ten months at the outside. Life had nothing to offer him at all.'

'So he thought that death might have a little more to offer, hey?' said Callaghan. 'You know, Miss Gardell, the fact that a man thinks he's fed up with life doesn't mean that he's going to commit suicide. A lot of people say they wish they were dead, but if they had the opportunity of dying they wouldn't take it.'

'That's true enough, Mr. Callaghan.'

She was smiling. He thought again that there was something extraordinarily attractive about Manon Gardell.

'If you knew anything about my uncle,' she went on, 'you'd know that he was tough in his mind. He wasn't the sort of man not to do anything he wanted to do, and he definitely wanted to commit suicide.'

Callaghan said: 'I see. That means he was going to get something out of committing suicide – something beyond shuffling off this mortal coil.'

'Yes,' she said. 'He was going to get something.'

Callaghan said; 'Miss Gardell, you tell me what he was going to get.'

She said: 'I wish you wouldn't call me Miss Gardell. I feel I've known you for years.'

Callaghan grinned.

'All right,' he said. 'I'll call you Manon. It's a nice name, but I'm glad that *I* don't feel as if I'd known *you* for years.'

She pouted prettily.

'That's not nice,' she said. 'Wouldn't you have liked to have known me for years?'

'I don't think so,' said Callaghan. 'If I had, I don't think we'd be sitting here as amiably as this.'

'You mean,' she said, 'something would have happened?'

Callaghan said: 'I think plenty would have happened. But let's get back to the Admiral, shall we?'

She took another cigarette.

'You asked me what the Admiral was going to get out of suicide besides possibly a peace that comes after shuffling off this mortal coil,' she said. 'He was going to get revenge.'

'I see,' said Callaghan. 'So it was like that. The old boy was feeling nasty, was he?' He held his lighter for her. As she lit the cigarette she looked at him through the first puff of smoke.

She nodded. The waiter appeared with liqueur brandies and coffee. She began to pour the coffee.

Callaghan said: 'Excuse me for a moment, please.'

He got up, went out into the hallway. In the little office on the other side, the night porter sat reading the evening paper.

'Can I telephone from here?' Callaghan asked.

'The box is at the end of the passage on the right of the hallway, sir,' said the porter.

Callaghan walked down the passage, went into the box. He looked at his watch. It was eleven-thirty. He dialled Effie Thompson's number. He waited, the cigarette hanging from the corner of his mouth. He was thinking about Manon Gardell. Effie's voice came through on the telephone. It was brisk.

Callaghan said: 'Hallo, Effie, are you in bed?'

She answered: 'Yes, Mr. Callaghan, but I think I'm going to give up going to bed. I think I'll just sit by the side of the telephone all night and wait for you to ring.'

'It's too bad, Effie.' He paused for a moment; then, 'Where's Nikolls?' he asked.

She said: 'I don't know. He's not at his flat. I rang him through half an hour ago. I wanted to know where you were.'

Callaghan asked: 'Why?'

She said: 'I thought it might be important. A Miss Gardell has been ringing the office. She wants to see you urgently.'

Callaghan grinned.

'The Gardell family are all inclined to be urgent, aren't they. Effie?' he said. 'Do you know what she's being urgent about?'

'I don't,' said Effie. 'I imagine it's something to do with her father's death.'

Callaghan said: 'Where was she speaking from?'

'The Grange at Chipley,' said Effie. 'She said she could come up to town to-morrow if you could see her, but that you might like to go down there. She didn't mind which. She wants to talk to you as soon as possible.'

Callaghan said: 'Thanks, Effie.'

He hung up. He came out of the box, walked along the passage. Manon Gardell was waiting in the hallway. She said: 'Do you know, I didn't realise what the time was. I've got to go. I've quite a distance to drive to-night.'

Callaghan said: 'That's too bad. I was just beginning to appreciate you. Incidentally, I thought there was something you wanted to tell me?'

She said: 'I don't know. I've been thinking things over. I want to sort them out in my mind. I'll be able to talk to you much better when I've done that. Come and see me.' She held out her hand.

Callaghan said: 'All right. Maybe I will one day. Where do I come?'

She said: 'I live at a place called The Cottage. It's near the little village of Valeston in Sussex – about ten miles from Chipley. I'd like to see you. Good-night.'

Callaghan grinned at her.

'Good-night,' he said. 'If I still want to hear what you've got to tell me in a day or two, maybe I'll come down.'

She laughed.

'Don't you think you will?' she asked.

Callaghan said: 'That depends.'

'On what?' she queried.

'On the week,' said Callaghan.

After she had gone, he walked back into the dining-room, paid the bill, got his hat and overcoat, and went out to the garage. She was just backing out her car. He watched it as she swung it expertly round and drove towards the old-fashioned gates leading on to the dirt road.

She stopped the car just outside the gates, turned towards Callaghan. She was smiling. Her face, in the moonlight, seemed oddly shaped, attractive.

A man came quickly through the gates, passed the car, moved towards Callaghan. He was wearing a well-fitting blue suit and a black soft hat.

Callaghan began to grin. He leaned against the garage doors. He said softly:

'Well, Nicky, what is it brings you down here at this time of night?'

Starata lit a cigarette before he answered.

'What do *you* think? he said.

'I suppose you want to talk to me,' said Callaghan, 'and you must have wanted it pretty badly to have had me tailed the whole evening. How did you know I was here?'

Starata smiled. He showed his white teeth.

'Naturally I've been taking an interest in your movements since last night, Callaghan. I've got to talk to you.'

Callaghan said: 'All right. Go inside and wait. I'll be with you in a minute.'

'O.K.,' said Starata. He walked away in the darkness.

Manon Gardell called out: 'Good-night, Mr. Callaghan. Happy landings!'

Callaghan walked over to the car.

'And to you,' he said. 'But then I should think most of your landings would be happy ones.'

'You think a lot of things about me that aren't quite true,' she said. 'And I think your friend is *very* good-looking.'

Callaghan smiled.

'You mean the one who's just gone into the inn,' he said. 'I wouldn't call him a friend of mine, but I agree with you he's good-looking. I don't think I like him a lot.'

'That means, I suppose,' she said, 'that you're looking forward to the interview. You seem very happy about it.'

'I am,' said Callaghan. He grinned. 'He's almost too good to be true,' he said.

She sighed.

'And what is Mr. Callaghan going to do about *that*?' she asked.

Callaghan said: 'I've got enough on that boyo in the drawer in my office desk to blow him sky-high, and I'm going to take great pleasure in doing it.'

She said: 'You're rather tough, aren't you. I think I like that. Good-night, Mr. Callaghan.'

Callaghan said: 'Good-night.'

He watched the rear light of her car disappear in the darkness; then he turned slowly, walked back to the inn.

Starata was waiting in the hallway. He said:

'This place isn't bad, is it? A nice sort of place to come to in the summer.'

Callaghan nodded.

'Very good,' he said. 'Providing, of course, that you're still in circulation in the summer.'

Starata grinned.

'Don't be old-fashioned, Callaghan,' he said evenly. 'I'll be in circulation in the summer all right, *and* the summer afterwards . . .'

'Yes?' said Callaghan. 'Well . . . I suppose you know.'

They sat down at one of the tables in the dining-room. Starata signalled to the waiter, ordered two large whiskies and sodas. He produced a thin, platinum cigarette-case, offered it to Callaghan. When his cigarette was lit he drew the smoke down into his lungs with obvious pleasure.

Callaghan thought: Nicky's pretty sure of himself; he's almost happy. Any one would think he was on the good end of the stick.

He said: 'What do you want Starata?'

Starata drew on his cigarette. He smiled at Callaghan. He said:

'You couldn't guess, could you?' His voice was pleasant.

Callaghan said: 'That warehouse job?'

Starata nodded.

'That's right,' he said. He leaned back in his chair. 'You know, Slim,' he said, I've been pretty successful most of my life, and not because I'm particularly clever. There's another reason.'

Callaghan said: 'I suppose I have to evince interest and ask what the reason is. All right. What is it?'

Starata shrugged his shoulders.

'You're a tough egg, aren't you?' he said. 'You wouldn't give a guy a chance.'

Callaghan said: 'Why should I? But you were explaining the reason why you'd been successful.'

Starata said: 'If I've had any success it's because I know my limit-
ations.'

Callaghan said: 'You mean you know when you're licked.'

'All right, you have it your way,' said Starata. He blew a smoke ring.
'Let's agree that I know when I'm licked. On the other hand, I might be
one of those people who are never licked. You know, the guy's dead but
he won't lay down. Get it?'

'I've got it,' said Callaghan. 'All right. You're dead but you won't lie
down. Well, what am I supposed to do?'

Starata said: 'Why don't you be sensible about this? Why do you have
to be so damned unpleasant?'

'I wouldn't know,' said Callaghan. 'Possibly I might get a kick out of it.'

Starata said: 'Let's get down to hard tacks. I got a feeling that that
heel Lagos is a canary.'

'Right,' said Callaghan. 'He's sung. He's made a statement. So then
what?'

Starata said: 'I'd like to stop things where they are. If that statement gets to the Public Prosecutor's Office, I'm for the high jump.' He
smiled at Callaghan. 'You see, I've got no false ideas about the way I'm
placed,' he said.

Callaghan said: '*I* see. So I'm to stop the Lagos statement going to
the Public Prosecutor's Office, am I?'

'Wait a minute,' said Starata. 'Don't be in such a hurry.' He stubbed
out his cigarette, took out his case, and lit a fresh one. He said: 'You work
for the Sphere & International, don't you?'

Callaghan said: 'I'm retained by the Sphere & International. I work
for any Insurance Society that wants me. I've specialised in that sort
of business.'

Starata said: 'I know. I've heard plenty about you. You're pretty good
at your job.' He sighed. 'Too good!'

Callaghan grinned.

'Thanks,' he said. 'That from you *is* a compliment.'

There was a pause; then Starata said amiably:

'Look, what do the Sphere & International pay you, or is that a rude
question?'

Callaghan said: 'No, it's not rude. They paid me a thousand a year
up to a few months ago; then they doubled my retainer.'

'I know,' said Starata. 'That was after the Vendayne case. So they
pay you two thousand now?'

'That's right,' said Callaghan. 'Don't you think it's enough?'

Starata shook his head.

'What's the good of forty pounds a week for a guy like you?' he said. 'Be your age! Now, look . . . I've got a proposition. I'm in bad and I know it. There's only one person can help me. That's you. All right. Well, I'm not mean. I want to get you on my side. So, as far as I'm concerned, the sky's the limit.'

Callaghan said amiably: 'I like that. I could do with a little loose change.'

Starata threw his unfinished cigarette across the intervening tables into the fire. He leaned forward.

He said: 'Listen, Callaghan . . . If the Public Prosecutor goes for me over that warehouse fire, what do I get?'

'Seven years,' said Callaghan evenly. 'Maybe ten . . . but I'd say seven. If you were very lucky it might be five.'

Starata nodded. He said: 'No . . . I think seven would be the stretch.'

Callaghan smiled.

'All right,' he said. 'We agree on seven.'

'Seven years in the can wouldn't amuse me a bit,' said Starata. 'It'd cramp my style. By the time I came out, even if I got remission for good conduct, I'd be too bored to want to do anything.'

'That's right,' said Callaghan. 'And the strawberry blonde of yours would have forgotten you too.'

Starata nodded. He showed his teeth in a quick smile.

'That strawberry blonde and a lot of other blondes too,' he said. 'I wouldn't like that.'

Callaghan said: 'What's the proposition?'

'The proposition is this . . .' said Starata. 'I take it *you've* got the statement from Lagos?'

'I wouldn't go so far as to say *that*,' said Callaghan. 'The statement is in existence and it's in a safe place. But you can take it we've got it. Lagos has sung the whole piece.'

'All right,' said Starata. 'Well, if that statement disappeared, and if Willie Lagos disappeared too so that it wouldn't matter about his squealing, the Sphere & International would pay, wouldn't they?'

Callaghan nodded.

'That's right,' he said. 'Beyond the Lagos evidence the claim looks all right. It was nicely done.'

Starata said: 'That means the Sphere & International would pay out on that warehouse nearly a quarter of a million.' He leaned across the table. The light from the shaded table lamp reflected on his diamond cuff buttons. 'You play this the way I want to,' he said, 'and you're on a hundred thousand pounds.' He paused. 'That's money, isn't it?' he said. 'You can have fifty thousand pounds within a few days and the balance when the Sphere & International pay out on that claim. Well, does that sound like sense to you?'

Callaghan got up. He said:

'No soap. I just wanted to hear what you were prepared to offer.' He smiled. 'You're going to do the seven years, Starata,' he said. 'It'll probably do you a lot of good.'

Starata shrugged his shoulders.

'Well,' he said, 'if that's the way it is, that's the way it is.' He finished his drink.

They walked back into the hallway. When they got to the garage, Starata said:

'I suppose there's no chance of you reconsidering this?'

Callaghan said: 'Not a hope. Let's say I'm old-fashioned.'

'That's a pity,' said Starata. He opened the door of his car; then looked over Callaghan's shoulder and smiled suddenly. He said: 'Well . . . that's funny . . .'

As Callaghan turned his head Starata kicked him in the stomach. Callaghan crumpled and fell to the ground in a heap. He lay there retching.

A man who had just come through the gates walked slowly towards them. Starata said:

'Leon, take the mug into the garage. Fix him so that he doesn't bother me for a bit.'

Leon nodded. He shifted his cigarette to the other side of his mouth. Starata got into the car.

Leon said: 'Wait for me outside. Something funny happened. It'll make you laugh.'

'O.K.,' said Starata. He let in the clutch and drove on to the dirt road.

Leon bent down and put his hand inside Callaghan's shirt collar. He began to drag him towards the garage. Callaghan, holding his stomach with one hand, hit Leon with the other.

There was no strength in his blow.

Leon said: 'Just a minute, smarty, an' then I'll fix you. Just now you couldn't hurt a baby.'

He propped him against the wall at the far end of the garage. 'The trouble with you is you're too smart,' he said pleasantly. 'One of these fine days you're going to catch up with yourself.'

Callaghan tried to get up. He got as far as his knees and fell back. His head hit the wall behind him with a thud. He began to be sick.

Leon said: 'You take it easy for a bit. Just try minding your own business, pal . . . just for a little while . . . see?'

Callaghan put his hands on the floor and tried again. Leon stepped back, measured his distance carefully, kicked hard. When his shoe hit Callaghan's side it made an unpleasant thud. He bent down, pulled at the collar of the inert form on the floor, raised the head and smacked it back against the wall.

He stood away and lit a cigarette. Then he went out of the garage. He walked slowly over to the car. He said to Starata:

'I took care of the mug. He's quite happy.'

Starata looked at him sideways.

'I bet he is,' he said.

III

It was nearly two o'clock when Callaghan came to, propped himself against the garage wall. He felt as if he had been run over by a lorry.

He edged along until he came to the corner of the garage. From there, in the darkness, he dragged himself towards the old car he had noticed. He rested his head on the running board and, inch by inch, stretched himself out straight.

He rested for a while, then drew out his cigarette-case and lighter. He lay in the darkness smoking.

He was thinking about Manon Gardell; wondering just what she would have to say when she decided to say it. He thought about her for some time. Then he thought about Starata.

Nicky was being very brave, thought Callaghan. Damned brave. He'd pulled something tough at a time when there wasn't any getaway because there was no place to make a getaway to. But what else could he do?

Callaghan began to blow smoke rings. Quite obviously, Starata was taking no chances. He knew that the Lagos statement would finish him and he was prepared to go the whole hog. And what was he going to pull now? In any event, it ought to be interesting.

He began to get up. It took him a long time. When he got on to his feet he discovered that he could not stand up straight. But he could walk. Holding his stomach with one hand, he snapped on his cigarette lighter and fumbled his way out of the garage. Outside, he rested a while, leaning against the outer wall.

After a bit he began to move towards the entrance of the inn. It took him a long time to make it. When he eventually arrived he leaned against the doorpost and kept his finger on the bell-push.

He kept it there for ten minutes.

Then the door opened. The hall-porter, in trousers and shirt, regarded him curiously.

'Sorry, sir,' he said. 'You can't come in now. We're closed and we don't take residents.'

Callaghan said: 'You don't say?'

He pitched forward, cannoned off the hall-porter, fell into the hallway.

CHAPTER THREE
STRAWBERRY BLONDE

I

IT WAS four o'clock when Nikolls went into the office. He stood just inside the doorway, a look of mild surprise on his face. He said:

'Jeez! They had a sweet game around here, those boys!'

Effie Thompson said: 'Well, it's no good looking at it. What shall I do?'

Nikolls said: 'Does the boss know about this?'

'I don't know where he is,' she said. 'I've rung upstairs. He's not there. He telephoned to me last night, but I don't know where from. I tried to check with the Exchange. All I could discover was that it was outside the London area. Shall I telephone to the police?'

Nikolls began to laugh.

'Be your age Effie,' he said. 'He'd just love that, wouldn't he? What a line! "Ace Investigator asks police to discover office thieves" . . .' He sucked at his cigarette. 'He'll be plenty pleased when he knows about this.'

He went into Callaghan's room. He stood in the doorway, looking about him. The safe let into the wall immediately behind Callaghan's chair had been cleverly blown. Two or three of the cabinets containing files and records had been forced – obviously with a jemmy. Nikolls walked over and examined Callaghan's desk. The one drawer with a lock was open; the papers inside disordered. He looked at the lock. It had not been forced. It had been opened with a key.

He went back into the outer office. The steel filing cabinets behind Effie Thompson's desk had been jemmied open. Even the lock of the towel cabinet in the corner had been forced.

Nikolls said: 'Where was that Lagos statement?'

'In Mr. Callaghan's draw,' said Effie. 'I told him I'd put it there.'

Nikolls nodded. 'That's what they were after,' he said. 'It's stickin' out a foot this is Mister Starata. That boy's a pip, ain't he? Nothin' stops him.'

She said: 'Wait till Mr. Callaghan hears about this.' She smiled. 'I wouldn't like to be Mr. Starata . . . !'

Nikolls said: 'Maybe. But he's winnin' this hand, ain't he. That Lagos statement ain't goin' to be the only thing that's gone. Willie Lagos will have gone too.' He stubbed out his cigarette, lit a fresh one. 'That's not so good,' he said.

Effie said: 'So there's nothing to be done?'

'Not that I know of,' said Nikolls. 'You'd better get the place straightened up.'

He went into Callaghan's office, sat down behind the desk. After a moment he put his feet up on the desk, tilted his hat over his eyes, folded his hands across his ample stomach, went to sleep.

II

The afternoon sun illuminated the chintz curtains in Callaghan's room at the Blue Cloud Inn. The doctor, busy repacking his bag in the corner of the room, looked over his shoulder. He said:

'It *can* be serious. The stomach muscles and the kidneys are badly bruised. You'll have to keep quiet for a week. Keep to the treatment I've ordered and don't get up. You ought to be fairly well then. But you've got to rest.'

He picked up his hat.

'Good-afternoon,' he said. 'I'll look in and see you again in a day or two.'

Callaghan said good-afternoon. When the doctor had gone he rang the bell by his bedside. A moment or two later there was a knock at the door. It was the hall-porter.

Callaghan said: 'If you feel in the right-hand pocket of my waistcoat you'll find some pound notes. Take two of them. One's for you and the other's for a bottle or half a bottle of whisky. Don't tell me you haven't got any because you never know what you can do till you try.'

The man grinned and went out. Five minutes later he came back with a tray. On the tray were a bottle of Johnnie Walker, a siphon and a glass. He put the tray down; went away.

Callaghan swung his legs out of bed. He put his feet on the floor gingerly; then he sat there feeling the bandages that strapped up his side and stomach. A sharp pain shot from his abdomen up to his stomach. He felt terribly sick, put out his hand to steady himself. He sunk his head between his knees as another wave of nausea swept through him. He stayed in that position for a little while . . . talking softly to himself . . . telling himself just what he was going to do to Starata and Leon one day . . . especially Leon.

After a minute or two he tried standing up – walking. He found he could manage it. He uncorked the bottle of whisky, put the neck in his mouth, took a generous swig. Then he walked round the room. He repeated the process two or three times, discovering that the more whisky you drank, the more easily you could walk.

He looked at his wrist-watch. It was four-thirty. He found his cigarette-case and lighter, sat on the edge of the bed, lit a cigarette. He sat there for five minutes, blowing smoke rings. Then he picked up the telephone, rang the office. Effie Thompson answered. She said:

'I'm glad you've come through. The offices were broken into last night. The place is in a terrible state. I'm just trying to clear things up.'

Callaghan asked: 'Is Nikolls there? If he is, put him on.'

Nikolls came on the line. Callaghan said:

'Windy, what's going on there?'

Nikolls yawned.

'Starata's goin' on, I think,' he said. 'Somebody came here pretty early this mornin' an' gave the offices the once-over. They knew what they were lookin' for too.'

Callaghan said: 'The Lagos statement . . . ?'

'That's right,' said Nikolls. 'The rest of the job was a frame. The guy who came in here knew what he was lookin' for and knew where he was goin' to find it. They jemmied open the filin' cabinets in Effie's room, blew the lock out of your wall safe – looks like nitro-glycerine. But the drawer in your desk where Effie had put the Lagos statement was opened with a key – a spider, I should think. Do we do anything?'

Callaghan said: 'No! Let it ride.'

Nikolls yawned again. He said:

'These guys took a bit of a chance. Somebody phoned through to Wilkie, got him out around the block on a fake excuse. They musta got in while he was round there. But they still took a chance. If you'd been upstairs you'd have heard 'em maybe.'

Callaghan grinned.

'They knew I wasn't upstairs,' he said. 'Starata took care of me personally last night.'

'No?' said Nikolls. 'You don't say? Anything serious?'

'Nothing much,' said Callaghan. 'They just pushed me around a little . . .'

'I bet they did,' said Nikolls. 'Those boys don't sorta like you, do they? Did they break anythin'?'

Callaghan said: 'No . . . nothing broken. They kicked me in the stomach and kidneys a little, that's all.'

Nikolls said: 'Oh, that ain't really anythin' much, is it? But it's sorta inconvenient. Did I tell you about that baby who kicked me while I was asleep in Palm Springs?'

'You did,' said Callaghan. 'The one who had spurs on when she did it . . . I remember.'

Nikolls said: 'O.K. . . . O.K. . . . Are you comin' back here?'

Callaghan said: 'Yes . . . probably. Maybe to-night or to-morrow morning. In the meantime do a little leg work. Starata had a place at 22 Chapel Street. He used to keep his latest girl friend there – a strawberry blonde. Have a look round there and see what you can get. Find out who the strawberry blonde is and where she's gone to if she's moved. You'll probably find that place is closed down.'

'O.K.,' said Nikolls. 'Anything else?'

'Yes,' said Callaghan. 'I want to know who Admiral Gardell's lawyer was. Possibly you can find out in London. Try anyhow, and if you can't, call through to Miss Desirée Gardell at Chipley Grange and ask her.'

'O.K.,' said Nikolls.

He hung up. He went into the outer office. He said to Effie:

'Desiray's a nice name. Effie. What does it mean?'

She looked interested. She said:

'Desirée . . . it means desired, I suppose. Why?'

'Oh, nothin',' said Nikolls. 'We got a client named Desiray now, that's all.'

'Have we?' said Effie. 'Well, what am I supposed to do about it?'

'Nothin',' said Nikolls with a grin. 'There ain't anything you *can* do, is there?' But it's a goddam pretty name. It sorta inspires me. I could write a hot number about a dame with a name like that. Look! I got an idea for it already . . .'

An expression of pain – intended to denote deep concentration – appeared on Nikolls's face. He began to sing:

'Oh, honey dame, you lit a flame,
You got me all excited with your name

That's the beginnin' of the verse,' continued Nikolls, 'an' the chorus is gonna start:

'Oh, Desiray, Desiray,
You're the baby for a tumble in the hay . . .'

Effie said: 'Mr. Nikolls, you're fearfully common, aren't you? Haven't you any ideals at all?'

'Yeah,' said Nikolls 'I'm practically all ideals. I got so many they run outa my ears on cold mornin's. Me . . . I'm a child of the people . . .'

'Really,' said Effie. Her voice was a little supercilious. 'In a moment you'll tell me you're the rough-and-ready type . . .'

'You got it, Effie,' said Nikolls archly. 'Any time you wanna get rough – I'm ready!'

Effie said: 'I think you're fearful. Don't you ever think of anything worth while. Haven't you any desire for Culture?'

'I never heard of her before,' said Nikolls. 'You give me her telephone number, and I'll go around an' slip her one of them "Look-me-over-kid-I'm-hard-to-get" looks.'

Effie said: 'You're impossible. You think of only two things – whisky and women.'

'You're all wrong Effie,' said Nikolls. 'I never think about whisky. How can a guy *think* about whisky. But dames is a different subject. Say, did I ever tell you about that Russian lady Commissar?'

She said: 'No . . . I've never heard *that* one.'

'Well,' said Nikolls, 'this baby was a dyed-in-the-wool Russian countess with pearls an' everything. She went all Red and became a Commissar. I met her in Moscow when I was workin' for the Transatlantic. There was a dame for you. If I was to tell you that baby's hipline . . .'

Effie said: 'You can skip that bit.'

'O.K. . . . O.K. . . .' said Nikolls. 'Well, this baby fell for me in a big way. She thought I was the kangaroo's dress stud. So I started work on her.'

'Yes?' said Effie. 'What did you do?'

'I usta look at her in a sorta longin' way,' said Nikolls. 'I bought myself a dictionary, but the mug who wrote it hadn't put in any proper sorta colloquial phrases like 'Baby, you're the goods,' or anythin' like that, so I couldn't do much talkin'. Well, then a touch of stark drama stepped in.'

'No?' said Effie. She was interested in spite of herself. 'What happened?'

'One night in the Hotel Stepanza,' said Nikolls dramatically, 'I was standing in the foyer lookin' all sorta soulful, an' she eased over to where I was standin'. She was dressed all in black an' she was wearin' a perfume that woulda hit you a home run. Every time I took a sniff I nearly passed out. Well, she put her hand on my arm an' she sorta hissed in my ear:

"Nikoleovitch," she says, sorta very low an' vibrant, "I shall be on the terrace at midnight. Come to me there. But be prepared." '

' "For what?" ' I asked her.

' "The worst," she says. "And remember this. I will have no failure. Two things may be yours. To-morrow you will either be a Hero of the Soviet Republic or a convict in the salt mines. It depends on you." '

'What happened then?' asked Effie.

Nikolls said: 'Well . . . I'm here, ain't I? I never went to the salt mines . . .'

III

Callaghan stopped the Jaguar in Dover Street. He walked a hundred yards down the street, turned into a doorway, ascended the stairs. On the first floor a door bore the sign of the Silver Bee Club. Callaghan went in, crossed to the bar, where a thin blonde was dispensing drinks. He ordered a double whisky and soda, carried the glass to a table in the corner and sat down.

His head ached. The lower part of his body felt as it he had been knifed. He lit a cigarette; began to think unpleasantly about Nicky Starata.

After a while he got up, went into the telephone-box. He dialled Nikolls's number. A glance at his wrist-watch showed him it was nine-thirty. When Nikolls came on the line Callaghan said:

'What about the Admiral? Did you get the lawyer's address?'

'Yeah,' said Nikolls, 'I got it. The lawyer is a guy named Vane, of Vane, Fleming, Searls and Vane, of Lincoln's Inn. The Vane we want lives at 27 Mount Street.'

Callaghan said: 'Where did you get the address from?'

Nikolls said: 'I got it from Desiray. Say, that's a helluva name for a dame, ain't it, that Desiray? It means "desired". Which reminds me of something . . .'

Callaghan said: 'Did you do anything about 22 Chapel Street?'

Nikolls said: 'Yeah, I went around to 22 Chapel Street. I've been pretty busy. I went there soon after you came through. There is a dame there an' she's goin' to scram.'

'Who is she?' asked Callaghan. 'The strawberry blonde?'

'That's right,' said Nikolls. 'An' she's some baby. I'm tellin' you. She's gettin' out of there in a hurry. Are you all right?' Nikolls went on. 'I've been a bit worried about you.'

'You're breaking my heart,' said Callaghan.

'I know,' said Nikolls. 'Well, maybe before we're through, we'll push that mug Starata around a bit.'

Callaghan said: 'Maybe!' He hung up.

He went down the stairs, started up the car, drove to Chapel Street. With the double summer-time dusk was only just falling. A motor-van with an East End address on it was outside No. 22. The front door was open.

Callaghan went up the stairs. He looked into the room in which the poker party of two nights before had taken place. It was bare. He went up the next flight. The door of the room facing the landing was half open. He went in. Two men were just carrying out a dressing-table. He stood on one side to let them pass.

The woman in the middle of the room said: 'Well, what can I do for you?'

Callaghan looked at her and smiled. She was about twenty-eight, of good figure – a natural strawberry blonde. She was beautifully clothed in a grey tailored suit that was almost too well cut. Everything about her was expensive.

Callaghan said: 'My name is Callaghan. I'm a private detective.'

She raised her eyebrows.

'So what?' she said. 'What am I supposed to do – curtsy?'

Callaghan said: 'You couldn't – in that skirt.'

He took out his cigarette-case, offered it to her. She thawed a little.

She said: 'Thanks.' She looked at him with an expression that seemed a mixture of suspicion and amusement. Callaghan thought that she was pretty certain of herself, but that, in any event, Nicky was unlikely to run a woman who wasn't. He thought that Starata's treatment of a woman would be on the 'treat 'em rough an' tell 'em nothing' lines. Mixed with a separate sporadic generosity when he had pulled something that seemed profitable.

He lit the cigarette for her. She stood leaning against the bare mantelpiece, looking at him appraisingly. After a moment she said:

'Well, why don't you get it off your mind?'

Callaghan leaned against the doorpost. He said:

'I think it's a damned shame.'

'Meaning what?' she said.

He smiled at her.

'You wouldn't know, would you?' he said. '*I'd* be feeling bad if I were you. When did Nicky give you the air? I suppose you got your marching orders some time this morning?'

She said: 'I don't know what the hell you're talking about.'

Callaghan grinned. He said:

'I know how you're feeling. But I wouldn't be too scared of Nicky if I were you. The bigger they come the harder they fall. You know, one of these fine days, you'll have to talk. Why not now?'

She laughed.

'I never talk to coppers,' she said, 'not even when they're only half-baked ones like you are.'

Callaghan inhaled. He blew the smoke slowly from his lungs. He said:

'All right. You have it your way. One of these days when you're feeling in a different frame of mind I'll be glad to see you. My office is in Berkeley Square. You'll find the number in the telephone book.'

'What a hope you've got,' she said. 'I've done a lot of things, but I'm no canary. I don't squeal easily.'

'You will,' said Callaghan cheerfully, 'especially when you find that Nicky's taken you for a ride. It wouldn't be so bad if the stuff he's pulled on you was true.'

She put one hand on her hip. She looked at him sideways. There was a gleam of interest in her eye.

'You know an awful lot, Mister Callaghan, don't you? Perhaps you're a mind reader. By the way, just what *did* Nicky tell you, since you know so much?'

Callaghan flipped the ash off his cigarette. He waited while the removal men came in and took away the last two chairs. He said:

'Nicky's had to do some quick moving during the last forty-eight hours. He knew I'd got that statement from Willie Lagos about the warehouse fire. He had to get a ripple on, and in spite of the fact that he didn't want to do anything too drastic he just had to, hadn't he?'

The strawberry blonde said: 'I'm not saying anything. But go on if it amuses you.'

'It does,' said Callaghan. 'Last night he had me tailed. He and Leon – that cheap muscle-man of his – pushed me around a little bit, got me out of the way whilst they broke into the office and got the Lagos statement. When we look for Lagos we'll find he's disappeared too. Nicky thought that, although the Insurance Company wouldn't pay on the claim after they'd heard what I'd got to say, the police couldn't take any action – not without Lagos and that statement. So, although he wouldn't get his quarter of a million, he'd be safe. So he told you that you'd have to pack up here. He told you that he was going to lie low for a bit until things blew over, and you believed it, didn't you?'

She said: 'Nuts to you, Mr. Callaghan. Even if he did tell me something like that, and I'm not saying he did, why shouldn't I believe him?'

Callaghan smiled at her easily. He was thinking of one of the sayings of Confucius: 'The woman who loves remains silent, but she who is jealous talks like the running stream!'

'Why don't you use your head?' he said. 'Even if all this was true, what's it got to do with *you*? Just because Nicky had to duck there's no reason why you should, is there? The very fact that you're packing up here and getting out, only a month or two after he took this place, furnished it and paid the rent for you, is something that isn't going to do *you* much good, is it? Quite obviously the police, who wouldn't be interested in you, will be now. For one thing, they'll think they might have a chance of finding Nicky by keeping an eye on you.' Callaghan went on: 'I don't see any reason why you shouldn't have stayed here except one – ' He grinned. 'And a damned good one too,' he concluded.

The strawberry blonde said: 'You slay me with curiosity. What's the damned good one?'

Callaghan said: 'What do you think? Nicky's found himself another girl, I should think.'

She stiffened.

'More nuts to you,' she said. 'You're trying to make me talk. That won't work.'

Callaghan said: 'I'm not even bothering whether you talk. You'll talk one day. You'll have to.' He laughed. 'You know Nicky,' he went on. 'No woman – not even one as good-looking as you are – ever lasted more than a couple or three months with Nicky.'

She said: 'I don't believe it, and if I did, I wouldn't do anything about it.'

Callaghan said amiably: 'That's where you're wrong. You'll want to do something about it. Nicky's told you to go off some place and lie low until you hear from him. He's probably told you you can join him in two or three weeks. But from now on all the time you'll be worrying about that other woman. You probably won't hear from Nicky again. You're "out" as far as he's concerned from this minute.'

'Yes?' she said. 'I'll take a chance on that.' She yawned. 'Is there anything else?'

'That's all,' said Callaghan. 'Only in the meantime you'll probably want to contact Nicky and find out if it's true or not – about that other woman, I mean. But you won't be able to do that.'

'No?' she said. 'You're fearfully bloody clever, aren't you?' Her voice was icy. 'Why not?'

Callaghan lied easily.

'Because from the time you get outside this house I'm going to have a tail on you,' he said. 'Every time you use a telephone you'll wonder if someone's listening in, and if you go out to see Nicky you'll lead us to him.' He paused. 'I want to see him particularly.'

She laughed.

'You don't like Nicky very much, do you?' she said.

Callaghan grinned.

'Not awfully,' he said casually.

She yawned again. 'Why?' she asked. 'What's he done to you?'

He raised his eyebrows.

'You wouldn't know, would you?' he said. 'Anyhow, he did enough for me to be wearing a four-inch bandage wrap-around that my figure didn't need before he took an interest in it.'

She smiled.

'No!' she said. 'Well, for a man who's been pushed in the guts you don't look so bad. Anyhow, I hope it hurts.'

Callaghan said: 'Don't worry. You've got your hope. Well, ring me up when you want to.'

'What for?' she asked. 'I've got nothing to tell you, and there's nothing I want to see you about.'

Callaghan smiled.

'Oh yes, you do,' he said. 'You'd like to know who that woman is. At the moment you don't believe she exists. You think I'm bluffing you. Well, when you're ready to talk to me, I'll talk to you.'

She said: 'I hope you've got something interesting to tell me.'

'I will have,' said Callaghan. 'I'll tell you who that woman is. So long!'

He turned and walked down the stairs. The strawberry blonde leaned against the mantelpiece for a few minutes. Then she threw her cigarette in the grate. Then she said a very nasty word.

IV

Mr. Aloysius Vane, of Vane, Fleming, Searls & Vane, was a short thin individual who peered at life over the tops of gold-rimmed pince-nez and even then did not believe it.

He was a lawyer of the highest integrity; found it convenient to believe that his clients must, of necessity, possess the same attribute. And he did not like private detectives.

During his forty years' experience of the law, he had, on occasion, been forced to use the services of these gentlemen. He had found them inclined to be grubby, salacious of mind – due, no doubt, to continuous activities in connection with what he called 'the more sordid type of divorce case' – and unreliable. Their expense accounts were inevitably, thought Mr. Vane, as unreliable as their reports, and their addiction to bitter beer, consumed in great quantities in small and ill-lit bars, provided an adequate obstacle to any sort of straight thinking.

And he was unable to 'place' Callaghan. Used to typifying, immediately on sight, the people who passed within his short-sighted orbit, he found that the proprietor of Callaghan Investigations possessed an elusive personality and certainly did not run true to what the lawyer considered 'form' in the world of private detectives.

Callaghan was well and quietly dressed. His shirt and tie were expensive. His gloves were of the best quality. His attitude towards Mr. Vane was also very odd. There were, in fact, moments when the solicitor thought that Callaghan was mildly amused.

He said: 'I don't mind your disturbing me at this hour, Mr. Callaghan, because, obviously, you must have something important to tell me. So perhaps you'll state your business as quickly as possible, and then I can go back to bed. Now . . . what can I do for you?'

Callaghan asked: 'Do you mind if I smoke?' He lit a cigarette, slowly regarded the end of it for some seconds before he answered. 'I don't think it's so much a matter of what you can do for me, Mr. Vane,' he said. 'Possibly I'm doing something for *you* – or the Gardell family.'

Mr. Vane raised his eyebrows.

'Really?' he said.

Callaghan went on: 'Did you know that Admiral Gardell, who was murdered early yesterday morning, tried to see me the night before?'

Vane said cautiously: 'Don't you think it would be better for both of us if I knew just where these questions are leading? And may I ask who you are representing? I don't *know* that your services have been retained by any member of the Gardell family.'

Callaghan thought for a moment. He decided to chance it. He said:

'Mr. Vane, I specialise in Insurance business. I've worked for most Insurance Companies. I take it that you're aware that Admiral Gardell carried a heavy insurance on his life?'

The solicitor said: 'I know about the insurance. I suppose there is no suggestion that the Insurance Company are going to query the claim that I propose to put in within the next two or three days?'

There was a pause. Callaghan wished that he knew what the company was. He realised he had to steer this conversation carefully. He said:

'I wouldn't go so far as to say that. But you can take it from me, Mr. Vane, that any questions I asked you are in the mutual interests of the Insurance Company and the beneficiary under the policy, who is, I think . . .'

Vane said: 'Miss Desirée Gardell, the Admiral's daughter, is the beneficiary.'

'Exactly,' said Callaghan. 'My questions are just as much to her advantage as that of the Insurance Company. When did you see the Admiral last, Mr. Vane?'

'The night before last,' said the lawyer. 'After he'd been to your office he came here. He knocked me up and asked to examine the policy. I got it out of the safe and gave it to him. He sat in the chair in which you are now sitting and examined it . . . Well, I should qualify that. He did not *examine* it – he merely glanced at it. Then he gave an exclamation – whether of pleasure or annoyance, I couldn't say. But there is no doubt that he changed his mind about something.' The solicitor put his finger-tips together, looked searchingly at Callaghan.

Callaghan said: 'I see. Did he by any chance decide that he was *not* going to commit suicide?'

'So it seemed,' said Vane cautiously. 'Because after he had handed the policy back to me, he asked if he might use the telephone. Whilst I was putting the policy back in the safe I heard him talking. He was talking to someone at Chipley Grange – I imagine to his daughter Desirée. I heard him say: "I've changed my mind. I'm not going to do what I intended to do – it would be useless. I shall be back in an hour or so. But I haven't finished with this business. I shall come up to-morrow and see Callaghan. I'm going to see this thing through to the bitter end now." '

Callaghan said: 'I see. What happened then?'

'He went away,' said the lawyer. 'I was very relieved.'

Callaghan asked: 'Did you know before this visit that he intended to commit suicide?'

The lawyer shook his head.

'It was the first I'd heard of it,' he said. 'I was surprised. He told me he'd been to see you, that you weren't in; that he'd left a note for you telling that he was going to commit suicide. When I asked him why, he said I'd know soon enough. I didn't pursue the subject, because the Admiral was an irascible sort of man.'

Callaghan said: 'I see.' He got up.

Vane said: 'If there's anything else you'd like to know, I'm at your disposal.'

Callaghan thought for a moment. Then:

'There are two or three questions I should like to ask you, Mr. Vane...'

The telephone on the desk jangled. Vane answered it. He said 'Yes' several times. Then he hung up.

Callaghan went on: 'There are two or three things I'm rather curious about. They are these: First of all...'

Vane interrupted:

'I'm sorry, Mr. Callaghan,' he said. 'But I can't answer any more questions.'

Callaghan raised his eyebrows.

'No?' he said. 'What's happened to make you change your mind so quickly?' He smiled suddenly. 'That was Miss Desirée Gardell on the telephone, I suppose?' he hazarded. 'And she'd told you to keep quiet. Is that right?'

Vane said softly: 'Mr. Callaghan, I don't *have* to answer your questions.'

Callaghan said: 'I know, but you've answered that one all right. The most important one. Good-night, Mr. Vane.'

He picked up his hat, went out.

Callaghan walked slowly back to the car. He was intrigued with the late Admiral Gardell, with Miss Manon Gardell, with the family lawyer, and possibly, he thought, with Miss Desirée Gardell. He wondered just how Callaghan Investigations were going to fit into the scheme of things.

That Callaghan Investigations *were* going to fit into the scheme of things was a certainty in the mind of the proprietor of that organisation. The fact that his services had *not* been retained by any one, and that the likelihood of a retainer was practically *nil* since the death of the Admiral, mattered little to Callaghan.

There were more ways than one of killing a cat...

He wondered why Desirée Gardell had found it necessary to instruct Vane to hold his tongue. Had Manon talked to Desirée? This seemed the obvious solution. Manon had constituted a scouting party of one, sent to spy out the land, to find out just what sort of person Callaghan was.

Desirée had instructed Vane not to talk to Callaghan. Why had she not taken this step earlier? She must have known when Nikolls telephoned for the lawyer's address that Callaghan intended to see him.

Quite obviously, thought Callaghan, because she had not then seen Manon; because since then she *had* seen Manon, was probably with her when Callaghan was talking to Vane. Something had been said which made it imperative that in no circumstances should the lawyer talk to Callaghan.

Callaghan started up the car and drove slowly towards the garage at the back of Berkeley Square. His mind was made up. He intended to cut Messrs. Callaghan Investigations in on the Admiral Gardell claim.

And he knew just how he was going to do it.

CHAPTER FOUR
A NICE PIECE OF GLAMOUR

I

NIKOLLS said: 'It's funny, but every mornin' around eleven o'clock I come over sorta dizzy. I wonder why it is.'

Callaghan said: 'I don't. It's happened ever since Effie removed the Bourbon from the drawer in my office desk. Help yourself.'

Nikolls said: 'Thanks!' He went to the sitting-room sideboard, took out a bottle and a glass, poured a stiff one. He swallowed it in one gulp. He said: 'That's better. It's funny how a little whisky clears the head.'

Callaghan put his hands behind his head and looked up at the ceiling. He was lying on the settee. He wore pillar-box red silk pyjamas. He looked almost Mephistophelean.

He said: 'Which Company was it covered the Admiral's life insurance?'

'The Globe & Associated,' said Nikolls. 'The Managing Director is a guy called Phelps. Maybe you remember him. We did some sleuthin' for them about three years ago.'

'I remember,' said Callaghan. He got up, went to the sideboard, poured a stiff shot of whisky, drank it. He lit a cigarette.

Nikolls asked: 'Howya feelin'?'

'Not too bad,' said Callaghan. He went on: 'When you go downstairs, get through to the Globe & Associated, speak to Phelps. Tell him I'd like to see him; that I'll come along some time this afternoon, on the off-chance.'

'O.K.,' said Nikolls. 'That all?'

'No,' said Callaghan. He was smiling a little. 'Tell him that there'll be a claim in from Vane of Vane, Fleming, Searls & Vane within a couple of days, on the Admiral's life policy for forty-five thousand pounds. Tell Phelps that my advice is to stall it.'

Nikolls said: 'What's the matter with that claim? It's O.K., ain't it? The Admiral's dead. The Globe & Associated have gotta pay, haven't they?'

Callaghan said: 'Not necessarily!'

Nikolls said: 'So you're pullin' a fast one, hey? The Admiral never retained you, did he? He was dead before he could see you. Are you workin' for *anybody* on this case?'

'No,' said Callaghan. 'But I'm going to be.'

Nikolls grinned.

'I see,' he said. 'Were cutting in on the deal, are we?'

'Yes,' said Callaghan. 'We're cutting in.'

Nikolls nodded. 'Well, you know! But if you tell me how an Insurance Company don't have to pay on a life policy when the guy's dead, I'll be learnin' something.'

Callaghan said: 'Every life insurance policy bears a clause that the policy isn't payable if the insured person commits suicide within two years from the date of issue.'

Nikolls whistled.

'I get it,' he said. 'So the two years ain't up, an' your story is that the Admiral committed suicide?'

'No,' said Callaghan. 'When we check the policy, we'll find the two years were up, possibly by only a few days, so even if the Admiral did commit suicide, the Insurance Company would have to pay.'

'All right,' said Nikolls. 'Well, you're arguin' against yourself. How can you stop 'em payin'?'

Callaghan drew on his cigarette.

He said: 'Gringall says the Admiral was murdered. Well . . . he ought to know. I'm laying a shade of odds that if the police say a man is murdered they're right. But I'm concerned with the niece – Manon . . .'

'Yeah?' said Nikolls. He poured himself another shot – almost absent-mindedly. 'Is she tryin' to pull somethin'?'

Callaghan said: 'She's certain the Admiral committed suicide. She was so certain that it's evident she wants to believe it and wants every one else to believe it too. She's made sure that I knew the Admiral had a motive for killing himself.'

Nikolls said: 'Every guy who commits suicide has a motive. The motive is he wants to die.'

'Not in this case,' said Callaghan. 'The Admiral intended to commit suicide in order to be revenged on somebody.'

Nikolls fished in his pocket. He produced a packet of Lucky Strikes. He extracted one, lit it. He said:

'We'll, it's a funny way to get revenge on a guy. I don't see how it'd work.'

Callaghan said: 'Use your imagination, Windy. Supposing the Admiral thought that the two years weren't up? If he committed suicide within that period the Insurance Company wouldn't pay, so he'd be revenged on whoever was going to get the money, wouldn't he?'

Nikolls said: 'I've got it. So that's the story. But it wouldn't work if he was murdered. They'd have to pay anyway if he was murdered.'

'Not necessarily then,' said Callaghan. 'The law says that nobody can make a profit out of a criminal action.' He looked at Nikolls. He was smiling.

Nikolls whistled through his teeth.

'For cryin' out loud!' he said. 'So your story is that whoever murdered the Admiral was the person who was goin' to get the benefit under the policy. Therefore they can't draw. Is that it?'

Callaghan said: 'That's not my story. That's just a *suggestion*. But it's good enough to stop the Company from paying that claim too quickly.'

Nikolls said: 'You ought to be head of the Brains Trust. So that's how you're goin' to cut in. Who're you goin' to work for?'

Callaghan said: 'I don't know. We'll find a client in a minute. Go downstairs to the office and get through to Phelps. Tell him I'll be seeing him this afternoon. Then get through to Gringall at Scotland Yard. Ask him if he could spare me a few minutes about a quarter to one.'

'O.K.,' said Nikolls. He went out.

Callaghan began to dress. He took lots of time over the process. He was thinking. By the time he was dressed his plan of campaign was settled.

He looked in at the office on the floor below on his way out. Effie Thompson was at work at her typewriter. The morning sunshine illuminated her neat red head. She said to Callaghan:

'There are some things you ought to know about. There's a woman wants you to keep observation on some man.'

'Write and tell her I don't want it,' said Callaghan. 'What are the other things?'

'Somebody's been stealing the petty cash in a cement factory,' said Effie. 'You wouldn't want to handle that, would you?'

'No,' said Callaghan. 'Tell 'em to keep it locked up.'

'Lastly,' said Effie primly, 'Miss Vendayne called through from Devonshire. She wanted to know how you were. She said the country down there was looking wonderful. She said if you felt you wanted a rest . . .'

Callaghan said: 'What did *you* say?'

She looked at the typewriter. She said:

'I told her you were busy.'

Callaghan said: 'Call through to her and tell her I'll telephone her as soon as I have time. Say I'm glad she called.'

'Very well,' said Effie. She hoped that Miss Vendayne – who was very beautiful – would develop a squint.

Callaghan went on: 'And you might call through to Miss Desirée Gardell at Chipley Grange. Tell her that I'd like to see her. Suggest that any time after six o'clock this evening would be suitable.'

Effie said: 'Should I make it seven o'clock, Mr. Callaghan? She might ask you to dinner then.'

Callaghan paused, his hand on the door-knob. He said:

'Do you think that would be a good idea, Effie?'

'Why not?' said Effie.

Callaghan said solemnly: 'Perhaps you're right. Make it seven, Effie.'

'Will you be back to-night?' Her tone was casual.

He looked at her and smiled.

'I wouldn't know,' he said. 'But you needn't wait. This is where you get a chance to go to a movie . . .'

She sighed. 'I've told you so often, Mr. Callaghan, that I'm not awfully keen on movies. I'd much rather read a book.'

'Well,' said Callaghan with a grin, 'read a book, Effie. A *good* book.'

She said: 'If I read anything it will be a thriller. I like reading about the wonderful things that happen to girls who work for private detectives.'

Callaghan said: 'I bet that makes you laugh.'

She flashed her green eyes at him.

'And *how* . . .' she said.

II

Chief Detective-Inspector Gringall was occupied with his favourite game of drawing fruit on the blotter. Years of practice had made him a considerable artist in this process. His pineapples and water-melons were the pride of the Central Office, had even been passed from room to room as examples of sheer unadulterated concentration. At the moment he was busy on a banana. It was half-finished when a detective-constable brought in Callaghan.

Gringall said: 'Hallo, Slim. It's nice to see you. Sit down. Something on your mind?' He finished off the banana quickly, started on a tangerine.

Callaghan said: 'I'm in a fix, Gringall. I don't quite know what to do. And you know my motto: "When in doubt ask a policeman."'

Gringall looked up. He dropped his pencil in the tray before him. He produced his pipe, began to fill it.

'I didn't know *that* was your motto,' he said. 'I always thought the motto of Callaghan's Investigations was, "We get there somehow, and who the hell cares how." But what's the trouble?'

Callaghan lit a cigarette. He leaned back in his chair and watched a smoke ring as it sailed across the office.

He said: 'It's this Gardell thing. Gringall. I don't like it.'

Gringall said: 'No? What don't you like about it?'

Callaghan said: 'You think the Admiral was murdered. Well, you might be right, but I don't.'

Gringall, who was in the act of lighting his pipe, allowed the match to go out.

'You *don't*?' he repeated. 'Well, what's your alternative?'

Callaghan considered for a moment. Then:

'Gardell was *planning* to commit suicide,' he said. 'He told one or two people that he intended to commit suicide. He had a definite motive for *wanting* to commit suicide. He left a note for me, when he came round to see me a few hours before he died, saying that he was *going* to commit suicide.'

Gringall said: 'Very interesting. But the fact remains that we think he was shot.'

Callaghan asked: 'Would it be in order to ask why?'

Gringall shrugged his shoulders.

'One very good reason,' he said. 'If there'd been a gun it might possibly have been a case of suicide. He might have shot himself by holding the gun as far away from his head as possible. With a small-calibred weapon there wouldn't necessarily have been burn marks round the wound. But there was no weapon.'

He lit his pipe, put the match carefully in the ash-tray, picked up his pencil and began work on a lemon. He said casually:

'What was his motive for suicide?'

Callaghan said: 'Revenge. He was insured for forty-five thousand pounds. If he committed suicide before two years from the issue of the policy the Insurance Company under their usual ruling wouldn't pay, so the beneficiary under the policy would get nothing. Have you got it?'

Gringall raised his eyebrows.

'I see,' he said. 'So your theory is that the Admiral planned to keep that policy going for nearly two years so that somebody thought they were going to get forty-five thousand pounds, and then, just when the two years were nearly up, he'd shoot himself and do 'em in the eye. Is that it?'

'That's it,' said Callaghan.

Gringall said: 'I'd believe it if we'd found a weapon. But the Sussex police and our own people believe it's a clear case of murder. By the way,' said Gringall, 'who are you working for?'

Callaghan said: 'I'm not working for anybody at the moment. I never saw the Admiral, so I don't know what he wanted to see me about.'

Gringall said: 'I see. Have you seen any one else?'

'No,' said Callaghan, lying cheerfully. 'Well, no one except Vane, his lawyer.' He sighed. 'I don't think he likes me a lot,' he said.

Gringall said: 'Possibly not. There are a lot of people don't like you, Slim.' He smiled at the private detective. 'So you're not working for *any one*?' he asked.

Callaghan said: 'Not at the moment. I expect to be this afternoon.'

Gringall grinned broadly.

'That tells me that you're going to see the Globe & Associated, the Company that wrote the policy,' he said. 'You're a clever devil, Slim.'

Callaghan said: 'So are you. It didn't take you long to find out who the Company was.'

'A mere matter of routine,' said the police officer. 'What are you going to tell 'em, Slim? Are you going to pull this suicide thing on them?'

'It wouldn't work if I did,' said Callaghan.

Gringall raised his eyebrows again.

'Why not?' he asked. 'If the Admiral had, as you suggest, committed suicide within the two years, they needn't pay, and they'd be glad if you could prove that he did commit suicide. They'd probably pay you a very handsome fee.'

Callaghan said: 'Probably they would, but I'm not going to try that with them.'

Gringall said: 'I see. Well, as a matter of curiosity, I'd like to know how you can get them to stall on the payment of that policy.'

Callaghan said: 'You know the only thing I can do.'

Gringall thought for a moment; then he said:

'The only other thing you could do would be a suggestion that the beneficiary under the policy was in some way connected with the murder of the Admiral, and was therefore not entitled to make a profit out of a criminal act.' He took his pipe out of his mouth; looked quickly at Callaghan. 'Is that it?'

Callaghan said: 'I didn't say I was going to put *that* up to the Globe & Associated. All I suggested was that they might like to employ me. I might be of use to them.'

Gringall said: 'Slim, you wouldn't hold out on me, would you?'

'Certainly not,' said Callaghan with a grin. 'When I know anything that's worth knowing I'll let you know. By the way, do you know anything about this murder – as between friends?'

'As between friends, I don't,' said Gringall. 'I'll be quite candid with you. At the moment all we have is a corpse and nothing else. We hadn't even got a motive until you suggested one.' He thought for a moment, then: 'I must get the Globe & Associated to let me know the date they issued that policy.'

Callaghan got up.

'I'll save you the trouble about that, Gringall,' he said. 'The Admiral didn't commit suicide.'

Gringall sighed.

'I wish I knew what you were playing at,' he said. 'I wish I knew what was going on inside that head of yours. So he didn't commit suicide? You tell me how you know that.'

Callaghan said: 'Listen to this: The Admiral intended to commit suicide, because he wanted to be revenged on somebody who was going to get the money, or some of it, from that policy when he died. But before he did the job he decided to see me. He came to town immediately, taking a chance as to whether he'd get me in the small hours of the morning. Now why should he come to see me?'

Gringall said: 'I might be able to answer that one. The Admiral had heard that you were a private detective who specialised in investigations for Insurance Companies. He wanted to be certain that the Company wouldn't pay if he committed suicide.'

'Right,' said Callaghan. 'That's my idea too. Well, he arrived in town, but couldn't see me because I wasn't in. So he went off, intending to come back. Then he got an idea. He began to wonder about the date of that policy. So he went round and knocked up Vane, his lawyer, who produced the policy. Vane told me that the Admiral merely glanced at it then obviously changed his mind about something.'

Callaghan shrugged his shoulders.

'There's the answer,' he went on. 'He took a glance at that policy and saw the date on it. He knew the two years were up. *He knew that even if he committed suicide within an hour the Insurance Company would still pay because the two years were up.*'

'I see,' said Gringall. 'And the murderer, knowing that the Admiral *intended* to commit suicide, thinking that here was a first-class chance of getting away with it, was lying in wait for the Admiral and shot him.' Gringall yawned. 'I don't think much of that murderer,' he said. 'What an imbecile he must have been. If your theory is correct, Slim, all he had to do was to shoot the Admiral, wipe his fingerprints off the gun, stick it in the Admiral's hand, and get out. If he'd done that we might well have believed that Gardell had killed himself. But the murderer doesn't do anything sensible like that. He just walks off the takes the gun with him.'

Callaghan said: 'That's the worst of you policemen. You take a really good-looking theory and you pull it to pieces.' He yawned artistically. 'So long, Gringall. I'll be seeing you.' He walked to the door.

Gringall said: 'I wonder what you really came here for?'

Callaghan said: 'I told you if I had any information I'd give it to you. Well, I've done my best, and look at the thanks I get.'

Gringall put his pencil down. He said:

'What you really came here for was to tell me that you're going to see the Globe & Associated and get yourself taken in on this job. You wanted to see my reaction. You wanted to see whether I wouldn't like the idea.'

Callaghan said evenly: 'And do you?'

Gringall said: 'I'm not saying anything. If the Globe & Associated like to employ you, well . . . they're entitled to. You might even find something out – who knows?'

'Quite,' said Callaghan. 'I might even come to you and talk to you about it.' He sighed. 'The amount of work I've done for this office during the last six years is just nobody's business.'

Gringall smiled. He said.

'You've got the most appalling nerve I've ever met. The work you've done for us! Damn it . . . look what we've done for *you*. You ought to be grateful to us for not slinging you inside on a charge of obstructing the police on half a dozen occasions. Look at that Riverton case . . . look at that Vendayne business. In both those affairs you skated on such thin ice that we could almost hear it cracking. You're incorrigible! By the way, d'you ever hear anything of Audrey Vendayne?'

Callaghan said: 'She called through to the office to-day. She said Devonshire was looking wonderful . . .'

Gringall said: 'It beats me how your clients can even bother to speak to you. You charge the most terrible fees. You're uncouth. You're cunning. Your methods are unspeakable. And yet charming women like Audrey Vendayne call you up and tell you that Devonshire is looking wonderful. I can't understand it.'

Callaghan opened the door.

'Of course you can't,' he said airily. 'You're just another policeman. You're much too coarse to understand the really fine relationship that exists between Callaghan Investigations and its clients.'

He grinned at the astonished police officer.

'Women have intuition,' he said. 'They have an additional sense. They *know* that they're safe with Callaghan's Investigations.'

Gringall said: 'My God . . . safe with Callaghan Investigations . . . I'd rather be in the hands of the Gestapo. If I were a client of yours I'd probably shoot you . . .'

'If you were a client of mine I'd probably shoot myself,' said Callaghan. 'So long, Gringall. And work *hard*. Otherwise they'll send you back to that beat where you *really* belong . . .'

The door closed behind him.

Gringall got up and went to the window. He stood there for some time looking out on to the Embankment.

When he returned to his desk he was smiling. He picked up the telephone, asked the operator to give him Inspector Maynes's room.

He said to Maynes: 'About that Gardell case. Apply for a fortnight's adjournment at the inquest. Give the usual reasons. And don't do anything – except routine – until I give you the word. Understand?'

'Very good, Mr. Gringall,' said Maynes. 'Has something happened?'

Gringall smiled into the transmitter.

'Callaghan's happened,' he said. 'He's going to cut himself in. He's on to something. He's at his old game of drawing red herrings all over the place.'

Maynes said gloomily: 'That means trouble for everybody. Is he working for any one interested?'

'He's suggesting that he's going to work for the Insurance people concerned,' said Gringall. 'That may be bluff. Perhaps he's working for somebody else. Who gets the money under the policy, Maynes?'

'Miss Gardell,' said Maynes. 'Miss Desirée Gardell – the daughter.'

'Ah!' said Gringall. 'Well . . . if she's going to get forty-five thousand pounds, you can bet next month's pay Callaghan will be working for her . . .'

Maynes said: 'I don't think so, sir. I don't think she's the type to use a private investigator. She's much too classy. I don't think she'd like Callaghan at all.'

Gringall sighed. He said:

'They never do at the start, Maynes. Mark you, I'm only guessing, but if Callaghan has made up his mind to work for her he'll do it . . .'

'Whether she likes it or not?' asked Maynes.

Gringall said: 'Maynes . . . when you know Callaghan as well as I do, you'll know that when he works for a client the client stands for it *and* likes it.'

Maynes said: 'Well . . . if that's so, Mr. Gringall, he *must* have something.'

'He's *got* something all right,' said Gringall. 'He's got a system. He just follows his nose. And he can do all sorts of things and say all sorts of things that we *can't*.'

'That's all very well, sir,' said Maynes. 'But if he interferes . . . I shall be very tough with him if he interferes.'

Gringall said: 'You be tough, Maynes, and see where it gets you. and Callaghan never *interferes* with the police. Oh no! He just *helps*. Personally I'd rather be assisted by the devil himself.'

'I see,' said Maynes. 'Thanks for the tip. I'm keen, as you know, Mr. Gringall, on making a good job of this Gardell business. It's my first job since I got my stop . . .'

Gringall said: 'If I can do anything, just let me know. In the meantime ask for that adjournment and see that you get it. I want a little time before you move at all drastically.'

'You think something will happen?' asked Maynes.

Gringall laughed.

'I'm damned certain it will,' he said. 'If I know anything of Callaghan he's going to *make* something happen. We might as well see what it is.'

He hung up. Then he relit his pipe and began to draw a water-melon.

III

Callaghan followed the ancient butler along the oak-wainscoted corridor that led through the house towards the rear lawn. Over the shoulder of the old man he caught a glimpse, in the distance, of the flower garden.

They came out into the fading sunlight. In the far corner of the garden Callaghan saw Desirée Gardell, a trowel in her gloved hand, busy transplanting. She saw them, dropped the trowel, stood waiting, relaxed and smiling.

Callaghan thought here's a hell of a woman. Manon had not exaggerated. Desirée presented a picture calculated to make any normal man catch his breath.

She was a little taller than Manon – a brunette. She wore an olive-green coat and skirt of corduroy velvet, with a primrose-yellow jumper. Her hair, severely dressed, was bound in a scarf that was a mixture of green and orange and olive. Her stockings were light sun-tan, and her small feet were exquisitely shod in well-polished oxford shoes.

The butler said, 'Mr. Callaghan,' and went away. They stood looking at each other. Then she smiled. It was an easy, casual sort of smile. It might have meant anything.

He was waiting for her to speak. He wondered what her voice would be like. He thought that a woman with a face and figure like that *must* have a poor sort of voice. It would be *too* much if that was as beautiful as the rest of her.

It was. It was low – like a husky flute, Callaghan thought – and soft and casual. She said:

'I'm glad to see you, Mr. Callaghan. I hope you'll stay to dinner, and I hope we shall be able to feed you adequately. At any rate it ought to be better than the nearest inn.'

'Thank you,' said Callaghan. 'I'm sorry to arrive at such an inconvenient time. But I thought you might like to see me as soon as possible.'

She said: 'I don't know now . . . possibly the cause of urgency has disappeared. One can't say. Well have to talk about it. Please smoke if you want to.'

He offered her his cigarette case. She shook her head. Callaghan lit a cigarette and took a long time over the process. He was smiling to himself.

A sweet set-up, he thought. So the 'cause for urgency' had disappeared, 'possibly . . .' Like hell it had disappeared. Manon Gardell, having done her scouting act and reported to Desirée, that lady had now decided that any urgency had disappeared. The decision being based on the fact that Manon had concluded that the time was not ripe to talk to Callaghan . . . possibly never would be ripe.

He drew the tobacco smoke down into his lungs and took a long look at Desirée Gardell. Here was a nice piece of glamour. Definitely an alluring picture – a picture that made the most of a superb figure, a perfect poise. She was shading her eyes with her hand, looking into the distance towards the wood that topped the hill a couple of miles away. A nice attitude, thought Callaghan. It suited her.

He said: 'Well, Miss Gardell, if you think there's nothing important for us to talk about I might as well go back. There are lots of things I can do . . .'

'Are there?' she said. She did not alter her position or turn towards him. Her voice was *very* casual. Callaghan swore under his breath. It was obvious that Miss Gardell could be very difficult – if she wanted to be, and it seemed, at the moment, that she wanted to be.

She said: 'I always think this view is so beautiful at this time in the evening. I like looking at it.' She turned towards him. 'I expect you've *lots* of important things to do in London,' she went on. 'So, if you like, you can go back immediately after dinner – and we needn't talk at all. Perhaps you think there isn't anything that needs talk.'

Callaghan thought: You'd be surprised if you knew just how much talk there *is* going to be. You've got everything cut and dried, haven't you, madame . . . ?

But he said evenly: 'That's for you to decide, of course.' His voice became a trifle humble. 'I thought that possibly you wanted to make use of the service of Callaghan Investigations; that you had thought we might help you?'

She smiled at him. She said:

'Do you know, I haven't really thought very much about it . . .'

Callaghan thought: You're a damned liar, Desirée. You've thought plenty about it. He could hear Manon saying: 'We've got to be careful of this Callaghan person, Desirée. He's quite intelligent. At moment he *almost* appears to have brains. Not a bit like one's ideas of a private detective, my dear. He's *almost* possible . . .'

He said: 'Anyhow, my journey won't have been wasted. There are one or two questions I'd like to ask you . . .'

'Are there?' she said. She smiled again. He noticed that her teeth were quite perfect and that her eyes were changed from violet to blue. 'I do hope I shall want to answer them . . .' Her voice was mildly sarcastic.

You'll answer them and like it, thought Callaghan. But he said smilingly:

'That, of course, depends on you.'

She said: 'Of *course*. Will you forgive me if I leave you now. I'd like to change. Please ask Grant for anything you want. I'll tell him to bring you a cocktail here. You might like to stay and admire the view . . .'

She flashed another smile at him, went towards the house. Callaghan watched her. He felt happy . . . he was almost contented . . . This, he thought, is going to be good. Damned good!

IV

Grant, the butler, brought coffee into the little sitting-room with french windows that overlooked the terrace. Out of the corner of his eye Callaghan was watching Desirée Gardell, wondering about her. A clever one, he thought. For once, here was a beautiful woman who had brains. She looked exquisite. She wore a plain black crêpe-de-chine dinner frock with a small diamond buckle at its belt and soft beige ruffles at throat and wrists. Her hair, loosely but artistically dressed, was tied at one side with a black water-silk ribbon.

During dinner she had been smiling and attentive, a perfect hostess, indulging in generalities of conversation. Now she sat silently, a cigarette between her fingers, looking towards the sunset.

Callaghan said: 'This is delightful. A wonderful contrast to the humdrum existence of a private detective.'

'Is it, Mr. Callaghan?' she said. 'I was afraid that this rusticity might have bored you.'

Callaghan said: 'It doesn't bore me a bit. I like looking at things and people. I can be very patient.'

'Can you?' she asked. She said suddenly: 'Mr. Callaghan, what do you expect to get out of this business?'

Callaghan said evenly: 'I don't think I *quite* understand.'

She laughed – it was a delightful laugh. She said:

'Oh yes, you do. You don't mean to tell me that you came down here for your health?'

Callaghan said: 'I came down here because you gave my office to understand that you wanted to see me urgently. Naturally we don't expect to work for nothing, and I wasn't to know that since you rang my office something had happened to make you change your mind.'

She said, with a hint of impatience in her voice: 'So I've changed my mind. You seem to add thought-reading to your other attributes, Mr. Callaghan.'

'Not always,' said Callaghan. He was smiling as pleasantly as she was. 'Only sometimes. Are you trying to tell me that you haven't changed your mind?'

She said: 'I'd rather ask you a question. Since you say I've changed my mind, perhaps you'll tell me what was responsible for the process.'

'I could make a guess,' said Callaghan.

'May I know what it is?' she asked.

'Certainly,' he said. 'I should say that your cousin Manon is responsible for your change of mind.'

She said casually: 'So you've seen Manon?'

'You *know* I've seen Manon,' said Callaghan. 'I imagine she was a scouting expedition sent forward in advance to see what sort of person I was. Apparently she didn't consider that I was quite the type. So she talked a lot and said nothing.'

She looked away over the terrace and lawns. She said: 'Ah!' There was a long silence, then: 'Mr. Callaghan, you thought that I might want to use your services. Well, that's true – I might. When I telephoned your office, I did want to see you urgently. I wanted you to tell me about the interview you had with my father.'

Callaghan said: 'And now you know I've nothing to tell you. Your lawyer's already told you that I didn't see the Admiral?'

'Yes,' she said. 'That's true enough. But even so *you* think that you can help me in some way.' She smiled charmingly. 'I like being helped,' she said. 'Have you a suggestion?'

Callaghan said: 'You know that the County police and Scotland Yard have a very definite idea that the Admiral was murdered. Did you know that your cousin Manon was just as certain that he committed suicide?'

She said: 'Mr. Callaghan, you must have a very poor opinion of me. Do you think if I honestly thought my father had been murdered I should be as calm and collected over this business as I am?'

'I don't know,' said Callaghan. 'I don't know you well enough. So you think he committed suicide, and you can be calm and collected about it because you knew that his suicide was inevitable?'

She nodded.

'You know, Mr. Callaghan,' she said, 'in order to understand the way I think about my father's death you'd have to know me. Life hadn't very much to offer him. He was old, tired, irascible. If I thought that by dying he'd have lost anything, I should have been sorry. But I know he's gained peace. That was what he wanted more than anything else.'

Callaghan said: 'Then we need not be sorry for the Admiral. He got what he wanted. But the fact remains that the police believe he was murdered.'

She said: 'Does that matter?'

'It might matter considerably,' said Callaghan, 'to you.'

She raised her eyebrows.

'Really!' she said. 'How could it matter to me?'

Callaghan asked: 'May I have another cigarette?'

She nodded. He took one from the silver box on the table, lit it. He said:

'Miss Gardell, you've got an idea that within a few days the Globe & Associated Insurance Company are going to pay you the sum of forty-five thousand pounds, haven't you?'

She said: 'Yes, my father's life was insured for that amount.'

He said: 'Supposing they didn't pay the claim?'

She looked at him. Her eyes seemed a little larger. Also he was certain now that their colour was violet.

She said: 'But how ridiculous. They've got to pay the claim.'

Callaghan smiled.

'Oh no, they haven't,' he said. 'They haven't *got* to pay anything.'

She said: 'Mr. Callaghan, do you mean to tell me that an Insurance Company is in the habit of bilking its customers?'

Callaghan said: 'A policy is issued under certain conditions, Miss Gardell. If the insured doesn't keep to those conditions, or if there is any other legal angle that needs examination, the Company are quite entitled to hold up the claim until they are satisfied.'

She said: 'Oh, I understand. You mean the two years' clause about suicide? That a Company won't pay if the insured person commits suicide within two years of the issue of the policy.'

Callaghan's smile became broader.

He said: 'I imagine it was that clause in the policy that the Admiral wanted to see me about. But when he called on Vane he discovered that the period *had* elapsed; that committing suicide wouldn't do any good – that the policy would be paid.' He stopped for a moment. Then: 'Did you know that his idea in committing suicide was so that the policy should *not* be paid?'

She said: 'I didn't know, and I don't believe anything of the sort.'

Callaghan shrugged his shoulders.

'All right,' he said. 'You didn't know and you don't believe. So what?' His tone was nearly insolent.

She said: 'Well, in any event what does it matter? Can you give me another reason why the Insurance Company shouldn't pay?'

Callaghan said: 'I think there's an obvious reason, Miss Gardell, and I should have thought that you were intelligent enough to know what it is.'

She said coldly: 'Perhaps I am not as intelligent as you think, Mr. Callaghan. Also I would like to tell you that I don't awfully like your tone of voice.'

'Don't you?' said Callaghan. 'That's too bad. I wonder what I'm to do about that.'

She did not answer. Callaghan got up. He said:

'Miss Gardell, I should like to thank you for a very interesting evening and an excellent dinner. It's quite obvious to me that Callaghan Investigations aren't going to be of much use to you.' He smiled. 'I don't think you like us a lot, do you?'

'I hadn't thought about that, Mr. Callaghan. *Must* you go?'

He said: 'I ought to be getting back.'

She got up. They went back through the dining-room into the hall-way. Callaghan took his hat and coat from the butler. She came with him to the entrance steps.

He said: 'If there's anything I can do for you at any time, Miss Gardell, just give me a ring.'

She smiled.

'In spite of the fact that you have the idea that I don't like Callaghan Investigations?' she asked.

Callaghan said: 'Miss Gardell, quite apart from whether you like me or not, you may find you'll *have* to use my services.'

She raised her eyebrows.

'Really, Mr. Callaghan,' she said, 'you amaze me. If I might be presumptuous enough to ask one more question, I would ask why.'

Callaghan said: 'I'll tell you. You're certain the Admiral committed suicide. Your cousin Manon is certain of it too. But there is only one person who can *prove* that the Admiral *intended* to commit suicide.'

'Really!' she said. 'And who would that be?'

'Myself,' said Callaghan. 'I've got a note from him in his own hand-writing saying he was going to commit suicide.'

She said: 'Very interesting, Mr. Callaghan. But I still don't see the connection.'

Callaghan said: 'The connection is this. It doesn't matter what you say, or what your cousin says, or what any of us think. The police say the Admiral was murdered, and that must effect the viewpoint of the Insurance Company.'

She said: 'Mr. Callaghan, you seem to know a great deal about the viewpoint of the Insurance Company.'

Callaghan smiled beatifically.

'I ought to,' he said. 'I represent them . . .'

She gazed at him blankly for a moment. She said:

'You . . .'

Callaghan said: 'I've been working for Insurance Companies for a long time, Miss Gardell. I had an interview this afternoon with the Managing Director of the Globe & Associated. He decided, having regard to certain information I was able to give him, that they would like to retain me on this claim. They've also decided, after hearing what I had to tell them, that they're going to suspend payment on the claim until they are satis-fied that the claim is in order.'

Her voice was like ice. 'Mr. Callaghan, I must congratulate you on your effrontery.'

Callaghan said: 'Thanks!'

She went on: 'One fact remains, whether my father committed suicide or whether he was murdered does not affect the validity of the claim. In any event the Insurance Company must pay.'

Callaghan's tone was almost bantering. He said: 'Don't you believe it, Miss Gardell. You know, before you make these statements you really should talk to somebody who knows something about it.'

She made a little hissing noise. She was furious. She looked at Callaghan with eyes that were very hard. Now, he thought, they were definitely blue.

She said: 'I see. I suppose you know about it, Mr. Callaghan. I suppose you know *all* about it.'

Callaghan said: 'I know enough to know this, Miss Gardell, and I'll give you the information free, gratis, and for nothing. Under common law it has always been understood in this country that a wrongdoer cannot benefit from the results of his crime.'

She said: 'I still don't understand.'

Callaghan said: 'The police believe that the Admiral was murdered. That's what they say and they can very easily make it stick. Therefore in certain circumstances the Insurance Company need not pay, those circumstances being that they have reason to believe that the beneficiary under the Insurance policy might have had a hand in the murder of the Admiral. That's plain enough, isn't it, Miss Gardell?'

She leaned against the stone pillar of the portico. She was quite speechless.

Callaghan said: 'Good-night, Miss Gardell. Thanks once again for your hospitality. If you want me you'll find the number in the book.'

CHAPTER FIVE
LINE FOR TWO GIRL

I

CALLAGHAN drove the Jaguar into the garage in the Berkeley Square Mews. He switched off the engine, lit a cigarette, relaxed in the comfortable driving-seat. He was thinking about Desirée Gardell.

People had such damned funny motives for the things they did, thought Callaghan. Especially women. *Sometimes* women were much

more logical than men. If they were not they were difficult to analyse –
especially women who believed in their intuition or who were inclined
to be impulsive like Desirée.

She was much too beautiful to be logical. Beautiful women seldom
were. They started off by being beautiful, by knowing the fact, by expecting
rather nice things to happen to them. Only plain women realised that
life was a matter of reasoning, that if you hadn't got looks you'd got to
develop something else.

Desirée was impulsive to a degree. Callaghan was certain of that.
She had telephoned through to the office desiring to see him urgently.
She had wanted to see him to find out if he had seen the Admiral; to
find out what the Admiral had said; and, more importantly, to find out
if the Insurance Company would pay the claim quickly. She had probably asked Manon to see Callaghan and, not hearing from her that she
had seen him, had taken matters into her own hands. Then afterwards,
she *had* seen Manon; had been told by her that 'no change' was to be
expected from Callaghan. Then immediately, and on impulse, late at
night, she had called through to Vane, the lawyer, to ask him about the
insurance, had heard that Callaghan was there, had instructed Vane to
tell him nothing. Why? Obviously because she had now – just as impul-
sively – agreed to consider Callaghan as an enemy. Why?

He shrugged, knocked the ash off his cigarette, got out of the car and
walked slowly across Berkeley Square.

He went up in the lift, went straight up to his apartment floor,
unlocked the door and went in. Nikolls was sitting in front of the fire in
the sitting-room, smoking a cigarette. Callaghan looked at the sideboard.
The door was slightly open. He said:

'Help yourself to a drink any time you want to, Windy.'

Nikoll's eyes followed the direction of Callaghan's glance.

He said: 'I thought I shut that goddam door.'

Callaghan said: 'The trouble with you is you're careless over small
things. You can give *me* one anyway.'

Nikolls said: '*I'll* have another one too. I hate to see a guy drinkin'
alone.'

Callaghan said: 'That's nice of you, Windy.'

Nikolls got up, produced the bottle and two glasses. As he poured
the drinks, he said:

'Is Desiray as good as her name?'

Callaghan nodded. He sat down in the big armchair by the fire. Nikolls
carried the glass over to him. He said:

'How come?'

Callaghan said: 'Desirée is beautiful and she has allure. She's got that *something* – you know what I mean, Windy?'

Nikolls said: 'You're tellin' me – that little thing I've been chasin' all my life. It's marvellous, ain't it? It's got nothin' to do with looks or breedin' or anything else. A dame's either got it or she hasn't. That reminds me of a nice piece of homework I knew way up at Hotsprings. This baby . . .'

Callaghan said: 'I know. That's the one who was married to five travelling salesmen at the same time.'

Nikolls sighed.

'What the hell!' he said. 'One of these fine days I'm gonna produce a *new* one, and then somebody is goin' to die. So this Desiray dame is the berries, is she?'

Callaghan said: 'As you say, she's the berries! She's very beautiful. She has allure. She's intelligent.'

Nikolls said: 'An' that means trouble. All the trouble in the world is caused by beautiful dames. Shakespeare or some guy said something like that, didn't he?'

'Yes,' said Callaghan, 'if not in those actual words.'

Nikolls drank some whisky. He said:

'So what?'

Callaghan said: 'The Globe & Associated are going to stall payment of the claim – not for *very* long, because Phelps, the Managing Director, doesn't like the idea. It's bad business for an Insurance Company to hold up a claim too long, but they're entitled to wait a little while. They're entitled to know where the forty-five thousand pounds now payable by them is going. Normally, they wouldn't be, but now there's a suggestion of murder they're within their rights. Phelps said that anyway they'd hold it up for a week or two. Well, that suits us . . .'

Nikolls asked: 'Why does it suit us?'

Callaghan said: 'I saw Gringall this morning. I told him what I was going to suggest to the Globe & Associated. He didn't mind. Gringall knows that Desirée Gardell is the person who is going to get that forty-five thousand pounds. See?'

Nikolls said: 'No, I don't. Maybe I'm dumb to-night.'

Callaghan smiled.

'Gringall is going to think that we're after Desirée Gardell as a client; that we'll play the old game of working for two sides at once – of representing the Insurance Company and the Gardell family at the same time. In other words, we're either going to try and stop the Insurance

Company paying altogether, in which case we've got to produce a first-class reason, or we've got to inform the Insurance Company that they're perfectly in order in paying the claim, in which case we've got to be in a position to assure them that the person receiving the forty-five thousand pounds definitely had nothing whatever to do with the murder of Admiral Gardell.'

Nikolls said: 'I still don't get it. Are you suggesting that this Desiray baby knocked off the Admiral for the Insurance dough?'

Callaghan grinned at him.

'I'm not suggesting anything of the sort,' he said. 'All I'm suggesting is that the police say that the Admiral was murdered, and the Insurance Company are in order in stalling for a little time so as to be certain that they're within their legal rights in paying. I'm not making accusations against any one – certainly not against Desirée. Anyhow, *she* couldn't murder anybody.'

'No?' said Nikolls. 'That's what *you* think. You never know with dames. You never know what they're thinking an' what they're gonna do next.' He finished his whisky, poured out another. He went on: 'I knew some baby in the Ozark Mountains. She was the quietest, kindest, cutest sorta frail I ever come across. One night she was sittin' on my knee sorta bitin' my ear an' doin' a lot of lovin' stuff, when all of a sudden she says: "Excuse me. Windy . . ." Well, she went off, and when she came back after a coupla minutes she stuck a meat skewer four inches in my leg. An' why? Just because while she was sittin' on my knee she found a hair on my collar. An' she recognised this hair as belongin' to the ash blonde on the next form. I tell you, you never know nothin' about a dame until you marry her, an' then you don't *want* to know nothin' about her.'

Callaghan said: 'That's as may be. But Gringall will wait to see what the Insurance Company do about paying that claim. He won't do a thing until he knows how *we're* going to play this.'

Nikolls grinned.

'Well, you've talked the Insurance Company into it,' he said. His grin became broader. 'Do you mean to say you're havin' trouble with Desiray?' he asked.

Callaghan smiled.

'At the moment, yes,' he said. 'She doesn't like Callaghan Investigations a lot.'

Nikolls said: 'What is that dame playin' at?'

Callaghan said: 'I'd like to know. I'd like to know what she and Manon are playing at. Listen . . . the Admiral decides to commit suicide. He tells Desirée. Desirée tells Manon. Both these girls – one his daughter, one his niece – knows exactly what's in his mind. They know they can't stop him, because I take it that the Admiral was one of these irascible, tough-minded, stubborn old boys who, when they made up their mind to do something, go through with it, and *nothing* stops them. Also he was a sick man and had nothing particularly to live for.

'The two girls had become used to the idea of hearing that one day he'd done it. That's all right. I can understand that, but I can't understand what they're playing at *now*. Quite obviously, Manon got into touch with me for the purpose of finding out what sort of person I was, and, apparently,' Callaghan went on, 'I didn't come up to requirements.'

'I get it,' said Nikolls. 'I reckon these two babies are very deep.'

Callaghan said: 'I think so too.'

Nikolls stretched. He said:

'Well, it looks as if there ain't much to be done at the moment. What do we do – stick around and wait for somethin' to happen?'

Callaghan said: 'No . . . we might even try and *make* something happen.' He lit a cigarette, inhaled deeply. After a minute he said:

'There's another thing, Windy. I went to see Starata's strawberry blonde last night. By the way, what's her name?'

'She calls herself Stephanie Duval,' said Nikolls. He grinned. 'That's a helluva name.' He yawned. 'Look, Slim,' he went on. 'What's the good of you worrying about gettin' after Starata just because he pushed you around a bit. That job's finished because the Insurance Company won't pay on the warehouse claim, an' the cops will get after Nicky. Why worry your head about that guy? It looks to me like you're gonna have enough trouble with this Gardell business.'

Callaghan said: 'Perhaps I am. But I'm not laying off Starata. I owe him a lot and he's going to get it – all of it!'

'O.K.,' said Nikolls. 'You're the boss. Only it seems a helluva waste of time to keep on after that punk when there's bigger fish waitin' to be cooked.' He helped himself to a cigarette. 'An' how did you like little Stephanie?' he asked. 'What did *she* try an' do to you?'

Callaghan said: 'She didn't do anything. The furniture was being taken away by a firm called Leberk & Son, 264 Mile End, E. You get down to those people and find out where they moved that furniture to. You'll probably find it's gone to a store, and you'll probably find that the bill's being paid by the blonde lady. Nicky Starata's too wise to let anybody know where he's going to be. Use a little palm oil and find out where she's living.'

Nikolls said: 'O.K. You're sorta sore at Starata, aren't you? I suppose you want to find him so that you can push *him* around?'

Callaghan said: 'You never know. Well, good-night, Windy.'

Nikolls said: 'Good-night.'

He went out.

Callaghan smoked silently for some minutes. The he got up, threw his cigarette stub into the fire, lit a fresh one. He stood looking down into the flames for quite a minute. Then he went over to the writing-table; began to write a letter. He wrote:

Dear Manon Gardell,

I saw your cousin Desirée this evening, and did not, I am afraid, make too good an impression on her. Apparently she does not at the moment require my services. I'm writing to you because, candidly, I'm a little bit worried about the Insurance claim in regard to your late uncle.

This afternoon the Globe & Associated, the Insurance Company concerned, have asked me to represent them. I am afraid they're going to take quite a little time before they consider paying that claim, that is if they do eventually decide to pay it.

I went down to Chipley Grange to see Miss Gardell because I wanted to advise her as to the best course she could take in order to smooth out matters with the Insurance Company, but her attitude was not at all helpful.

I am writing to you, therefore, because you asked me to come and see you if anything turned up. If you'll ring through to my office and make an appointment, I'll come down to The Cottage. Candidly, I think someone ought to advise Desirée for her own good.

Sincerely yours,

S. Callaghan.

He folded the letter, slipped it into an envelope, addressed it to Miss Manon Gardell, The Cottage, Valeston, Sussex. He stamped the letter.

He went to the sideboard, poured himself another drink, carried it to the fireplace, stood looking at the amber liquid in the glass. The telephone jangled. Callaghan looked at the instrument for a moment, walked slowly over, picked up the receiver. A voice said:

'Is that Callaghan Investigations?'

Callaghan grinned. It was the strawberry blonde.

He said: 'Hallo, honey! So you've decided to talk?'

She said: 'I've decided nothing.'

'All right,' said Callaghan. 'You've decided nothing. You've just rung up to ask me how I am.'

'Look, you don't have to be tough all the time! Why don't you give a girl a break sometimes?'

Callaghan said: 'You can have a break any time you like. Listen, Stephanie . . . You don't sound so good to me. You sound depressed.'

She said: 'You're telling me. I feel as if I was walking over my own grave.'

Callaghan said: 'I know a nice little place near here where they still have a bottle of champagne and where the atmosphere's conducive to rest. Why don't you come along and get cheered up a little?'

She said: 'I might at that.'

Callaghan asked: 'Where are you at the moment?'

'I'm in a call-box at Piccadilly Circus Underground.'

Callaghan grinned.

'Still keeping your address a secret, hey, Stephanie?' he said. 'Never mind. I'll pick you up in ten minutes.'

She said: 'All right. I'll be waiting. But if you think I'm going to talk you've made a big mistake.'

Callaghan said: 'I don't think anything. I'll be seeing you.'

He hung up. He picked up the envelope addressed to Manon Gardell, took out the letter he had written her, read it slowly. He thought it was all right. He thought that Manon might fell for the line.

He stood in front of the desk, the letter in his hand, thinking about Manon and Desirée. He wondered if these two had ever disliked each other, if they had ever been jealous of each other. They were both beautiful, and it would be amazing if they had never suffered from a little mutual dislike. Callaghan wondered if it would be possible to drive a wedge between the two of them, to create a situation in which they would begin, actively, to become a little bored with each other. There was nothing like a spot of trouble, he thought, to make a woman talk. And if there was something on between Desirée and Manon . . . If there was some scheme . . .

Callaghan began to smile. He lit a fresh cigarette, went to the telephone. He dialled a Holborn number. He said:

'Is that Stevens? This is Callaghan. Listen . . . I'm going to take a woman – a good-looking strawberry blonde – to the Green Canary Club. It's just off Bruton Street. When we leave there she'll take a cab and go off on her own. You'd better have that two-seater of yours there. Go after her cab and tail her till she goes home. Directly you've got the address, ring through to Wilkie, the night porter in Berkeley Square, and tell him where it is. Have you got that?'

Stevens said he'd got it.

II

The Green Canary was one of those places. It was one of those places which occasionally break into the headlines with a sensational theft, a Mayfair case, a drug-peddling charge, or a food-hoarding prosecution. It was run by one Enrico Galdina – a young man with artistic leanings and of indeterminate sex. Some quite nice people went there – they didn't know why – and some very nasty people who were always perfectly certain of their reasons for going there. Believe it or not, there are lots of places like this in London even now, but they don't advertise. They don't have to.

The club occupied a well-furnished ground floor and basement. It was comfortable, and whilst you were sober the liquor was good. When you were not, it became very bad. There was a subdued orchestra of four, who sat on a small raised gold platform at one end of the room, and whose expressions belied the hot music they produced. They disliked Galdina, the club, it patrons, and each other. They looked like four men to whom life was almost redundant.

Callaghan and the strawberry blonde sat at a table in the corner farthest away from the band.

Callaghan said: 'Do you know it's the first time I've ever seen a *real* strawberry blonde.'

Stephanie got as near to a simper as she could. She was dressed for a killing. She wore a rather severe black frock with a very good line that was perhaps just a little too tight. A real pearl necklace was her only ornament. She relied mainly on her face, figure and intelligence. She was right. Usually those assets were all she needed.

She said seriously: 'I didn't expect to be talking to you so soon. As a matter of fact I wasn't so pleased with you the last time I saw you, but I've been thinking . . .'

Callaghan said: 'You've been thinking that there was quite a lot of sense in what I suggested?'

She nodded. She said:

'It's not only that.'

Callaghan raised one eyebrow.

'No . . . ? What else?'

She sighed. She picked up her glass of whisky and soda and looked at it. She said:

'I'm going to give you a big laugh. Well, if you want to laugh, the joke's on me. I suppose you think I'm pretty tough?'

Callaghan shrugged his shoulders.

'I haven't thought about it,' he said. 'But when I come to think about it, any woman who strings around with Nicky Starata has *got* to be tough.'

She nodded.

'I suppose that's right,' she said. 'Let's say that I *used* to be tough.'

Callaghan said: 'All right. You *used* to be tough.'

She went on: 'When I saw you last night I thought I didn't like you a bit. I thought you were trying to pull a fast one. But you put one or two ideas into my head. Since then I've done some quiet thinking on my own. I thought I'd like a talk with you; first of all because I think there's just an odd *chance* you might be right.'

Callaghan asked: 'What's the second reason?'

She said: 'Don't laugh, but . . . I'm crazy about you . . .'

Callaghan said: 'You don't say!' He signalled a tired-eyed waiter. He ordered two large whiskies and sodas He said: 'That calls for another drink. When a women like *you* tells a man like *me* she's crazy about him there just has to be another drink.' He grinned at her. 'Why are you crazy about me?' he asked.

She smiled. He realised suddenly that she was a *very* pretty woman. She said:

'I'll tell you. I've spent most of my life kicking around with pretty cheap people; I suppose Starata was an aristocrat compared to most of them. There's something about you I go for. You're tough, but underneath there's a streak of something I like. But that's not my main reason.'

Callaghan said: 'What's your main reason?'

She said: 'My main reason is that you wouldn't let anybody down. If you had a girl you'd look after her. She'd be safe enough.'

Callaghan asked: 'Is this an offer?'

She looked at him. Her eyes were very soft.

'Why not?' she asked.

He said: 'Let's shelve that part of the proposition for a minute.' He grinned at her. 'So you're wise to the fact that Nicky is leading you up the garden path?'

She said: 'I'm going to tell you something. I was never awfully stuck on Nicky. Oh, he's all right in his way. Let's say he's not my type. The thing is that I've got an idea that what you said about another woman is right, and I'm not the sort of girl who shares a man.'

Callaghan said: 'So you've decided to talk to me. You've decided to talk to me for two reasons – one that you think Nicky is giving you what is commonly called the run-around, and two because you're crazy about me. Is that it?'

She said: 'Yes.' She put her elbows on the table and leaned towards Callaghan. She said: 'When I said I was crazy about you that was only half the truth. I've never been so completely nutty about any man in my life. Has any woman ever told you that you've got something?'

'You don't say?' Callaghan looked thoughtful for a moment. 'So *that's* what they've been after . . . But let's come back to Nicky. What's the idea?'

'The idea is this,' she said. 'You're interested in Nicky, aren't you?'

Callaghan said: 'I'm interested in anybody who thinks they can push me around. I'm particularly interested in Nicky.'

She said: 'Well, why shouldn't you be? I think he's on the bad end of the stick.'

Callaghan said: 'I don't think about it – I know. *I* told you that.'

She nodded.

'He's made a mess of it this time,' said Callaghan. 'He's going to drop a whole hatful of money over that warehouse claim. He knows the Insurance Company won't pay. The best he can hope for is to lie low and take a chance that the police won't get their hooks on him.'

Callaghan drew his cigarette smoke down into his lungs. He was watching her. He was thinking that Stephanie might be *very* attractive if she wanted to be. He said:

'What's your real name, Stephanie?'

'My name's Rose,' she said. 'And my second name's Jones. I think it's a terrible combination, and I don't think I look like it.'

Callaghan nodded.

'You certainly don't,' he said. 'You look much more like Stephanie Duval.'

She said: 'I know that. That's why I picked that name.'

Callaghan said: 'So you're coming on to my side. You're going to work for me?'

'Why not?' she asked. 'Starata's washed up. I have to think of my future. I like to be on the side of the one that's going to pull it off.'

Callaghan said: 'Of course. Everybody likes to be on the side of the one who's going to pull it off. But when I saw you last you thought Starata was going to pull it off. What's made you change your opinion so suddenly. I suppose it was the idea of the other woman . . . ?'

'That's right,' she said. 'It was the *idea* of the other woman. I'd never thought there was any one else, and when you'd gone I began to think about it. I remember what you said about Nicky sticking to a woman for two or three months . . . I began to think about little things he'd said. Suddenly I was certain that you were right. I realised that just because all this business had happened with that warehouse business going wrong, there was no reason for Nicky to want to get rid of me so suddenly.'

'Right,' said Callaghan. 'You'd think that with things beginning to go wrong, Nicky would need you about the place more than ever. As it was, he simply used the warehouse job as an excuse to ditch you.'

She said: 'And there was something else. You said that you knew who the woman was. You said that you'd tell me.'

'Did I?' asked Callaghan. He changed the subject quickly. 'There was no need for Nicky to get so frightened,' he said. 'That boy scares too quickly. If he'd had any sense he would have realised that once the Insurance people knew that they hadn't to pay that warehouse claim, they wouldn't give a damn about chasing *him*. They'd leave it to the police, and the police are pretty busy these days. He might have got away with it. He might easily get away with it now.'

She smiled at him.

'You're telling me,' she said. 'Are you trying to suggest that he'll get away with it with you on his tail?'

He shrugged.

'I've something else to do besides chase after Nicky,' he said. 'Naturally I was annoyed when he started to get rough. But I'm on a big case just now with lots of money hanging on to it, and provided he behaves himself and doesn't try to pull anything else he might still be all right.'

She said: 'Like hell . . . If I know anything of you, you'll never leave Nicky until you've got him where you want him. *I* shouldn't like to do what Nicky did to you. I'd be scared for the rest of my life.'

Callaghan drew on his cigarette.

'So he told you about it?' he asked.

She nodded.

'That's right,' she said. 'He told me about it.' She looked at him along her nose. She said: 'I wouldn't like to be Nicky. You'll get him all right. You'll pull it off.'

'So you said before,' said Callaghan. 'So I'm going to pull it off, am I?'

'Aren't you?' she asked. 'I've been hearing things about you. They tell me you *always* pull it off one way or another.'

Callaghan said: 'I don't do so badly – sometimes.'

She put her hand over his. It was soft and white. She had long artistic fingers. Her nails were well manicured.

She said: 'Look . . . I don't expect you to believe everything that I say. Why should you? But you will. You will when you know me a little bit better. When you know that all I want is to feel that you have a good opinion of me. You tell me what I can do for you and I'll show you that I mean business.'

Callaghan said: 'And how much does that cost?'

She said: 'Well, I suppose you're entitled to say that. Now you can be surprised when I say – nothing!'

Callaghan grinned. He said: 'I *am* surprised.'

'I've got a little money,' she went on, enough to get by on. I'm not out to make money, but I've made up my mind that I'm going to make you think well of me.'

Callaghan said: 'I think a lot of you *now*, Stephanie. After all, you're *here*. You're doing your best.'

She said: 'Let's get down to hard tacks. You want to know where Nicky Starata is. Well, I don't know. But I think I can find out in two or three days' time.'

Callaghan asked: 'He'll be getting in touch with you?'

She shook her head.

'No,' she said. 'Nicky's not one to take any chances. But he'll *have* to see me. If I know anything of Nicky, within a week he'll arrange that somehow or other he and I meet. But he'll do it so that even I don't know where he's hanging out.'

Callaghan said: 'Well, if you meet him it'll be useful.'

'I think, if I play Nicky the right way, I might even find out where he's staying, and if there's anything else you want to know I might find that out too – see?'

Callaghan said: 'I see. This is fine, Stephanie. I think you and I can help each other.' He blew a smoke ring, watched it sail up into the air. He went on: 'I haven't quite decided how I want to play Nicky yet. But I've two or three ideas. I shall know something definite within two or three days, so I'm going to suggest that you ring me up the day after to-morrow. I'll make an appointment. We'll meet. I'll tell you what you can do. How's that?'

She said: 'That's wonderful. I'm getting a kick out of this.'

Callaghan said: 'So am I.' He signalled a waiter, ordered more drinks.

III

It was half-past twelve. Stephanie Duval and Callaghan stood in the hallway to the Green Canary Club. He said:

'I'd like to see you home, Steve, but if you don't mind I won't. I've a lot of work to do to-night.'

She said: 'Don't you worry. Anyway, do you think I'm fool enough to go back with you in the cab. If Nicky guessed I had anything to do with you he'd cut my throat.'

Callaghan nodded.

'That's what I was afraid of,' he said. 'I didn't like to put it that way.'

She said: 'I'm going now. I'll find a cab for myself. You follow in a few minutes. I'll ring you the day after to-morrow about seven o'clock in the evening. So long, Slim.'

She put her hand on his arm. She walked quickly out of the club. Callaghan watched her. He stood there leaning up against an ornamental pillar, smoking a cigarette. He waited for ten minutes. Then he got his hat, began to walk towards Berkeley Square.

IV

Wilkie was leaning against his glass office, smoking. As Callaghan came through the black-out curtain, he said:

'Oh, Mr. Callaghan . . . there was a phone call for you about two minutes ago – one of your boys – Stevens. He said the address was 22 Chapel Street, Knightsbridge.'

Callaghan grinned. He said:

'Thanks, Wilkie.'

He went back through the doorway. He walked across the square, found a solitary cab crawling towards Piccadilly. He said to the driver:

'Chapel Street, Knightsbridge. Drive like the devil – chance the traffic lights. Stop this end of the street. Get there in three minutes and there's a pound for you.'

Inside the cab he lit a cigarette. He was feeling almost happy. He paid off the cab at the Knightsbridge end of Chapel Street.

He walked quickly down the street, stood in the darkened doorway next to the entrance of No. 22. Ten minutes went by; then Callaghan heard the door open. In the half darkness he could see a short figure of a man as he descended the two steps on to the pavement. Callaghan stepped up behind him. He said:

'Hallo, Leon.'

Leon spun round. Callaghan thought his face was thin and drawn like a ferret's. He said:

'It's nice seeing you.'

Leon began to grin. Callaghan brought up his right arm quickly. He hit Leon between the eyes. Leon's knees crumpled; he subsided on the pavement. Callaghan lit a cigarette. After a minute or two he stirred the recumbent figure with his foot. Leon moved. Callaghan reached down, yanked him to his feet.

He said: 'You and I are going to have a little talk. You're going to like it. Don't let me have any trouble with you. If you annoy me I'm going to hurt you. Understand?'

Leon said nothing. He turned his head away from Callaghan. He brought up his knee suddenly. Callaghan was waiting for that. He side-stepped expertly. He raised his arm and, using his fist almost like a sledge-hammer, he hit Leon on the side of the jaw. Leon went down again.

Callaghan stooped, picked him up, held him against the railings of the house next to No. 22. He held Leon with his left hand; with his right he began to slap him across the face hard. Leon tried another kick, but he was too slow. He was tiring. Callaghan hit him in the mouth. Then he recommenced the slapping process. After two or three minutes he stopped. He said:

'Well, are you going to talk?'

Leon said he was. His face was not an attractive sight. He mumbled: 'Let's get out of here. I'll talk when I've had a drink.'

Callaghan said: 'You'd be surprised!' He smacked Leon across the face again. He said: 'I don't want to say much to you and I don't want to hear much from you. I just want two things. You'll say 'em now, and like it! Understand?'

Leon said he understood.

CHAPTER SIX
INVITATION TO SUPPER

I

MANON sat at an antique oak desk in front of the sitting-room window at her cottage. She was looking out of the window, over the little lawn bounded by the white fence, towards the orchard. On the left of the orchard, the country sloped gently upwards towards the Valeston woods.

The evening sun casting its final rays through the window caressed her blonde tresses. She did not appreciate the fact. Manon was not good-tempered. Life, she thought, could be quite lousy.

She yawned. Half-way through the yawn she made an attempt to stifle it with slender white fingers. Her eyes, cool and demure, rested on Callaghan's letter, which lay on the oak writing-desk at which she sat.

She thought: This Callaghan is a damned nuisance. He's made up his mind he's going to get something out of this business, and if I know anything of men, he'll get it. He could be unpleasant, I think. She folded her hands underneath her chin, looked out of the window.

Manon, who was not at all stupid where the male sex was concerned, decided that *really* she rather liked Callaghan. She thought he might be very amusing. She liked him too because he had a strong personality. He knew exactly what he wanted – just how he was going to get it.

She wondered why she thought that she *could* like Callaghan . . . Possibly because he was inclined to be a little insolent and because he hadn't taken her very seriously. So many members of the male sex *had* taken Manon seriously that it was almost a nice change.

And he could be a nuisance. Manon thought that Callaghan would be *very* tenacious – if he wanted to be; that he would be very hard to shake off. She wondered if one ought to try and play Callaghan a little or whether it would be better to get rid of him somehow.

She read the letter again. It was obvious to her that it wouldn't be easy to get rid of Callaghan. She wondered if she'd been stupid in getting in touch with him originally. In any event, she thought, Desirée had not been fearfully wise in getting his back up, which was obviously what she had done.

She wondered if the Globe & Associated would, in any event, have employed Callaghan to investigate the claim, or whether he had arranged that he should be so employed. If he had, Manon thought she would like to know what the *quid pro quo* was, what advantage the Company expected to get out of his employment.

There could only be one advantage, and that would be that they would not have to pay. Yet here was Callaghan representing the Company, writing to her suggesting that someone ought to 'advise Desirée for her own good' in order to 'smooth out matters with the Insurance Company.' So it *was* possible to smooth out matters with the Insurance Company. There was no situation at the moment in which the Company had suggested it definitely would *not* pay.

Callaghan was cleverly suggesting – practically telling her – that *he* had created the situation with the Insurance Company, that it could be smoothed out, and in order that that process could obtain he, Callaghan, must be employed. She shrugged her shoulders.

She got up, walked over to the old-fashioned fireplace, stood in front of it, her hands behind her back, regarding the cool pleasant interior of The Cottage sitting-room; subconsciously admired the passing sunlight reflecting on the chintzes.

The solution was, she thought, to employ Callaghan. She took a cigarette from the silver box on the mantelpiece. Suddenly she smiled. There might of course be another angle on Callaghan's interest – herself. Why not? Manon knew she was very attractive. Directly she had seen the private detective she had realised that he was not an unattractive man, and that therefore he was an experienced man. Many women, thought Manon, would fell very easily for Callaghan, so it would not be ridiculous to think that Callaghan would expect other women to fall for him. Why not herself? Would *that* be Callaghan's idea?

She regarded the end of her cigarette critically. Then she looked in the mirror on the wall opposite. You're not a bad-looking girl, Manon, she thought. The question is whether you've got sufficient brains for Mr. Callaghan. Somehow I think you have. Anyway, we'll see!

She was wearing a green velvet house-coat. It was a long coat, and her small feet, in green crêpe-de-chine slippers, peeped out attractively. Manon looked at them appreciatively. She liked nice clothes; she liked everything that was attractive and easy and comfortable. And, in order to have those things, one had to work very hard – to try all sorts of processes.

She shrugged. Life could be very difficult . . . She moved slowly across the room towards the telephone. When Desirée came on the line she said:

'Desirée . . . how are you, darling? I'm afraid Mr. Callaghan is being rather difficult.'

Desirée asked: 'Why?'

Manon said: 'Well, he's written me a letter. He says he saw you yesterday evening. He says he doesn't think he made a good impression on you. He seems to think you don't require his services. He says he's worried about the insurance claim.'

'Is he?' said Desirée. 'Manon, dear, why should he worry? I don't think I like Mr. Callaghan. I don't like his attitude or the way he talks. I like nothing about him, and I suppose, having tried to get me to use his services, he's decided to try his blandishments on you.'

Manon said: 'You *are* angry with him, aren't you, darling? And has he any blandishments? *I* didn't think he was a fearfully attractive person either. On the other hand, of course, he's a fearfully well-known investigator, and all the first-class Insurance Companies employ him . . .'

'You seem to know an awful lot about him,' said Desirée.

Manon said: 'Well . . . I talked to Mr. Vane. Darling, you *do* want that money paid quickly, don't you?'

'Yes,' said Desirée. 'You know that perfectly well, Manon. But I don't want anything to do with Mr. Callaghan. I don't see what the claim has to do with him.'

Manon said: 'But now apparently he's representing the Insurance Company. I think you *ought* to have him on our side, don't you? It seems as if he might make things a little difficult.'

Desirée said: 'How can he? Mr. Vane tells me that the claim is in order. He tells me that it is not unusual for an Insurance Company to take a little time to settle a claim. And he agrees with me about something else too, I think.'

Manon said: 'What's the something else?'

'I think this Callaghan man is a bluffer,' said Desirée. 'I think he's annoyed because he thought originally that I was going to employ him. Now that he knows that I don't require his services, he's trying to make things difficult.'

Manon said: 'I think you're right, dearest; but don't you think it would be more clever if you got this Callaghan on your side? Why don't you see him? Why don't you ask his advice? Men love having their advice asked. It makes them feel so strong. He's the sort of man who wouldn't be awfully attracted by self-reliant women, don't you think?'

Desirée said: 'I haven't thought about the sort of women who would attract him . . .'

Manon said: 'Haven't you, darling? *I* have. I think you can learn an awful lot about a man by trying to decide just what sort of woman he'd fall for. And he's got a *very* decided jaw. I think he'd be *very* selective about women.'

'Do you?' asked Desirée. 'Well . . . I don't care whether he's selective or not. What else does he say in the letter?'

Manon said: 'He said that he went to Chipley to see you, that he wanted to advise you as to the best course to take in order to smooth things out with the Company. He says your attitude wasn't helpful.'

Desirée said: 'I didn't intend my attitude to be helpful. Mr. Callaghan bores me. I don't think he can do anything to help. I think he's quite likely to do some things that would hinder. Besides, I don't see why we should pay him in order to get the money from the Insurance Company to which we're quite obviously legally entitled.'

Manon said: 'Darling, are you *quite* sure you're not allowing your dislike for this Callaghan person to interfere a little with your usual intelligence?'

There was a pause; then Desirée said:

'That's possible, Manon. But he offended me. I didn't like the way he spoke.'

Manon smiled.

'I know,' she said. 'When one feels like that about a man it is rather difficult, isn't it?'

Desirée said: 'What's difficult?'

Manon said: 'One isn't quite certain whether one isn't a little bit attracted, is one, darling?'

Desirée said: 'I certainly am *not*.' There was a pause. Then:

'Well, dearest,' said Manon, 'if you've made up your mind, of course there's nothing else to be done.'

Desirée said, a little impatiently: 'I haven't made up my mind about anything. Tell me, does this paragon suggest anything else in his letter?'

Manon said: 'Darling, you're not angry or anything because he wrote to *me*, are you?'

'I wish you wouldn't be ridiculous, Manon.'

'I'm sorry,' said her cousin meekly. 'I didn't mean to annoy you, Desirée. But I think you ought to know that he did suggest that he might come and see me. Anyhow, if he's got anything to suggest it won't do any harm if I pass it on, will it?'

Desirée said: 'No. If you'd like to see him, there isn't any reason why you shouldn't, Manon, is there?'

Manon said: 'Darling, I didn't say I wanted to see him. I said I thought it might be a good thing to do, for all our sakes.'

Desirée said: 'Very well. You do as you think best, Manon. Let me know what happens.'

'I will,' said Manon. 'I'll let you know. So long, darling.'

She hung up. She went back to her desk, stood there looking over it out of the window. After a minute she helped herself to another cigarette from the box, lit it slowly.

She thought: To hell with Mr. Callaghan!

Then she sat down at her desk, began to write him a letter.

II

Leon looked out of the window of his second-floor flat overlooking a Bayswater garden. In front of him, on the window-ledge, was an ash-tray. In it were the stubs of some twenty-five cigarettes, by which it will be gathered that he had been indulging in concentrated thought. He was thinking about Callaghan.

It would not be desirable to state exactly what Leon thought about Callaghan. The processes of the thinker's mind – never particularly beautiful – were on this occasion extended into the uttermost depths of obscenity. But, in the main, Leon was concerned with the fact that, so far as he was concerned, Callaghan was definitely dangerous.

Leon had had his finger in too many mysterious pies in the West End for the last decade not to know that the methods, the techniques, used by Messrs. Callaghan Investigations were as unusual as they were able. He had realised for a long time that Insurance claim rackets had always worked unsuccessfully as regards Companies which employed Callaghan as Investigator.

Leon had no use for failure. It seemed to him that this time Starata had asked for it and got it. On the other hand, Nicky was no mug. He had gotten himself out of a great many difficult situations; had not arrived at his present position of power and affluence without having something between his ears.

Leon stubbed out his twenty-sixth cigarette. Who was going to win the next round – Starata or Callaghan? It was sticking out a foot that the Sphere & International were not going to worry particularly about Nicky Starata now that they had not to pay the warehouse claim. If anybody was going to worry about Nicky, it would be the police. But the police were very busy these days. What with one thing and another – the war and all the other odd businesses that obtained – they had their hands full. There was quite a chance, thought Leon, that Starata would get away with it.

He sighed. And *if* Starata got away with it, and if Starata discovered that he, Leon, had been playing with Callaghan, it wouldn't be so good. On the other hand, it wouldn't be so good if he continued to play along with Starata and had Callaghan on his tail.

He stood looking out of the window with unseeing eyes. After a while he took a half-crown from his pocket. He spun it. While the coin was in the air, he said: 'Heads it's that bastard . . . tails it's Nicky.'

It came down heads.

So it was to be Callaghan. Leon heaved a sigh of relief. Now that fate, in the shape of a spun coin, had decided the matter, he realised that he felt considerably safer in being on Callaghan's side. In any event, Nicky was washed up. He'd had a good run and it was time that someone caught up with him.

He sighed again; fingered his swollen jaw gingerly. Perhaps he had been wise – even clever. At any rate there was no reason why Nicky should ever know that he, Leon, had spilled the beans; had told Callaghan where Nicky was to be found.

He wondered what else Callaghan would want. He hoped not too much. It might be as dangerous playing along with Callaghan as it had been with Nicky.

And the devil of it was that there was no pay-off with Callaghan. The best you could expect was a poke in the eye.

Leon lit a cigarette. He sat down in an overstuffed arm-chair and regarded the wallpaper morosely.

He began to think about Stephanie Duval. Stephanie had been a bloody fool, thought Leon. She had kidded herself that she could pull a fast one on Callaghan. And she would not know that she had not succeeded. Stephanie, who thought she was going to take Callaghan for a walk up the garden, stood a damned good chance of taking the mug's ride herself.

He shrugged his shoulders. To hell with it, he thought.

He tried to amuse himself by thinking just what he would *like* to do to Callaghan.

III

Callaghan and Nikolls sat on high stools at the ornate bar in The Black Lounge Club – on the first floor in Albemarle Street – drinking whisky.

Nikolls said: 'I found the guy who drove the van for Leberk & Co. They took practically all the stuff away from Chapel Street. But they left some of it.'

Callaghan said: 'You bet they did. That move was eyewash. Stephanie's still living there. I suppose they left the top two rooms furnished. Not a bad idea.'

Nikolls lit a cigarette. He flipped the dead match into an ashtray on a nearby table.

'Stephanie called me last night,' said Callaghan. 'I had a long talk with her.'

Nikolls said: 'Say, what the hell do you know about women after that . . . ?'

'You never know anything about women,' said Callaghan. 'You know just what they want you to know at any particular moment. All the rest is guessing.'

'Yeah,' said Nikolls gloomily. 'Maybe you're right.'

Callaghan finished his drink. He signalled to the hennaed siren in the five-inch heels at the other end of the bar. He ordered a large bacardi.

Nikolls said: 'I never saw a guy drink bacardi on top of whisky like you do. Didn't they tell you it takes the lining off a guy's stomach?'

'It hasn't taken the lining off my stomach,' said Callaghan.

'It might've,' said Nikolls. 'Maybe you wouldn't know. That's a helluva idea, hey? Maybe there's lots of guys walkin' around with no linin's on their stomachs.'

He relapsed into silence for a moment. Then: 'What the hell! Nobody's ever told me why a guy *has* a linin' on his stomach. Maybe it ain't even necessary. If it ain't necessary to have an appendix, why is it necessary to have a linin'? Anyhow, I'm gonna try the same poison.' He ordered a double bacardi. 'To hell with stomach linin's!'

He threw his cigarette away, fumbled in his waistcoat pocket, produced a small cigar.

As he lit it he said: 'What did Stephanie want? Did she try an' pull somethin'? Or is she scared?'

'She's not scared,' said Callaghan. 'It would take a lot to scare Stephanie. She's got a nice nerve – that one.'

'So she was trying to pull somethin'?' said Nikolls. He finished the bacardi at a gulp. 'That drink's gotta helluva kick, ain't it?' he said. 'Me . . . I'm gonna have some more. It makes me feel sorta relaxed.'

Callaghan ordered two more. The henna-haired one said:

'I'm sorry, Mr. Callaghan, but you know how it is about liquor. We only got so much to serve, and we try an' treat all customers the same. You an' your friend have had seven double whiskies an' sodas, four straight bourbons, and two double bacardis. I mean to say that's fair, isn't it?'

Nikolls blew a smoke ring. He watched it sail away and dissolve.

He said: 'What's fair?'

'You havin' all that drink,' said henna-hair. 'I mean to say we know that Mister Callaghan is a good customer here an' we always try an' treat our good customers right. We try to be fair – if you know what I mean.'

Nikolls said: 'I could tell you somethin' that would make you blink, sister, but I won't . . . see? Even if you *have* got the sorta shape that keeps me awake at night.'

'Now, Mister Nikolls,' she said archly. 'I don't know that I'd like to listen to it. What was it?'

Nikolls said: 'I'm an old-fashioned guy. I don't believe in married couples sleepin' in twin beds, do you?'

She said: 'I don't know. I've never slept in a twin bed.'

'That's what I thought,' said Nikolls. 'Just hurry up with those drinks, Gorgeous.'

She poured out the drinks. She said:

'You always say such funny things, Mister Nikolls. I never know what you're gettin' at.'

Nikolls said: 'I'm whimsical. That's what it is. I'm just a great big-hearted boy. An' if you wanta know more about me just call me some evenin' around nine o'clock.'

Henna-hair bridled. 'You are a one, Mr. Nikolls,' she said. She went to the other end of the bar.

Callaghan said: 'Starata put Stephanie in to find out what the next move was going to be. She told me she was scared and wanted to play in with us. She decided she was crazy about me. When she went off, Stevens tailed her back to Chapel Street. I waited round there and Leon came out. He's acting as contact between Stephanie and Starata.'

Nikolls grinned.

'Jeez!' he said. 'What did you do to that chiseller?'

'It didn't take much,' said Callaghan. 'Leon's not particularly tough. He only thinks he is. He talked. I know where Starata is.'

'So what?' said Nikolls. 'What good does that do you?'

Callaghan said: 'I wanted to know where he was. One of these fine days I'm going to get around to Nicky.'

Nikolls grunted. After a moment he said:

'If you want to even up with Nicky, it's easy. All you gotta do is to let the cops know where he is. That baby's goin' to get a stretch that's goin' to keep him plenty occupied for about seven years. So why worry?'

Callaghan said: 'I'm not worrying. I prefer Nicky to be where he is. Let him think he's getting away with it. I like it that way.'

'I got it,' said Nikolls. 'You're gonna give him his head an' let him think he's O.K., an' then you're gonna crack down on him.' He chewed on the end of his cigar. 'What're we gonna do about the other thing?' he asked. 'The Admiral – I mean. Are we goin' to stick around an' wait for somethin' to crack? What about Desiray?'

'I told you,' said Callaghan. 'Desirée doesn't like us a lot. Why should she? She thinks we're cutting in on something that doesn't concern us. Maybe she's right.'

Nikolls looked at him out of the corner of his eye.

'I don't get you over this Admiral thing,' he said. 'You sound sorta sentimental to me. Maybe this Desiray is a smart dish an' is aimin' to give you the big stall until she's got the insurance dough. Me . . . I just don't get this Admiral business at all. Everything smells bad to me.'

Callaghan said: 'What's the matter with it? It's all very simple.'

'Like hell it is,' said Nikolls. 'Look . . . you tell me something. Has anybody got around to decidin' whether the Admiral killed himself, or whether somebody fogged him? That's what I'd like to know.'

'Use your brains, Windy,' said Callaghan. He lit a cigarette, drew the smoke down into his lungs. 'What do you think happened to the Admiral?'

Nikolls said: 'Well the old boy insured his life for a bundle, an' Desiray gets the dough when he dies, an' he wants to be revenged on somebody an' he thinks that if he bumps himself off before the two years are up the Insurance Company won't pay, an' so Desiray won't get the dough. So it looks as if the Admiral wasn't so stuck on Desiray. It looks as if he was tryin' to gyp her out of the jack, don't it?'

'No,' said Callaghan. 'It doesn't.'

'O.K.,' said Nikolls. 'All right. Then it don't. You tell me.'

Callaghan said: 'In the first place the Admiral insured his life so that the money should go to Desirée. Then suddenly he decides that he'll commit suicide and thereby prevent the insurance money being paid to Desirée. He tells her this and she tells Manon. So it seems that Desirée is in the Admirals' confidence, and that doesn't look as if he disliked her, does it?

'Then he decides to come up to town to see me. I believe he wanted to see me to make certain about that suicide clause in the policy. He'd heard that I handled business for Insurance Companies and he thought I was the one to tell him. But he couldn't see me. So he left a note and then went round and saw his lawyer. He looked at the policy, checked on the date, and came to the conclusion that he was too late to nullify the policy by committing suicide. So he called through to Desirée at Chipley and told her that he'd changed his mind, that he hadn't finished with the business. He told her that he was coming up to town the next day to see me. He told her that he was going to see this thing through to the bitter end. Have you got that?'

'I've got it,' said Nikolls. 'An' what does he mean by all that?'

Callaghan said: 'It's obvious that if he had anything against Desirée he wouldn't be talking like that to her. Manon told me that the Admiral originally intended to commit suicide because he wanted to be revenged on someone. Now who would that someone be? Obviously somebody who was going to benefit by the insurance money – *apart from Desirée*; obviously somebody who might expect to get some of the money from Desirée after the Insurance Company had paid.'

Nikolls said: 'Maybe Desiray's got a boy friend an' the old boy thought he'd chisel some of the dough offa Desiray. Maybe the Admiral didn't like the idea.'

Callaghan said: 'Perhaps. But that telephone message puts Desirée in a bad spot. Remember Vane, the lawyer, heard what the Admiral said on the telephone. Well . . . he went back to Chipley and somebody killed him.'

Nikolls said: 'I got it. Desiray knew he was going back. *She* was the *only* one who knew he was going back. So it looks as if Desiray was the one who creased him.' He smoked for a minute; then: 'I reckon Gringall will be on to Desiray,' he said.

Callaghan grinned.

'Gringall doesn't know about the Admiral's telephone message,' he said. 'Therefore he has no more reason to suspect Desirée than any one else. Providing Vane, the lawyer, keeps quiet, who's to know about that telephone message?'

Nikolls said: 'Well . . . *you* know about it.' He considered for a moment. Then he said: 'I reckon Vane will be goddam sorry that he told you about that telephone message. It sorta puts you right on top of the heap, don't it?'

'Yes,' said Callaghan. 'It puts me right on top of the heap.'

'An' I reckon that Desiray is a mug to argue with you,' said Nikolls. 'That baby oughta want to be nice and friendly with you – that is if she's got any sense.'

Callaghan said: 'Maybe she'll get some sense.'

Nikolls nodded. He called to the henna-haired one; ordered two double bacardis. She came from the other end of the bar. She said:

'Look, Mister Nikolls, I always . . .'

'You always try to be fair,' interrupted Nikolls, 'an' we've had a whole lot of liquor, an' you're restricted about what you sell, an' we've had more than our share, an' if you give us another drink Lord Woolton is gonna sail around here in a chariot of flame an' smack you around like it was his birthday. O.K. O.K. *I* know. Consider it all said. An' cash in with two double bacardis before I jump over the bar an' send out a reconnaissance party to find out whether you're still wearin' that cork leg you usta tote around.'

She said: 'Well, I'm damned! That's a lie. I haven't got a cork leg.'

Nikolls said: 'Why should I take your word for a thing like that?' He grinned at her. 'Look, hurry up those drinks, honey-pot,' he said, 'or I'm gonna tell everybody around here that you got a cork leg an' keep your stockin's up with glue.'

She began to pour the drinks. She said:

'Mister Nikolls, you go too far.'

'I know,' said Nikolls. 'But when you first found that out, it was swell, wasn't it, Gorgeous? You remember that night in June, or was it July . . . with the wind sighin' in the trees? Remember, honey? That wonderful night when you said you was prepared to trust me an' give me your all . . .'

Henna-hair gasped. She said:

'Mister Callaghan, he's awful. He says the most terrible things. I never said anything of the sort. Do I look the sort of girl who would say a thing like that?'

Nikolls said: 'Never mind. That's my story, an' I'm gonna stick to it . . . unless you leave that bottle of bacardi on the counter where I can get at it any time I want it, instead of havin' a death struggle with you every time I need a drink.'

She said: 'I think you're impossible, Mister Nikolls. Sometimes I'm not even sure I like you.'

Nikolls said: 'That's just it. You're crazy about me. But you won't even admit it to yourself. Ain't that just how it is, honey?'

Henna-hair smiled. She sighed.

She said: 'It's no good. I can never get the better of him, Mister Callaghan.'

She went away. But she left the bottle.

Nikolls stubbed out his cigar butt, fished out a packet of Lucky Strikes, lit one, gazed ardently at the back view of henna-hair who, at the other end of the bar, was exchanging light badinage with a customer.

Callaghan said: 'That telephone call might mean a lot so far as Desirée is concerned and it might not. If she had an alibi at the time the Admiral was killed she has nothing to be scared about.'

Nikolls said: 'She ain't likely to have an alibi, is she? At the time the old boy was creased she oughta be in bed an' asleep. Well, bein' in bed an' asleep is not an easy thing to prove, is it? It woulda been easy for her to have got up an' slipped on a coat an' gone out inta the grounds an' waited for the old boy an' croaked him. She coulda gone back to bed afterwards an' finished her beauty sleep. Is that good deduction, or is it?'

'It's good enough,' said Callaghan.

'I reckon it's watertight,' said Nikolls. 'She was the only one who knew the Admiral was comin' back. Me – I think that Desiray is the baby. I reckon she fogged the Admiral because she just *had* to have that insurance dough. She knew that the two years were up. She musta guessed that was the reason for the Admiral changing his mind about killin' himself. She don't know that the lawyer guy heard what the Admiral said to her on the telephone. She thinks that everybody will think it's suicide. She thinks she's sittin' pretty.'

Callaghan got off the stool. He stood leaning against the bar. He said:

'Desirée has got enough sense to have cleaned her fingerprints off the gun and put it into his hand. She'd know that if somebody shoots themselves there has to be a gun. Well, there wasn't any gun.'

Nikolls said: 'Hell . . . I forgot. There wasn't a gun.'

'That's why Gringall and the Sussex police are certain it was murder,' said Callaghan.

'Why not?' said Nikolls. 'I reckon they're right. I think it was murder too. I reckon Desiray forgot about the gun. Maybe she ain't used to killin' guys all the time, an' she went a bit haywire and forgot to plant it. I reckon it was her all right.'

'No,' said Callaghan. 'It wasn't Desirée.'

'You got another theory?' asked Nikolls. He emptied the bacardi bottle into his glass.

'No,' said Callaghan. 'I haven't got any theories. Except that Desirée didn't do it. She's our client. Our clients never kill people.'

'O.K.,' said Nikolls. 'But this Desiray don't *want* to be our client, does she? She don't like us at all. If she *was* a customer it would be different. But she ain't.'

'You'd be surprised,' said Callaghan. 'She's going to be a customer all right.' He lit a cigarette. 'I'll be seeing you,' he said.

He went out.

Nikolls finished the bacardi. He drank it slowly. He was looking at henna-hair.

She came down to his end of the bar. She said:

'You're a one, talking to me like that in front of Mister Callaghan. I don't know what he must've thought.'

'I do,' said Nikolls. He grinned at her impudently.

She said: 'The trouble with you, Mister Nikolls, is that you're too fresh.'

'Yeah,' said Nikolls. 'I know. "Fresh" Nikolls. They usta call me that. There was a dame in Milwaukee usta call me that . . .'

'Well . . . I reckon she knew,' said henna-hair. She put a hand up to her back curls. 'Was she nice?' she asked diffidently.

Nikolls looked up and down the bar mysteriously. He sunk his voice to a hoarse whisper.

'She was a French countess,' he said. 'She was the berries. She was such an eyeful that if you looked at her without smoked glasses she got you dazzled. She was bughouse about me,' he added modestly.

'No . . .' said henna-hair. 'What happened?'

'It was terrible,' said Nikolls. 'She went to her brother and told him that she was crazy about me. She said if she couldn't marry me she was gonna cut her throat.'

Henna-hair gasped a little.

'What happened then?' she demanded.

'Her brother was a heel,' said Nikolls. 'He told her that if she wanted to cut her throat it was O.K. by him. He was sorta jealous of my appeal. He said he'd rather have his sister a corpse than me for a brother-in-law. A small-minded guy, that one.'

She nodded.

'There's drama for you,' she said. 'What did you do then?'

'The countess got sorta sentimental,' said Nikolls. 'She said that in death we would not be divided. She got a big idea about us committin' suicide together. She said that anythin' else but marriage was outa the question. So we committed suicide.'

Henna-hair was pop-eyed with interest.

'But you're not dead,' she said. 'Didn't you do it?'

'Yes an' no,' said Nikolls. 'She sorta worked out that we oughta do somethin' dramatic, an' while she was workin' it out I went off and had a stag party with the boys. By the time she had thought up the idea an' collected me I was so high I was game for anything'.'

'Yes,' said henna-hair. 'Go on . . . go . . . on . . .'

'She'd got it all fixed that we was to be run over by the midnight express,' said Nikolls, 'an' I was feelin' so bad after drinkin' Milwaukee beer on top of whisky and rum that it sounded good to me. So we went down to the railway an' tied ourselves across the permanent way with ropes, just outside the depot where the lines curve.'

'My God . . .' said henna-head. 'It must have been awful.'

'It was,' said Nikolls. 'Especially when we found she'd got the time wrong and there wasn't any train. I'd sobered up a bit by this time an'

I wasn't feeling so good. The countess wasn't worryin'. She said it was O.K. because there was another train at twelve twenty-one. It wasn't so bad for her because she was wearin' a fur coat. I was good an' cold an' I didn't think it was so good.

'Anyway, we stuck around there an' at twelve twenty-one the express comes roarin' along at about eighty miles an hour. I tell you it was terrible . . .'

'Well, what happened?' demanded henna-hair excitedly.

'Well,' said Nikolls, 'I'll tell you. The express come roarin' along an' when it was about six feet away it turned off on one of the curves. That baby had got us roped on the wrong line.

'It took all the romance out of it,' concluded Nikolls. He sighed heavily. 'I'll take another bacardi,' he added.

She opened a fresh bottle. The bar was empty.

She said: 'This one's got to be the last. I'm going to close up then.'

Nikolls drank the bacardi.

'Since I been here so long, I better see you home, honey,' he suggested.

She said: 'All right, Mister Nikolls. But you got to be good.'

Nikolls smiled at her.

'Don't give it a thought,' he said. 'If you knew how good I can be you'd be surprised.'

She looked at him. She put a straying curl back into place.

'I can guess . . .' said henna-head.

'That's what I thought,' said Nikolls.

IV

The Chinese clock on the mantelpiece struck midnight as Callaghan came out of the bathroom. He was wearing the top half of a pair of yellow crêpe-de-chine pyjamas and one bedroom slipper. As he looked for the other slipper the extension telephone from the office below jangled. He took off the receiver.

He said: 'Callaghan Investigations . . .'

A crisp voice said: 'This is Mr. Vane of Vane, Fleming, Searls and Vane. I want to speak to Mr. Callaghan.'

'You're speaking to him,' said Callaghan. 'What can I do for you, Mr. Vane?'

'It's about that conversation we had, Mr. Callaghan,' said Vane. 'Having thought things over, I've come to certain conclusions that I feel I should disclose to you. I . . .'

Callaghan began to grin.

'Don't bother,' he said. 'You can save your breath. I can guess the conclusions.'

Vane said: 'I don't understand you. I wished to tell you – '

Callaghan interrupted: 'You wished to tell me that our conversation of the other evening was based on a misapprehension. You wished to tell me that, having thought things over carefully, you could not be *quite* certain as to what the Admiral said when he telephoned to Chipley Grange, when he knocked you up to read that policy; that you have no idea as to the person to whom he was talking; that he was speaking so indistinctly that you could easily have been mistaken in thinking that you understood what he said. That's what you wished to say, isn't it?'

Vane said: 'Well, Mr. Callaghan, I must admit it was something on those lines.'

Callaghan said: 'Don't worry, Mr. Vane. You can call through to Desirée and tell her that she needn't worry. That I'm keeping that information about the Admiral's telephone call to myself.'

There was a pause. Then: 'May I ask why?' said Vane.

'You may,' said Callaghan. 'You can tell Desirée that I'm doing that because, at the moment, I feel like it.'

'Mr. Callaghan,' said Vane sternly. 'I must say that you speak rather disrespectfully of my client, Miss Gardell. I am sure she has *not* asked you to call her Desirée. I am sure – '

'Right,' said Callaghan. 'She hasn't asked me to call her Desirée. But she'll always be Desirée to Callaghan Investigations. We like to feel friendly with our clients.'

'Miss Gardell is *not* a client of yours, Mr. Callaghan,' said Vane. 'My instructions are – '

Callaghan said: 'Your instructions be damned. I don't know if you're a betting man, Vane, but if you are you can put your shirt on two things. One of them is that Desirée is our client – even if she doesn't like it – and the other is that you'll take your instructions from us.'

'Nonsense,' said Vane. 'I take instructions from Miss Gardell and from Miss Gardell only.'

'That's what *you* think,' said Callaghan. 'But she'll be writing you within a day or two on that point.'

Vane said: 'Mr. Callaghan, I resent your attitude and your impertinence. I shall advise my client – '

'Listen, Vane,' said Callaghan evenly. 'Let me give you some advice. Just don't advise your client anything at all. Did you ever hear the story of the fish with the big mouth?'

'I never did,' said Vane. 'And I fail – '

'It had such big mouth,' said Callaghan, 'that it not only swallowed the hook but the line and the sinker too. You ought to remember that fish. If it had kept its mouth shut it would have been all right.'

Vane said in an enraged voice: 'Mr. Callaghan, I refuse to talk – '

Callaghan said: 'That's the first clever thing you've said up to date. Just keep on refusing. Because you thought I was representing the Globe & Associated when I came to see you, you spluttered all that stuff about what he said on the telephone. Now, of course, you realise that what you said is evidence . . . *bad* evidence. You realise, now that it's too late, that every goddam bit of evidence in this case points straight at your client. I suppose Scotland Yard's been to see you and even your fat brain has grasped the fact that this is a murder job and that your client stands a damned good chance of being suspect. *She* was the only person who knew that the Admiral was going back home, wasn't she? And the obvious presumption was that she was going to meet him – '

Vane said: 'No . . . my client was in bed.'

'Nuts,' said Callaghan. 'Was she in bed when she answered the telephone?'

There was a long pause.

'Listen,' said Callaghan evenly. 'Remember the fish with the big mouth. Forget that telephone call *altogether*. Tell Desirée to forget it too and don't argue about it, because when you try to be clever it hurts.'

There was no reply. Callaghan replaced the receiver on the hook. He looked around for his slipper. He could not find it. He kicked off the one he had on, walked over to the sideboard, took out the bourbon bottle, indulged in a long swig.

He sat down in the big arm-chair in front of the electric fire. He put his bare feet on the mantelpiece, carefully avoiding the Chinese clock.

He thought the Gardell case was going to be very, very amusing.

He went to sleep.

CHAPTER SEVEN
LOVE IN A COTTAGE

I

THE telephone rang. Effie Thompson stopped typing, reached out for the instrument, took off the receiver.

She said: 'Oh, good-morning, Miss Vendayne.' Her voice was a trifle cold. 'Yes, Miss Vendayne . . . I gave Mr. Callaghan your message . . . Yes, I'll tell him again . . . that the country's looking *beautiful* . . . No, I don't think I can get him for you just now. We've rung his apartment several times this morning, but there was no answer. I don't think he's in . . . Good-bye, Miss Vendayne.'

Nikolls was sitting in Callaghan's chair in the inner office, his feet on the desk. He called through the open door:

'The boss ain't out. He's asleep.'

Effie said: 'Well, what do I do? There have been four telephone messages for him this morning. Every time I ring upstairs there's no reply. And there's a personal letter.'

Nikolls said: 'You'd better overcome that maidenly modesty of yours and go and wake him up.'

She said: 'Very well,' She went up to Callaghan's apartment, crossed the hall, went into the sitting-room. She stood on the threshold.

Callaghan was sound asleep in the big leather arm-chair in front of the electric fire. Effie could see his naked feet on the mantelpiece. She was glad it was a very low chair.

She went back to the office. She said to Nikolls:

'You'd better go up. He's asleep in his arm-chair in front of the sitting-room fire. I suppose he's been there all night. He's practically nude, I imagine.'

Nikolls said: 'What the hell d'you mean "you imagine." Why do you dames haveta be so coy. A guy is either practically nude or he ain't. There's no imagination about it.'

Effie said: 'If you *must* go into details, I didn't bother to look.'

Nikolls grinned at her. He said:

'I know . . . that's why you had to imagine . . . hey?'

She said: 'You're terrible. Whatever I say you twist. And you might tell Mr. Callaghan that Miss Vendayne's telephoned again. Remind him that he was going to call her. She keeps telling me that the Devonshire country is looking wonderful. I wonder why she keeps calling.'

Nikolls said: 'You'd be surprised . . .' He got up. 'Give me that letter.' He went upstairs.

II

Callaghan sat on the arm of the chair. He ran his hands through his thick, unruly black hair. His head ached.

Nikolls said: 'It's not so good – that bacardi on top of whisky, you know. I felt shockin' this mornin' until I took somethin' for it.'

Callaghan asked: 'What did you take?'

Nikolls said: 'I took some whisky. It put it right practically immediately.'

Callaghan said: 'You'd better give me some.'

Nikolls poured out four fingers of whisky, brought it over. Callaghan drank it at a gulp.

Nikolls said: 'Will you be wantin' me to-day?'

Callaghan asked: 'Why?'

Nikolls said: 'Oh, nothin'. I though of havin' a day in the country.'

Callaghan grinned.

'I bet you did,' he said. 'Some woman, I suppose?'

Nikolls said: 'Well, why not? A guy's gotta have relaxation, ain't he?'

Callaghan said: 'You get all the relaxation you want outside office hours. I want you in the office to-day.'

'O.K.,' said Nikolls. 'Is anythin' goin' to pop?'

Callaghan said: 'How should I know?'

Nikolls said: 'The trouble is you're gettin' bored. You want a change. That's what you want.'

Callaghan said: 'All right. Just get out, will you?'

Nikolls stopped at the doorway. He said:

Miss Vendayne's been through again this morning. She said Devonshire was looking lovely. Why don't you go down an' see that dame?'

Callaghan said: 'You go to hell and mind your own business.'

Nikolls went out.

Callaghan took off his pyjama jacket. He went into the bathroom, filled the bath, got in. He left the cold tap running. After five minutes he began to feel like a human being. He got out of the bath, dried himself, put on a bathrobe. He went into the sitting-room, took the letter off the table where Nikolls had left it. He opened it. It said:

Dear Mr. Callaghan,

Thank you very much for your letter. I was very glad to get it because as you can guess I've been very worried about all this business.

I am awfully sorry Desirée made you feel unhappy. I don't think she meant to. I think that just at this time she's a little overwrought, and when women feel like that they're not inclined to be awfully intelligent, are they?

Not being concerned in this business I take a more dispassionate view of things. I understand the position of the Insurance Company, and I was awfully glad to hear that you are representing them, because the first time I saw you I felt that you and I could be friends.

Of course if you feel you'd like to see Desirée again, please see her, although I think that just at the moment she may not be in a very receptive frame of mind, and I think too – and I am sure you will understand this – that any ideas you have about smoothing out things with the Insurance Company would perhaps come better through me.

Would you like to come and see me? I am sure you must be working very hard and it is very nice down here. Even a few hours would mean a rest for you. I shall be in all day to-morrow, when you will get this letter, and if by any chance you care to come down in the late afternoon or the evening, I should be very glad to see you. But please don't put yourself out in any way. Come just when you want.

Manon Gardell.

Callaghan flipped open the cigarette-box on the table, took a cigarette, lit it. He read the letter again. He went to the telephone, called through to the office. He said to Effie:

'Get through to Miss Manon Gardell at The Cottage, Valeston, Sussex. Say I was very glad to get her letter. Tell her I'll be down this evening about nine o'clock.'

'Very well, Mr. Callaghan,' said Effie. 'Shall you dine before you go?'

Callaghan asked: 'Why?'

'Oh, nothing,' said Effie. 'Only I expect Miss Gardell will have dined by nine o'clock.'

Callaghan said: 'Never mind. Perhaps she'll be able to give me supper. That's a good idea. You might ask her, Effie.'

Effie said: 'Very well.'

She hung up.

III

The grandfather clock, set in the corner of the stairway between the two floors of The Cottage, wheezily struck the half-hour. It was half-past eight. Manon looked at herself in the cheval mirror. She said:

'Manon, my dear, I don't think you look *too* bad.'

In fact she looked alluring. She wore a blue silk foulard frock with white pinspots. The bodice was tight; showed off Manon's delicate curves to the very best advantage. It had short puffed sleeves. The skirt was full and billowy. She wore sheer beige silk stockings, blue kid, high-heeled sandals. Her blonde hair, dressed carefully over one shoulder, was caught in a blue watered-silk ribbon.

She began to think about her visitor.

Callaghan, she thought, would be susceptible. Most obviously strong personalities in the male line *were* susceptible. They were affected very much more by atmosphere, by a woman's appearance and clothes, than they cared to admit. It was only weak men who were not greatly concerned with feminine atmospherics, mainly because they were too busy thinking about themselves. But strong men were quite a different proposition. If they fell, they fell quickly, easily and hard.

Manon sighed. She took a cigarette from her dressing-table, lit it. She went downstairs, cast an expert look at the dining-room.

She thought it looked charming – charming and delightfully old. When it was dark, thought Manon, the candles with their vieux-rose shades would cast a very flattering light.

On the sideboard were two bottles of champagne, brandy and the makings for cocktails. Manon thought she was lucky to have enough liquor in these hard days suitably to entertain her guest. She went to the sideboard, poured herself out a gin and bitters. She carried the glass into the drawing-room, stood in front of the fireplace holding it, her cigarette in the other hand.

She wondered what Callaghan was going to say – what his plan was. That he had some plan she had no doubt. Callaghan had a definite idea in his head. He had made his mind up that he was coming in on the Gardell insurance claim. Why not, thought Manon.

Desirée had handled him in the wrong way. She – Manon – would not make the same mistake. She looked at herself in the glass. She said:

'You always were delightfully tactful, weren't you, darling? Except perhaps just one or twice. And then, I'm afraid, you allowed your heart to run away with your head. Well . . . here's to you . . .'

She drank the gin and bitters. She felt she was going to enjoy herself.

IV

Callaghan, relaxed in the big chintz-covered arm-chair by the side of the brightly burning fire, warmed his brandy-glass between the palms of his hands. Manon, he considered, had a nice taste in brandy. He sniffed the bouquet appreciatively. Definitely *very* good brandy. Life, he thought, was rather like brandy. It was always amusing, very seldom bad, occasionally superfine.

He looked at Manon, snuggled into the chair on the opposite side of the fireplace. The grandfather clock on the stairs struck a wheezy eleven.

She said: 'Eleven o'clock. I'm so glad that you've got your car here; that I know you're a person who doesn't mind driving in the dark. I'm glad because it doesn't matter if it *is* eleven o'clock. And there are so many things I want to talk to you about.'

Callaghan smiled at her. He said:

'Do you realise that we haven't really talked at all – about anything that matters, I mean . . . ?'

'Oh, but we *have*,' she said. 'You've told me that you liked your supper – and that made me *fearfully* happy; that you liked the cottage; that it was nice being here. And I've been happy. Much happier than I've been for a long time. I don't know why. But I am.' She sighed audibly. 'Really, I suppose I *do* know why.'

'Do you?' said Callaghan.

She nodded.

'It's because I feel that you're being *friendly*,' said Manon. She shot him a glance under her long eyelashes. 'I'm feeling happier because, for one thing' – she hesitated for a moment – 'I'm not worrying about Desirée so much as I was.'

Callaghan asked: 'Why not?'

She said: 'I'm certain that you're going to do everything you can to help her. She needs help. Poor Desirée has had such a tough time with the Admiral. He was so very tactless, and he made life very difficult for her.'

Callaghan said: 'Perhaps it's better for her now that the Admiral's gone.'

She said: 'She doesn't think so, but I do. I think it's better for every one, including *him*.'

He said: 'When you first telephoned my office and said you wanted to see me, was that your idea or was it Desirée's?'

She thought for a moment.

'I can't remember,' she said.

Callaghan said: 'That means you two must have talked about it. Did you?'

She said: 'Yes . . .'

'Then it wasn't your idea.' said Callaghan. 'If you discussed it, it was *her* idea.'

Manon said: 'Yes, perhaps you're right. Perhaps it was her idea. This is awfully good fun,' she went on. 'Having you here, I mean. I think you're an *exciting* person.'

Callaghan drank some brandy. He thought: She's rather an artist. She knows I know she's putting on an act, but she still thinks it will achieve its purpose. He wondered what that purpose was. He said:

'Why do you think I'm an exciting person?'

She said: 'Well, you *look* exciting. And being a detective must be an exciting profession. I expect you've met all sorts of interesting men and women – especially women.'

Callaghan said: 'Why especially women?'

She leaned back in her chair; regarded the ceiling seriously, her hand behind her neck. She said:

'I don't know. But I should have thought women would have got into trouble – the sort of trouble that needs a private detective – more than men. Especially if they were beautiful women.'

Callaghan grinned. He said:

'You're a believer in the theory that a beautiful woman has to get into trouble?'

She said: 'Yes. Aren't you?'

He said: 'I suppose you're right, but if we accept that theory, both you and your cousin Desirée are liable to get into plenty of trouble. Or don't you regard yourselves as being beautiful women?'

She said primly: 'We like to think that we're not hard to look at. But as for the theory – well, we've proved it, haven't we? We're in trouble – at least Desirée is – and I am in it in a way because I'm trying to help.' She changed her tone suddenly. She leaned forward. She said seriously: 'Tell me something. You were awfully disappointed because you and Desirée didn't hit it off together. Very naturally Desirée thinks that's because you expected to work on this case; you expected her to employ your organisation about the claim. But *I* don't think so.'

Callaghan raised one eyebrow.

'No?' he said. 'Why don't *you* think so?'

She said: 'I'm quite certain that the mere fact of whether you were employed or not by the Gardell family wouldn't matter a tinker's curse to you. But there's something else.'

Callaghan said: 'You might be right.'

She said: 'I know I'm right.'

He smiled at her.

'Well, supposing you are right . . . ?' he said.

'I'm curious to know what your motive is, naturally,' said Manon. 'Even more curious because I believed you when you said that you might be able to smooth things out with the Insurance Company.'

Callaghan said: 'I wasn't thinking so much about smoothing things out with the Insurance Company as smoothing things out for Desirée.'

She said: 'Exactly what do you mean by that?'

Callaghan took a cigarette from the silver box on the little table at his elbow. She got up, struck a match for him. She stood near to him. He caught a breath of the perfume she was wearing. His nostrils twitched appreciatively.

Callaghan said: 'Perhaps I'll answer that question in a minute. In the meantime I'd like to ask you one. Why were you so keen on getting it into my head that the Admiral did commit suicide? Tell me that.'

She said: 'I told you both Desirée and I knew that he intended to commit suicide. We knew he'd do it some time or other. The only question was when.'

Callaghan said: 'Was that your real reason? You know that the County Police and Scotland Yard are both practically certain that the Admiral was murdered. So am I. If he'd committed suicide there'd have been a gun. *I* think he was murdered.'

She said: 'I'd agree with you if my uncle had been an ordinary sort of person. But the fact remains that he did *mean* to commit suicide . . .'

Callaghan interrupted. He said:

'He didn't mean to commit suicide. He telephoned through to Chipley Grange not very long before he was murdered to say that he'd changed his mind about that.'

She had gone back to her chair. She looked at him with wide eyes.

She said: 'My God!' There was a pause. Then: 'How do you know that?'

'Vane told me,' said Callaghan. 'After the Admiral had written me that note and left Berkeley Square, he knocked up Vane. He looked at the Insurance Policy; then he telephoned through to Desirée and told her that he'd changed his mind.'

Manon said: 'I see. That puts a different complexion on things doesn't it? That *makes* it look like murder.'

Callaghan said a little grimly: 'Yes. It also makes it pretty obvious that Desirée knew that he did *not* intend to commit suicide. That isn't very good for her, is it?'

Manon said: 'I don't understand. What do you mean by that?'

Callaghan said: 'Quite obviously the Admiral came up to London to see me on an impulse. It was quite obvious that he intended to stay in London until he did see me.' Callaghan paused. 'And there was only one person who *knew* he was returning,' he said.

She said: 'Oh, I see. You mean Desirée?'

Callaghan nodded.

'Right,' he said. 'I mean Desirée.'

She looked into the fire. Quite a long time passed before she said anything; then:

'It is quite ridiculous,' she said. 'Quite ridiculous that anyone could even *think . . .*'

Callaghan interrupted.

'You'd be surprised if you knew what people *could* think,' he said. 'There's another point too. Who is going to benefit under the Insurance Policy – Desirée. So if the Admiral decided not to commit suicide, but to go on living, there would be no money from the Insurance Company. And we come back *again* to the fact that there was only one person who knew that he did intend to go on living.'

Her face was sad. Callaghan thought her eyes were very soft. He said:

'You told me that the Admiral wanted to commit suicide because, amongst other reasons, he wanted to be revenged on somebody. Exactly what did you mean by that?'

She said: 'I'm not quite certain . . . I . . .'

Callaghan asked: 'Did you mean that the Admiral thought that, having got the money, Desirée might do something foolish with it; that there might be someone he didn't like who might unduly influence Desirée?'

'Yes,' she said. 'I suppose I did mean that, in a way.'

Callaghan said: 'That's not sense, is it? If the Admiral thought that, all he had to do would be to arrange that his lawyer held the money in trust; that he took steps to see that Desirée *didn't* do anything silly with it. That's all he had to do. It wasn't necessary for him to commit suicide to achieve that simple end, was it?'

Manon said: 'No . . . when you put it like that, it sounds as if it wasn't. Will you have some brandy? I wish you would.'

Callaghan said: 'Thanks, I'd like some.'

She poured out the brandy. She said:

'I wish I knew what you were *really* trying to do about this insurance business. I wish I knew whether you were on our side or not. I've a sneaking hope that you are.'

Callaghan smiled at her. He said:

'I'm not on any one's side. I'm acting for the Insurance Company. But that fact shouldn't worry you or any one else – not unless there *is* something for someone to worry about.'

She looked into the fire.

'Really,' she said. 'It's a little ridiculous of the Insurance Company, or any one else, to believe that poor Desirée had anything at all to do with Uncle Hubert's death. One has only to look at Desirée to know that such a thing is quite impossible.'

Callaghan said: 'I know. If you looked at most murderers and didn't know they *were* murderers, you'd think it impossible to believe that they had actually killed somebody. Killers seldom look the part.'

She said: 'You mean that – '

'I mean that the Insurance Company are concerned only with facts,' said Callaghan. 'They're stalling payment on the claim merely because they have reason – good reason – to believe that your uncle was murdered. Before they pay the claim they want to know that any one connected – in any way – with the murder is not going to benefit directly or indirectly from the fact. If Insurance Companies were knowingly to pay out insurance claims to murderers they'd be making themselves accessories *after* the fact. Wouldn't they?'

Manon nodded. She said:

'I suppose they would. Are you trying to tell me that the Insurance Company think that Desirée had *anything* to do with my uncle's death?'

'No,' said Callaghan. 'They haven't any reason to think that, have they? They don't know anything about the Admiral's telephone message to Desirée. They're not likely to know unless Vane tells them – and he won't – or I tell them.'

Manon asked softly: 'Are you going to tell them.'

'I don't know,' said Callaghan. 'I don't know what I'm going to do.'

She said: 'Why not? Does that mean that you haven't made up your mind about something?'

'Right,' said Callaghan. 'I haven't made up my mind about Desirée.'

Manon said: 'Well . . . perhaps I can help you. If there's anything you want to know – '

'There are quite a few things I want to know,' said Callaghan.

'Are there?' she said.

She slipped quickly out of the chair, knelt on the hearthrug in front of the fire, her foulard skirts billowing about her. Callaghan thought that there was something pathetic in her attitude and in her eyes.

She said: 'Tell me . . . What are you going to do about Desirée? Are you going to go on being offended with her, or are you going to see her again and talk things over and see if you can help?'

Callaghan said: 'I don't see the use of worrying Desirée just now, do you? Quite obviously she doesn't think that I can be of much use to her.

Candidly, at the moment, I don't think I can. On the other hand, I think you could help – if you wanted to.'

She looked at him with wide eyes.

'Of course I want to,' she said. 'Of *course*. Just tell me what it is you want.'

He grinned at her. Manon thought: He's a damned attractive man, this Callaghan. He's got something. I could fall for him very easily, that is if I was that sort of girl . . .

She said: 'You make me vaguely uncomfortable, Slim. And I'm going to call you Slim because I like you and trust you awfully. I feel I've known you for *ages*. Just ask me anything at all and I'll do my best to help.'

Callaghan said: 'All right . . . I suppose you *can* tell the truth – when you want to.'

She looked at him reproachfully. She said:

'Now you're not suggesting – '

Callaghan interrupted: 'I'm suggesting that practically ever since I've met you you've been busy putting on an act. Personally, I think you're scared sick about Desirée. I think that your one idea is to prevent Desirée and me from seeing too much of each other – just in case we get on one another's nerves. I think you're trying like hell to cover up for Desirée somehow or other, and I don't think you're doing so well either. I think you'll get tired of remembering what it is you want to forget in a minute, and then you'll slip up and make a mistake, and I shall be on it like a cat jumping on a mouse.'

She looked at him pitifully. She moved a little closer to him on her knees. She was near enough for him again to be aware of the peculiar and very attractive perfume she was wearing.

She said: 'Damn you, Slim. . . . You're *such* a good guesser. I haven't much chance against you, have I?'

Callaghan lit a fresh cigarette. He said nothing.

She said eventually: 'Why do you accuse me of putting on an act?'

'It's obvious,' said Callaghan. 'Right from the first you've been acting as scout for Desirée. She asked you to get in touch with me. She wanted to find out if I had seen the Admiral. If I'd done my stuff and been a good boy, and cashed in with any information I had, then everything would have been O.K. But I wasn't. And Desirée doesn't like that. She likes getting her own way.'

'Everybody likes getting their own way,' said Manon. 'But it doesn't mean that the fact makes them murderers – or murderesses.'

'Quite,' said Callaghan. 'But it's a help, isn't it?'

'I suppose it is,' said Manon. 'I wish I knew what to think and what to do.'

'I can help you there,' said Callaghan amiably. 'I suggest that you stop putting on an act and that you let me in on this thing that's troubling you. You'll feel a lot better afterwards.'

She looked into the fire for a long time. Then she said:

'How do you know that something's troubling me?'

Callaghan said: 'You've got all the symptoms. When a woman as beautiful as you are, as attractive as you are, kneels in front of the fire, after having given me an excellent meal, three or four glasses of superb brandy, and just talks round the subject – as you are at the moment – I know she's really only waiting for a chance to talk . . . providing she can do it on *her* terms.'

She said in a low voice: 'My God, you're clever, Slim. They said you were clever, and now I know they are right. You're damned clever.'

Callaghan grinned at her. He said:

'You're telling me! I have to be. The sort of people I deal with sharpen my wits.'

She said: 'If only I knew that I was going to be *safe* in talking to you.'

He said: 'That's what the girl said to the sailor.'

'No!' said Manon. 'Did she – the forward hussy! And what did the sailor say?'

Callaghan said: 'He told her he couldn't *guarantee* anything.'

'So she didn't talk?' said Manon.

'Wrong,' said Callaghan. 'She talked . . . and liked it. Just as you'll talk because you've got to talk.'

She sat up. She looked at him with wide eyes.

'Now you're being really interesting,' she said. 'So I've *got* to talk, have I? *Really*, Mr. Callaghan . . . tell me why.'

Callaghan drew cigarette smoke down into his lungs, expelled it slowly and expertly. He watched her during the process. She sat back on her heels, her lips parted in a small smile . . . waiting.

He said: 'I've made up my mind. I'm going to advise the Insurance Company not to pay that claim. I've made up my mind to get them to write Vane and tell him they're not going to pay – '

Manon said: 'My God! You *can't* do that, Slim. You *can't* do it.'

'Can't I?' said Callaghan. 'Well, you watch me . . .'

'After eating my expensive food,' complained Manon. 'After drinking my very best *Biscuit* brandy that I save for my very *dearest* friends. After my being so nice to you and thinking so much of you, and very nearly being *quite* silly about you. You don't mean it, Slim. You can't. And anyhow, why?'

Callaghan said: 'I'm going to force your hand. Or rather I'm going to force Desirée's hand. If the Company advise Vane that they don't intend to pay, then Vane can do one of two things. He can either issue a writ against the Company and try and make them pay or he can do nothing and like it. I think he'll have to do nothing and like it.'

'Why?' asked Manon.

Callaghan grinned.

'If he wants to be funny, I'll force his hand,' he said. 'I'll make him divulge that telephone conversation he overheard between the Admiral and Desirée. He may say he can't remember what it was now, but he remembered it all right when he told me.'

She said: 'You're like a limpet, aren't you? You stick to one point and keep on sticking to it. That damned telephone conversation between Uncle Hubert and Desirée. You keep coming back to it.'

Callaghan said: 'It's the only point I've got at the moment.' He grinned amiably at her. 'I'm making the most of it,' he said.

'You definitely *are*,' said Manon. 'Again . . . why?'

'There's something connected with that telephone conversation that *you* know,' said Callaghan, making a shot in the dark. 'That's why you stall directly I get on to the point. Well . . . I shall find it out one way or another.'

She said: 'I believe you will. You *are* a creature, aren't you, Slim? You'll keep on ferreting and worrying and asking questions and annoying me until you find out. I wish to God I could tell you.'

'So it's like that, is it?' said Callaghan. 'That's how you feel about it. Well . . . that makes it easier . . .'

'What do you mean?' she asked quickly.

'Quite obviously if you wish it was something you could tell me and can't, it's something else in connection with that telephone message and Desirée that makes the case look even worse against her. The fact of the matter is you're between the devil and the deep sea, Manon. You know damned well that if you *don't* talk and I find out, it's going to be very much worse for her than if you *do* talk and I keep quiet about it.'

Manon said: 'But how *could* you keep quiet about it? If you thought it was going to help that damned Insurance Company *not* to pay, then how could you keep quiet about it?'

Callaghan looked at her. His eyes were half closed. He said:

'You'd be surprised how quiet I can keep when I feel like it.'

Manon came a little closer on her knees. As she moved, Callaghan could see her silken knees. She put her hand on the arm of his chair. She said:

'I'll make a bargain with you, Slim. Tell me the truth and I'll do my damnedest to tell you the truth.'

'That's fair enough,' said Callaghan. 'I promise you I'll give you as good a deal as you give me. What is it you want to know?'

She said: 'What's the *exact* position with the Insurance Company? Are they going to pay or aren't they?'

Callaghan said: 'They're stalling because I told them to. They won't pay until I give them the O.K. I'm their legal and proper investigator. If I tell 'em to-morrow that so far as I'm concerned everything's in order, they'll pass the claim for payment.'

She said: 'If you tell them that the claim's in order, exactly what does that mean? Does it mean that you know who killed my uncle?'

Callaghan shook his head.

'The Insurance Company don't give a damn who killed your uncle,' he said. 'All they want to know is that the person to whom the insurance is payable to properly entitled to receive it; that there is no possible connection between that person and the murder.'

She nodded.

'I see,' she said. 'Well . . .' She hesitated. Then: 'This is difficult for me,' she said. 'I don't know how to put it . . .'

Callaghan said: 'Is it important?'

'It's important enough,' said Manon miserably. 'It's too damned important for my liking.'

'What's worrying you, then?' he asked.

'*You're* worrying me,' she said. 'I like you an awful lot, but I don't know if I can trust you.'

'I know,' said Callaghan. 'That's what the girl said to the sailor.'

'Did she?' said Manon in a little voice. 'And what did the sailor say?'

Callaghan looked into her eyes. They were very blue and misty. 'The sailor said she'd have to take a chance some time,' said Callaghan.

She came even closer. She put her hand on his knee.

She said: 'I'm going quite mad. If I don't get this off my mind I shall go mad.'

Callaghan said nothing. She put one arm round his neck. She drew his face down towards hers. She kissed him on the mouth. She said in a trembling voice:

'Listen, you nasty detective person . . . I'm a little bit crazy about you. So I'm going to take a chance. I'm going to trust you. If you want to take advantage of the fact, then you can. But I'm making a bet with myself that you're too decent to do it. If you *do* take advantage of the fact then you'll have another case on your hands because *I* shall kill myself. It would be the only thing I could do. D'you understand, you nasty, cynical, mercenary, rather good-looking, rude pig? She kissed him again . . . and again. Then she stopped. She sat back on her heels and looked at him. Her eyes were wet, her cheeks scarlet.

'Well . . . what did the sailor say to that?' she demanded.

Callaghan said: 'He didn't say anything. He was too busy collecting himself. Come here, Manon.'

She got up. She sat on the arm of Callaghan's chair. He put his arm round her waist. He said:

'Look, Manon. This business has gone too far for you. You need help.'

She said: 'If I "come clean" – as they say on the films – will you give me your sacred word of honour that you'll never divulge what I tell you?'

'Certainly not,' said Callaghan. 'But I'll give you my word that I won't take any particular action on it. Any action, that is, that I wouldn't have taken normally, supposing I hadn't been told. How's that?'

Manon said: 'Well . . . I suppose that'll have to do. It sounds safe enough.' She sighed. 'Life's amazing,' she said. 'I asked you down here thinking you'd have your meal, and a drink, and allow me to pick your brain in an hour or so. Instead of which you eat my food, drink my brandy, and pick *my* brain. I suppose a lot of women have told you that you're a fascinating sort of low-life type?' asked Manon, adjusting a straying curl.

Callaghan said: 'Come down to brass tacks, Manon. The sooner you say it the better you'll feel.'

She put her arm round his neck. She said:

'This is damned awful.' She began to cry. Callaghan could feel her tears on his cheek.

He said quietly: 'Cough it up, Manon,'

She said hoarsely: 'The night uncle went up to town. Desirée didn't know he was going. She telephoned me very late – about twelve o'clock. She asked me if I'd like to drive over and spend the night at The Grange. I said no . . . I was tired. I asked her where uncle was. She said she didn't know. I went to bed and then I began to worry. I suffer from an imagination. I wondered if he was going to carry out his threat and kill himself. I got into an awful state.

'I telephoned Desirée at two o'clock. I asked if Uncle had come in. She said no. She was in a terrible state too. I went back to bed but I couldn't sleep. I got up about three, and put on some slacks and a fur coat, and made myself some coffee. Then I got out the car and drove over to Chipley. When I got there I noticed the Admiral's car standing at the end of the lane that runs round the flower-garden at Chipley and through the coppice at the back of the house. I pulled the car into the road, and walked along the lane. I had a fearful feeling that something awful was going to happen.

'I skirted the coppice – there's a little path runs round it. If I hadn't skirted the coppice I should have walked straight into Uncle's body. He must have been lying there then. So you see . . . so you see . . .'

'Get on with it,' said Callaghan brusquely.

She gulped.

'When I came to the end of the path I could see the back of the flower-garden and the little bridge that runs over the lake at the bottom. I could just see as far as that. It was a lovely night. I saw Desirée . . . she was just at the end of the bridge. She was wearing a fur coat over her nightgown. Just a fur coat and her nightgown, and a pair of high-heeled shoes . . . I suppose she'd put them on in a hurry. I thought . . .'

'Never mind what you thought,' said Callaghan. 'What was she doing?'

'She dropped a pistol into the lake,' said Manon. 'I saw it in her hand distinctly . . . and I knew what she'd done . . .'

'You knew she'd killed the Admiral,' said Callaghan coolly.

'*No*,' said Manon. '*No . . . No . . . No* . . . I guessed she'd heard his car arrive. She'd heard him come home. She'd heard the shot. *I tell you he shot himself. I know he did. He said he was going to . . .*'

'To hell with that,' said Callaghan. 'Stick to Desirée . . .'

'She heard the shot,' said Manon. 'So she flung on a coat and shoes and came down. She found him. I'm certain she found him there with the pistol in his hand – dead. She knew it was suicide; that he'd killed himself.

But she was afraid. She was afraid of the same thing that he feared. She was afraid that Uncle had killed himself before the two years were up; that the Insurance Company wouldn't pay. She knew that Uncle had always wanted that money paid. I don't care what any one says, that's what he wanted, and because Desirée knew that, and because she knew what he wanted done with the money, she did the only thing she could do . . .'

Callaghan whistled quietly through his teeth.

'I've got it,' he said. 'She picked up the gun and threw it in the lake so that it looked like murder. If it was murder the Insurance Company would pay . . .'

'Yes,' said Manon. 'Yes . . . that's right.'

Callaghan said: 'It was a pity that Desirée didn't know that the two years *were* up, that in any event, suicide or murder, the Company would have to pay.'

'I know,' said Manon. 'I know that now. So does she. But she didn't know it then.'

Callaghan said: 'Let's have some brandy, shall we?'

Manon said: 'That's a grand idea. I feel like death.'

She got up, poured out some brandy. She said:

'And I'll make some coffee. You're going to play the game with me, aren't you, Mr. Callaghan?' She smiled at him wistfully.

Callaghan said: 'Don't worry . . .'

She said: 'I'll try not to worry too much.' She smiled suddenly. 'I suppose the girl said *that* to the sailor too?' she asked.

He grinned.

'No,' he said, 'she didn't say that. You go and make the coffee and when you've done that – '

'What?' said Manon. She looked at him. Her eyes were very bright.

'When you've done that,' said Callaghan, 'we can have a really serious discussion. We can definitely decide something.'

She nodded.

'You mean about Desirée?' she asked.

'No,' said Callaghan. 'I mean about what the sailor said.'

'Oh,' said Manon. She went to the door. She turned, her hand on the door-knob. 'I think it's funny,' she said. 'Desirée was afraid that we might have to pay you and she didn't see why.' She sighed dramatically, 'The woman always pays,' she said.

She threw him a quick, alluring smile. 'But sometimes she pays – and likes it. *Au revoir*, Slim . . .'

'*Au revoir*,' said Callaghan.

He poured himself out some brandy. He stood looking into the fire. His expression was amiable. He was thinking that even private detectives get a break – sometimes.

When Manon returned with the coffee, she set the silver tray on the small table by Callaghan's arm-chair. She said:

'It's half-past twelve. It's amazing how quickly the time goes.'

Callaghan said: 'I've noticed that too. But if it's twelve-thirty my holiday is up. I've got to get back. I've some very important work to do.'

'Well . . . drink your coffee first,' said Manon. 'I'm sorry you have to go. Is it *very* important?'

He stood with his back to the fire. He was smiling. She thought that when he smiled he was *really* rather handsome.

He said: 'I've got to think up some scheme for making the Insurance Company pay that claim – quickly.'

She came over to him. Her eyes were shining. She said:

'Slim, you positive *jewel*. I almost adore you. So you're really on our side. You're really going to *help* Desirée?'

He said: 'Yes . . . definitely. It just shows you how weak we detectives can be, doesn't it?'

Manon said: '*You'd* never be weak. You'd never do anything that you really didn't want to do. I'm fearfully pleased to think that perhaps I've helped to make you change your opinion about things . . .'

He nodded.

'You have – definitely,' he said.

She handed him his coffee. He drank it quickly. He said: 'Well . . . I'm going. So long, Manon.'

She put her arms round his neck. While she was kissing him Callaghan was thinking that one could fall, very easily and very hard, for Manon.

She said: 'I'm damned *good* to you, aren't I?'

'First-class,' said Callaghan. 'I think you're wonderful. But I expect you've heard that before.'

'Perhaps,' said Manon. 'But I've never listened with quite so much attention.' She sighed. 'I hate you going,' she said. 'But if you must . . . I'll go and get your things. In a way, I suppose I'm rather glad you've got to go.'

He asked why.

She shrugged.

'I could be *very* foolish about you,' she said.

Callaghan smiled at her. He said:

'I'll remove the cause of temptation.' He lit a cigarette. He said: 'Now you listen to me, my dear. There are two points of interest about the Admiral's death; both of them concern Desirée. One of them is the telephone message from the Admiral to Desirée. Who knows about that? You know about it; I know about it; Desirée knows about it; Vane know about it. Well, none of us is likely to talk. The other is a fact known to three of us – you, Desirée and me – and that is that she threw that pistol in the lake. Now, you've got to be a very clever girl.'

Manon said: 'Have I? What have I got to do?'

Callaghan said: 'To-morrow morning I want you to go up to London and see Vane. I want you to tell him what you have told me about seeing Desirée throwing that pistol in the lake. You've got to do it. You understand?'

Manon said: 'I've told you I trust you. If you say I'm to do it, I'll do it, but I'd like to know why.'

'You're entitled to know why,' said Callaghan. 'Ever since the Admiral died Desirée's kept very quiet. She's kept very quiet about things that are important. For instance, *she* never said anything about the Admiral's telephone message. I learned that almost by accident from Vane. She didn't tell Vane, and she's told nobody about this business of dropping the pistol in the lake. She hasn't even told you.'

Manon nodded.

'That's true,' she said.

Callaghan said: 'I think the normal thing for Desirée to have done would have been to have told Vane or someone else she could trust about the Admiral's telephone message, to have told him about dropping the pistol in the lake, even if only to relieve her mind. Well, she hasn't done so.'

'No,' said Manon. 'And you want me to?'

'Quite,' said Callaghan. ' My reason is obvious. If Vane knows that story that you told me, it is almost as good as if she told him, isn't it? In other words, it is no longer a secret.'

Manon said: 'I see! You're a clever person, aren't you, Slim?'

Callaghan said: 'Don't let's worry about my cleverness. Let's worry about our story. We'll probably never have to use it. I hope it won't ever be necessary, but if it is this is our story, and we'll stick to it . . .'

She said: 'Go on, I'm listening.'

Callaghan said: 'Nobody can be certain about the Admiral's telephone message to Desirée. In other words, that telephone message could have been about anything. The rest of the story you know. Desirée heard the shot, threw on a few clothes, dashed out to the coppice, found the Admiral shot; naturally concluded that he'd carried out his threat and killed himself. At the same time thinking that the two years were not up, and that the Insurance Company wouldn't pay the money which she knew the Admiral wanted paid. She picked up the gun, threw it in the lake, because the Company would pay if they thought the Admiral had been murdered.

'In other words,' said Callaghan, 'Desirée was only trying to do what the Admiral wanted done.' He grinned. 'There's no one on earth could disprove that story,' he said.

Manon said: 'I'm going to do what you say, Slim.'

'That's right,' said Callaghan. 'Go up to town tomorrow. See Vane, tell him the story and tell him that I advised you to tell him.'

Manon said: 'You want him to know that you know?'

He smiled at her.

'I want him to know that I know,' he said. 'I want him to realise that I'm on your side. Now I must be off.'

She pressed his hand. She said:

'I knew I wasn't wrong about you.'

She went for his hat and coat.

V

It was half-past one when Callaghan put the car away in the Berkeley Square garage. He went straight up to his apartment; walked across to the house telephone.

He said: 'Wilkie, give me a ring at four-thirty, and keep ringing until I answer.'

Wilkie said: 'Right, Mr. Callaghan.'

Callaghan said: 'Get through to Trunk Directory and get me the number of Chipley Grange, Chipley, Sussex. You can give that to me at four-thirty.'

Wilkie said he'd do that.

Callaghan went into the bedroom, undressed, got into bed. He lay there, looking at the ceiling, smoking.

He switched off the light; went to sleep.

He was awakened by the jangling of the telephone bell. He sat up in bed, cursing quietly, consigning everybody and everything to perdition.

He got up, walked into the sitting-room, took off the receiver of the house telephone.

Wilkie said: 'It's just four-thirty, Mr. Callaghan. And the number you want is Chipley 072. Shall I ring it for you?'

'No,' said Callaghan.

He hung up. Wandered across to the electric fire, turned it on. He went across to the sideboard, helped himself to four fingers of bourbon and a cigarette.

He sat in the arm-chair in front of the fire and thought about Desirée. He wondered why the hell he should sit about at four-thirty in the morning, dressed in the top half of a pair of violet silk pyjamas, thinking about Desirée. The idea amused him.

He threw his cigarette stub away, looked at the Chinese clock on the mantelpiece. It was quarter to five. He went to the telephone, called Trunks; asked for Chipley 072.

He could hear the bell ringing at the other end. He wondered if any one would bother to answer it.

Exchange said: 'I'm ringing your number. But there isn't any answer. Shall I call you?'

'No thanks,' said Callaghan. 'I'll just hang on. I can hear their bell ringing. Maybe somebody's coming.'

Exchange said: 'Here they are.'

A man's voice said: 'Hallo . . . this is The Grange, Chipley. Who – '

Callaghan said: 'Is that Grant, the butler?'

'Yes, sir,' said Grant.

Callaghan grinned. He thought it a damned shame to get the old boy out of bed.

He said: 'This is Mr. Callaghan. You remember me, Grant?'

'Why yes, sir,' said Grant. 'But . . .'

'All right,' said Callaghan. 'Where were you when the telephone bell rang, and where are you speaking from?'

Grant said in a surprised voice: 'I was in my room, sir, on the floor above – the third floor. When I heard the telephone I put on a dressing-gown and came down to the library on the floor below. I took your call on the extension line. It's always put through the library at night. Shall I . . .'

Callaghan said: 'Did you answer any telephone calls the night the Admiral died?'

Grant said: 'Yes, sir, I did. But you see – ' There was a pause, and the sound of another voice; then Grant continued: 'Miss Gardell's here, sir. Would you like to speak to her?'

Callaghan said: 'If you like. I don't mind.'

Desirée came on the line. Her voice was very low, almost caressing. Callaghan thought she had a hell of a voice. He liked it. He said: 'Hallo!'

She said: 'What do you want, Mr. Callaghan?'

Callaghan said: 'I don't want anything. Do you?'

He heard an exclamation of annoyance. She said:

'If you don't want anything, why are you telephoning at this unearthly hour?'

He said: 'I don't want anything *now*. I did want to speak to Grant. I've spoken to Grant. So now I'm quite happy.'

She said: 'I suppose it's part of your technique to telephone people's servants in the small hours of the morning?'

'Quite,' said Callaghan cheerfully. 'We do practically nothing else all day.'

She said: 'You're gratuitously insolent, aren't you, Mr. Callaghan? Will you please ring off. I don't want to talk to you.'

Callaghan said: 'You don't *have* to talk to me. Will you put Grant back on the line?'

She said: 'No . . . I will not. He's gone. And I refuse to have the household disturbed by you.'

'As a household disturber I'm unequalled,' said Callaghan. 'Tell me. Do you find me very disturbing?'

She said angrily: 'I find you very rude, and very boring and quite – ' She hesitated for the word.

'Despicable,' suggested Callaghan.

'Thank you,' she said. 'Despicable was the word.'

He heard the receiver replaced.

He sighed. He hung up, lit a fresh cigarette, walked about the sitting-room thinking until his feet began to feel cold.

Then he went back to bed.

CHAPTER EIGHT
NEAT STUFF

I

IT WAS three o'clock in the afternoon when Callaghan was shown into Vane's office. The lawyer looked at him over his pince-nez. He said, almost cheerfully:

'Good-afternoon, Mr. Callaghan.'

Callaghan said: 'Good-afternoon.'

He put his hat on the corner of the solicitor's desk, sat down, lit a cigarette. He felt a little sorry for Vane.

He said: 'Have you seen Manon?'

Vane said: 'Yes! She came in to see me this morning. She told me a rather extraordinary story. I gather she told it to you too?'

Callaghan said: 'Yes, she told me. It's not so good, is it?'

Vane said: 'I don't think I quite understand. What isn't so good?'

Callaghan said: 'Look, supposing you and I stop making circles round each other and get down to hard tacks? If the Insurance Company *and* Scotland Yard knew about the telephone conversation the Admiral had with Desirée, and the rest of the story that Manon's told you, it wouldn't look so good for Desirée, would it?'

Vane said: 'I'm sorry I can't agree with you, Mr. Callaghan. As I told you before, I could not swear to that telephone conversation.'

'Right,' said Callaghan. 'But *I* could swear to what you told me about that conversation.' He grinned. 'A jury would love that, wouldn't they?' he said. 'You going into the box and saying you couldn't be certain of what you heard, and then my going into the box and repeating quite plainly what you told me you heard. That would be evidence all right. You know the court would allow it, more especially as obviously you're an interested party.'

Vane said: 'Really, Mr. Callaghan!' He raised his eyebrows.

'Of course you are,' said Callaghan. 'Your firm's represented the Admiral and his family for years. Naturally, *you'd* do your best for Desirée.'

Vane said: 'Mr. Callaghan, I'm concerned only with the truth. Neither I nor Miss Gardell have anything to be afraid of.'

'That's right enough,' said Callaghan, 'so far as you're concerned. Whether Miss Gardell's position is as good is a question that none of us can answer at the moment – '

Vane interrupted. He said:

'I really can't allow you to make such extraordinary statements, Mr. Callaghan. I – '

Callaghan said: 'How d'you propose to stop me? In certain circumstances which you can easily guess, her position wouldn't be enviable. Although I must say you could, at least, produce a coherent story now – and that's a damned sight more than you could before.'

The lawyer put his finger-tips together.

He said: 'You seem to know exactly what the story would be, Mr. Callaghan.'

Callaghan said: 'I can make a good guess. The story would be that the Admiral rang through to Chipley Grange with some quite unintelligible message. The fact that it was unintelligible, you will suggest, would show his state of mind at the moment; would show that he was not quite himself. He then goes back to Chipley and kills himself, which he's told his daughter that he intended to do. She hears the shot. She discovers her father's body. She *says* she knows perfectly well that the Admiral was keen on the Insurance being paid, so she removes the gun and drops it in the lake in order that the Insurance Company shall pay in the belief that the Admiral was killed.'

Callaghan drew on his cigarette.

'The story has sequence; it would be easily believable. Unless something else turns up, it is ten to one that the prosecution wouldn't be able to disprove it. And we have to remember,' said Callaghan, with a glance at the lawyer that was almost arch, 'that in murder cases the prosecution have got to prove their case, and the accused hasn't got to prove his or her innocence.'

Vane said: 'Mr. Callaghan, where is all this leading? I should like to tell you that up to the moment I believe that you have been well disposed towards the Gardell family. I think, for instance, the advice that you gave to Miss Manon Gardell to come to me and tell me this story was good advice. I appreciate it. Now I want you to be frank with me and tell me exactly what it is you are trying to get at?' Vane continued, pursing his lips together and looking out of the window. 'You represent the Insurance Company. Would it be out of order if I asked what your report to them is likely to be?'

Callaghan said: 'It would be in order. I'll tell you. I'm going to advise the Insurance Company to pay that claim directly the ordinary normal formalities are completed.'

Vane nodded. A little smile appeared on his thin lips.

He said: 'That means, Mr. Callaghan, that you believe the Admiral *did* commit suicide.'

Callaghan said: 'Not exactly. Let me put it another way. It means that I, as Investigator for the Globe & Associated, have no reason to believe that the beneficiary under this Insurance policy has been connected with the death of the Admiral. It means that I consider the claim may be paid by them.'

Vane said: 'I approve your attitude, Mr. Callaghan. I appreciate it. You may rely on the fact that we, on our side, hope to show our gratitude in a practical form at some future date.'

Callaghan said: 'That's fine. But I want you to show your gratitude in a more practical form now, Mr. Vane.'

Vane said: 'I see . . .'

Callaghan said: 'Don't misunderstand me. You're thinking I want a *quid pro quo*. You're right. I do, but it is not what you think.'

The lawyer said: 'No? Then what is it, Mr. Callaghan?'

Callaghan said: 'The inquest on the Admiral has been adjourned for a fortnight. Chief Detective-Inspector Gringall is handling this case.'

He grinned. 'Gringall's pretty good. I know him well. He thinks this is a murder case. He'll go out to prove it. He thinks he can get sufficient evidence in a fortnight. If he can't, he'll ask for another adjournment.' He inhaled, blew the smoke out slowly through pursed lips. 'I don't think he'll need it,' he said.

Vane said: 'You mean by that . . . ?'

Callaghan said: 'I think this case will be tied up in the next fourteen days, but whatever happens I don't why see the Globe & Associated shouldn't pay that claim as soon as possible. I'll make a bargain with you – '

Vane interrupted: 'I'm sorry, Mr. Callaghan. I don't make bargains.'

Callaghan said: 'You'd be surprised. This is where you do make a bargain.' He went on: 'I'm going to advise the Globe & Associated to pay that Insurance claim. I'm not doing that because I like your face. I'm not doing that because I like Desirée Gardell's face – although I think it's a very handsome one.'

The lawyer asked: 'Why are you doing it?'

'I'll tell you,' said Callaghan. He grinned mischievously. 'Gringall's got an idea that I know something about this *murder* that he doesn't. That's why he's asked for that adjournment. He wants to see what I'm going to do. If I advise the Insurance Company to go on stalling and not pay this claim, Gringall will think that I have some definite evidence that I'm sitting down on. He'll find some means of prising it out of me. If, on the other hand, I advise the Company to pay the claim, he will think I know nothing. He will think I know of no reason why the claim shouldn't be paid. I want him to think that.'

Vane said: 'Mr. Callaghan, what is the bargain exactly? What is the *quid pro quo*?'

Callaghan said: 'I take it, Vane, that your one desire is to carry out the wishes of the late Admiral, isn't it?'

Vane nodded. Callaghan went on:

'Manon Gardell told me that one of the reasons why the Admiral originally intended to commit suicide, believing that the two years' period mentioned in the policy *had not expired*, was so that he might be revenged on somebody who would benefit by his death. In other words, he wanted to stop the Insurance claim being paid. You understand that?'

'I understand perfectly,' said the lawyer. 'I'd heard nothing about *this* angle before.'

'That's all right,' said Callaghan. 'You didn't have to hear about it, but I'm telling you now.' He went on: 'I want to do what the Admiral wanted done. You'd like that too, wouldn't you, Vane?'

The lawyer nodded.

'Of course,' he said.

'All right,' said Callaghan. 'I'm going to advise the Globe & Associated that this claim is in order, on the condition that you give me your word that, if and when that cheque for forty-five thousand pounds is paid over, you're not going to let Desirée or any one else handle one penny of it until I give you the word. In other words, you're going to hold it in trust until . . .'

Vane raised his eyebrows.

'Until when, Mr. Callaghan?' he asked. 'This is – '

Callaghan smiled amiably.

'Until I discover who murdered the Admiral,' he said. 'Well, what about it?'

Vane looked out of the window. It was some seconds before he said: 'And if I say no?'

Callaghan said: 'If you say no. I'm going to advise the Globe & Associated to refuse payment of that claim. I'm going to suggest that there is information in your possession which should rightly be laid before the authorities.'

Vane thought for a moment; then he said:

'Mr. Callaghan, I see nothing extraordinary in your request. In carrying it out I should be carrying out the wishes of my deceased client, and quite candidly, although I'd never before heard of this idea of his of stopping any benefit going, through Miss Gardell, to some other person, I'm prepared to take your word for it. I am prepared to hold this money in trust on my own responsibility as Executor of the Admiral, as and when it is paid, until such time as it is obvious that it may be handed over with – shall we say – complete safety.'

Callaghan said: 'That's fine.'

Vane said: 'Of course there should be some sort of time limit. A lawyer can't hold up the payment of money for ever, even if he is an Executor.'

Callaghan said: 'You should worry. I'll look after that. So long, Vane.' He went out.

II

Effie Thompson was pouring out tea when Callaghan walked into the office.

He said: 'Where's Nikolls?'

She said: 'He's with the head porter, Mr. Callaghan – Jarvis.' She smiled. 'The ex-Sergeant-Major.'

Callaghan asked: 'What's the joke?'

Effie said: 'It seems that Mrs. Jarvis had to go and see a sick cousin the other night, and it was perhaps unfortunate that Jarvis saw her and Nikolls coming out of a cinema just about the time she would have been with the sick cousin. But I've no doubt Mr. Nikolls will talk his way out of it.'

Callaghan said: 'Of course. He loves situations like that. He'll make Jarvis feel so bad about it that he'll probably *ask* Nikolls to take his wife out next time.'

She said: 'Yes, it's peculiar how rather uncouth and unattractive people like Mr. Nikolls get away with things.'

Callaghan said: 'Uncouth possibly – unattractive no, Effie. You've got your psychology wrong.'

She said: 'Probably Mr. Callaghan, but then I've never been particularly interested in psychology as regards sex.'

'No?' said Callaghan. 'You ought to be really.'

She said: 'May I ask why, Mr. Callaghan?'

'Oh nothing,' he answered. 'But you might be more of a match for Nikolls if you were. Let me have some tea, Effie,' he went on. 'And when our plump Lothario comes back, tell him to come in and see me.'

He went into his office. Nikolls arrived ten minutes later. He was looking quite pleased with himself.

He said: 'What's cooking?'

Callaghan said: 'I wish you'd keep your affairs of the heart away from this building. I understand there's been a little trouble with Jarvis and his wife?'

An injured expression appeared on Nikolls's face.

He said: 'What the hell! It's a funny thing, but every time a man has a decent motive about bringin' a little pleasure into some hard-workin' woman's life, everybody gets it wrong.'

'I know,' said Callaghan. 'It depends on what you mean by pleasure. Just lay off the head porter's wife, will you, Windy?'

Nikolls grinned.

'I've already fixed to do that,' he said. He sat down, produced a packet of Lucky Strikes, lit one. 'Have I gotta go to work?' he said.

Callaghan nodded.

'Don't make any mistakes about this,' he said. 'You've got to play this carefully. There's a butler at Chipley Grange by the name of Grant. He's a nice old boy. I imagine he's been with the family for a long time. He's probably the soul of loyalty. I want you to go down to Chipley and pick him up,' Callaghan went on. 'He has to go out sometimes. I want you to find out from him exactly what happened so far as he knows at Chipley on the night the Admiral died. I want you to pay particular attention to any telephone calls that came through and who answered them.'

'O.K.,' said Nikolls. 'When do I start in on this?'

'Now,' said Callaghan. 'I want you back to-night or early to-morrow morning.'

'I got it,' said Nikolls.

He went out.

Callaghan threw his cigarette into the fireplace, put on his hat. As he went through the outer office, Effie Thompson said:

'Do you know when you'll be back?'

Callaghan said: 'No. But if I'm not back by six, don't wait. I don't think anything's likely to happen to-day.'

Effie smiled. She said:

'I know! Its always on the days that you think nothing's going to happen that something does happen.'

'Meaning what?' asked Callaghan.

'Meaning that I'd better wait till you come back, or I hear from you,' said Effie.

Callaghan had opened the door. He turned. He said:

'That's an idea. Has any one told you, Effie, that you're a first-class secretary?'

She said: 'Several people, but where does it get me?'

Callaghan looked at her.

'Where do you want to get, Effie?' he asked.

She said: 'Mr. Callaghan, you ask the most ridiculous questions.' She began to work her typewriter.

III

Gringall was sitting at his desk, smoking his short briar pipe, when Callaghan was shown in. He said:

'Hallo, Slim. How are you?'

'Not too bad,' said Callaghan. 'All the better for seeing you.'

Gringall said: 'I'm glad you feel that way.' He picked up a pencil, began to draw a lemon on the blotter.

Callaghan said dramatically: 'Oh, hell . . . !'

Gringall looked up.

'Why that?' he asked.

Callaghan said: 'Whenever I come into this office and you begin to draw fruit on the blotter, I always know that means trouble for somebody.'

Gringall put the pencil down. He smiled. He said:

'Who are you expecting trouble for – you?'

'Oh no,' said Callaghan. 'Nobody can make any trouble for me . . . well, not yet.'

Gringall said: 'Well see. You never know your luck. What did you want to see me about, Slim?'

Callaghan said: 'It's about this Gardell claim. I think it's all right.'

Gringall raised his eyebrows.

He said: 'Is that what you came in to tell me?'

Callaghan said: 'Yes and no. The fact that I do tell you that, asks a question, doesn't it?'

Gringall said: 'You mean as to whether I think you're justified in reporting to the Globe & Associated that it's all right for them to go ahead and pass the claim?'

Callaghan said: 'Will you give me any reason why the Globe & Associated shouldn't pass the claim?'

Gringall grinned. He picked up the pencil again.

He said: 'So that's what you really came to see me about?'

Callaghan said: 'Well, what's the answer?'

Gringall leaned back in his chair. He relit his pipe.

He said: 'What do you care? If you honestly and sincerely believe that you're justified in telling the Globe & Associated to go on and pay that claim, why worry about us?'

Callaghan said: 'Why don't you have a heart, Gringall? You've asked for the inquest to be adjourned for fourteen days so that Maynes, who's handling this case, could get busy. Very naturally,' he went on, 'I don't want to make a fool of myself.'

Gringall said caustically: 'Is that possible?'

Callaghan said: 'Very easily. I've checked on all the angles on this Gardell claim, and I can't see any reason why it shouldn't be paid, but I haven't got the facilities that the police have; I haven't got all the majesty and power of the law behind me.'

Gringall whistled.

'I like that,' he said. 'Surely you don't think we've got any advantages on a case like this that you haven't. We can bribe and corrupt people, draw red herrings all over the place, make false statements, suborn witnesses like – '

'Like who?' Callaghan asked blandly.

'Some private investigators we know,' said Gringall. He put his pipe down on the desk. 'Anyhow,' he went on, 'as, in this particular case, Messrs. Callaghan Investigations seem to have behaved themselves – at least up to the moment – fairly well, I don't mind telling you what I know. I don't think it'll affect your report to the Globe & Associated one way or another. It's just interesting, that's all.'

Callaghan sat down. He lit a cigarette. He said:

'If it interests you, it's good enough for me. What is it, Gringall?'

Gringall said: 'That Insurance policy of the Admiral's was a rather interesting piece of business. The policy has only been in existence for a couple of years, and, having regard to the Admiral's age, and the state of his health, the premiums were heavy.'

Callaghan nodded.

'I know all that,' he said.

'The interesting question was,' said Gringall, 'Why he should suddenly decide to take out that policy. Do you know the answer?'

Callaghan said: 'No. That isn't part of my business.'

'I agree it isn't,' said Gringall. 'But nevertheless its interesting.' He began to refill his pipe. 'It seems,' he went on, 'That the Admiral was a gambler. As far as I can see he'd gambled most of his capital away. It seems that the old boy couldn't keep away from any sort of card game. Practically every roulette party in the West End knew Admiral Gardell – the big ones, I mean. He must have lost thousands during the past ten years.'

Callaghan nodded.

'All right,' he said. 'So what?'

Gringall said: 'About two years ago, Gardell lost about thirty thousand pounds in one night playing *chemie* and roulette. It seems he'd got in pretty bad at the beginning of the game, doubled his stakes, kept on doubling them, and kept on losing. Eventually he cut his main creditor double or quits and lost.'

'Nice going,' said Callaghan.

Gringall nodded.

'The devil of it was,' he continued, 'The Admiral couldn't pay. He couldn't pay without cleaning out the Gardell estate, and he didn't want to do that. Apparently he was decent enough to want to leave something to his daughter.'

'I see,' said Callaghan. 'So what did he do?'

'He managed to scrape up ten thousand,' said Gringall, 'which he paid over on account of his losses, and arranged to settle the balance as soon as he could. But he just couldn't raise the money. Then, apparently, he evolved a scheme which would enable him to satisfy his conscience and eventually satisfy this debt of honour. He took out that policy with the Globe & Associated for forty-five thousand pounds. The money, as you know, will go to the daughter. Then he gave a formal note, certified by his solicitor, Vane, in which he instructed his daughter, Miss Desirée Gardell, to pay over the balance of twenty thousand pounds due on the gaming debt as and when she received the forty-five thousand pounds from the Insurance Company.'

Callaghan said: 'But – '

Gringall interrupted: 'I know . . . I know if it was a gaming debt it would be illegal. But the Admiral looked after that point in the note. It said, "in consideration of services rendered." '

Callaghan said: 'Where did you get this from – Vane?'

Gringall nodded. 'He told Maynes the whole story.'

'Pretty good,' said Callaghan. He paused for a moment; then casually: 'Had he got anything else of interest to tell him?'

'That was all,' said Gringall. He began to draw a watermelon. 'So if your idea about the Admiral thinking he was committing suicide before the two years stipulated in the policy were up is right, it might look rather as though he was trying to stop somebody getting that twenty thousand pounds.'

Callaghan said: 'Yes. So it seems.' He stubbed out his cigarette, opened his cigarette-case, took out a fresh one. He took a long time about lighting it; then he said:

'Did Vane say who the individual holding the note was?'

Gringall said: 'He didn't know. The wording of the note concealed the identity of the individual who would benefit. It talked about "the bearer of his note." '

'Quite,' said Callaghan. 'That's why the Admiral took the trouble to get Vane to certify. Vane would recognise his own certificate and handwriting.'

Gringall nodded.

'That's all Maynes has got up to date,' he said. 'It's interesting, but it doesn't seem to affect the case very much.'

'You mean – ?' asked Callaghan.

Gringall said: 'I mean that we haven't altered our opinion that the Admiral was murdered.' He smiled at Callaghan. 'That doesn't affect any report that you, in your discretion, may care to make to the Insurance Company.'

Callaghan said: 'You're playing funny devils with me, aren't you, Gringall? Are you trying to give me a tip-off?'

Gringall sighed. He said:

'It's not my business to give you tip-offs, but I'd like to remind you of one or two things in that hectic career of yours. You remember that Vendayne business? Well, you were right about that. But you didn't know you were going to be right. You just did what you did because you fell like a ton of bricks for that Audrey Vendayne.' He grinned. 'Not that I blame you . . . Then there was that Riverton case – the same sort of story.'

Callaghan said: 'Why don't you say what you mean?'

Gringall said: 'I've heard that Desirée Gardell is an extremely beautiful young woman.'

Callaghan said: 'I've got it. So you think I'm fool enough to tell the Globe & Associated to pass that claim for payment just because Desirée Gardell is a beautiful young woman. Let me tell you something. She hates my guts.'

Gringall said: 'Well, that's a nice change!' He went on: 'I'm only telling you what I know, but if you think the job's all right, put your report in.'

Callaghan said: 'Listen. The trouble with you is that you're not half so clever as you think. Either that or you're not half such a damn' fool as you *look*.'

Gringall bowed. He said: 'Thank you for nothing.'

Callaghan went on: 'Will you do something for me?'

Gringall sighed.

'I knew it was coming,' he said. 'Well, what is it? But understand this. Maynes has already told me he'll be very tough with you if there's anything that looks like obstruction.'

Callaghan smiled: 'You tell Maynes to teach his grandmother how to suck eggs. That one hasn't got enough brains to come in out of the rain.'

Gringall said: 'I wouldn't tell him that if I were you. He thinks he's rather good. Well, what is it you want, Slim?'

Callaghan said: 'I want you to sit on Maynes's head for a bit. The fact that I'm reporting to the Globe & Associated that they can pass that claim means just nothing at all.'

'Nice work,' said Gringall. 'So you're playing hooky with your own clients now. It's wonderful what depth you private detectives will sink to. What is the big idea?'

Callaghan said: 'You mind your own business. I don't have to divulge my brilliant and scintillating methods to a lot of flatfeet. I'm reporting to the Globe & Associated that the claim's all right for passing for payment. Well, it's going to be some time before they pay it, isn't it? There are the usual formalities, and then, when they're through, the money will go to Vane, the executor.'

Gringall nodded.

'That's right,' he said.

'I've got an arrangement with Vane,' said Callaghan. 'He's not going to part with that money or any part of it until I give him the O.K. Understand?'

'I understand,' said Gringall. 'And that means that if later you were to find the claim wasn't quite in order, the money would still be available for return to the Globe & Associated?'

'That's right,' said Callaghan.

Gringall said: 'Well, that's very interesting.'

Callaghan said: 'You tell me something. Are you going to tell Maynes to lay off for another week or so?'

Gringall said: 'There's no reason to do that. Maynes – who, in my opinion, is a most efficient officer – is doing his damnedest, but his damnedest can't be very much.' He laid down his pencil. He went on: 'This is a damned funny murder. I've never known a murder with less motive or less evidence.'

Callaghan raised one eyebrow.

'Less motive?' he said. 'I can see the hell of a motive.'

'Such as?' queried Gringall.

'What about the boyo who's going to get the twenty thousand pounds?' said Callaghan. 'Supposing that boyo wasn't quite certain about the date on the Insurance policy. Supposing he thought that the Admiral was going to kill himself in order to prevent that policy being paid. He might get annoyed, mightn't he?'

Gringall said: 'That's what I thought.'

Callaghan got up. He said:

'Well, thank you for nothing, Gringall. I'll be on my way.'

Gringall said: 'Do. I've got work to do. And thank *you* for nothing.'

At the door, Callaghan said: 'The trouble with you is, you don't realise the terrific amount of assistance you get from private individuals like myself.'

Gringall said: 'No. And the trouble with you is that you don't know how lucky you are not to be in Portland with about seven years to go.'

Callaghan said amiably: 'All right. Nuts to you.'

Gringall took up his pencil.

'And to you,' he said as pleasantly.

He began to draw a pineapple.

IV

The Chinese clock on Callaghan's mantelpiece struck ten. Callaghan, who was pouring himself a whisky and soda, paused as he heard the key in the door of his apartment. Nikolls came in.

He said: 'I could do with one of them, Slim.'

Callaghan said: 'Help yourself.' He sat down in the armchair. He said: 'Well?'

Nikolls finished the whisky. He sighed; poured out another. He said:

'It looks to me like all this stuff about the Admiral's having called through to Chipley is a lot of hooey. I reckon Vane musta been dreamin'.'

Callaghan asked: 'Why?'

Nikolls said: 'Look, I talked to this butler guy – Grant. He's a nice old boy too. I met him down at the local in Chipley. We had two, three drinks together. Me – I like these old-time butlers. They got class. They – '

Callaghan said: 'Never mind the atmospherics. Get down to hard tacks.'

'O.K.,' said Nikolls. 'Well, Grant says this: He was sleeping in his room on the third floor the night the Admiral was creased. He hears the telephone ringin'. The time was about three o'clock. So he starts gettin' up. He put on his dressin' gown an' went down to the library, which is on the floor below, where's there's an extension line that you can talk on. It takes him some little time to get down there, an' he was worryin' because he thought he might not make it in time. He also thought it might be the Admiral comin' through. When he gets into the library the telephone is still ringin'. He takes off the receiver an' he says: "Hallo!" Well, there ain't any reply, so he says: "Hallo, Exchange . . . are you callin' me?" An' the girl at the Exchange says: "I don't want you . . . Sorry you've been troubled." So he hangs up the receiver an' goes back to bed. An' that's that.'

Callaghan lit a cigarette.

Nikolls went on: 'Grant says if there'd been any other telephone calls he'd have heard 'em. His hearin's very good. He says there wasn't any other calls. He says that it's the only call there was that night.'

Callaghan asked: 'Did he say where Desirée was?'

Nikolls said: 'Yeah. She musta been in her room, because next mornin', after she'd sorta got over the shock of the Admiral's death, she asked him who the telephone call was from. She'd heard the bell ringin'.'

Callaghan nodded.

He said: 'That's all right.'

Nikolls said: 'How come? Don't it sorta bust your theory? Maybe the Admiral wasn't speaking to Chipley Grange at all. Maybe he rang somewhere else. Maybe Vane only thought he was speakin' there.'

Callaghan said: 'Maybe, but I'm satisfied.'

Nikolls looked at his wrist-watch. He said:

'Do you want me any more?'

'No,' said Callaghan.

'O.K.,' said Nikolls. He grinned. 'I gotta date,' he said. 'I gotta date with a very nice little number. I oughta tell you about this number. It's a funny thing, but maybe you remember me tellin' you a story about some dame in Saskatoon – a dame with honey-coloured hair – '

Callaghan said: 'Look, Windy, do you think that story could wait?'

'O.K.,' said Nikolls. 'O.K. I'll be seein' you.'

He went out.

Callaghan lit a fresh cigarette. As he threw the match away, the telephone rang. It was Stephanie.

She said: 'Hallo, Slim. Remember me?'

Callaghan said: 'Of course, Stephanie. How could I forget you?'

She said: 'Remember I said I'd ring you up in a couple of days? Well, here I am.'

'That's nice of you, Stephanie,' said Callaghan. 'Have you got some news for me?'

'Maybe yes – maybe no,' she said. 'It depends on what you call news.'

Callaghan said: 'What are you doing?'

She laughed.

'At the moment I'm waiting to be asked out by you,' she said. 'Didn't I tell you that I was a little crazy over you?'

'That's right,' said Callaghan. 'I remember that too. I expect you're talking from a call-box, aren't you?'

'Yes,' said Stephanie. 'When I talk to private detectives I *always* talk from call-boxes.'

Callaghan said: 'How'd you like to meet me at the Green Canary Club in half an hour?'

'That'd suit me fine,' said Stephanie. 'I'll be seeing you.'

Callaghan hung up. He sat down in the big arm-chair; put his feet on the mantelpiece; smoked violently.

He felt almost contented.

CHAPTER NINE
THE CUSTOMER IS ALWAYS RIGHT

I

CALLAGHAN and Stephanie sat at the corner table furthest removed from the band platform at the Green Canary. It was one o'clock in the morning. Stephanie, casting a practised eye on Callaghan, came to the conclusion that he was a little high. And why not! During the last hour he had consumed enough liquor for four men. Brandy, whisky and bacardi had followed each other in succession. Most men, Stephanie thought, would have been unconscious. Callaghan must be pretty good to be only high.

She said; 'You're pleased with yourself about something, aren't you, Slim?'

He looked at her. His eyes were a little glassy.

He said: 'Why?'

'Oh, nothing,' said Stephanie. 'But I thought you'd be excited about hearing if I'd got anything to report.'

Callaghan said: 'About what?'

'About Nicky,' said Stephanie.

Callaghan shrugged his shoulders.

'Oh, that . . .' he said. 'I've got bigger fish to fry than that.' He had a little difficulty in speaking clearly. 'I've a great big fish, much more important than that poor sap Nicky.'

'So it's like that! Anyway, you're right about Nicky. That's what he is – a poor sap.' She looked at him quizzically. She wondered whether he was sufficiently far gone. She said: 'Let's have another drink.'

'Why not?' said Callaghan. 'The night is still young.'

He signalled the waiter, ordered more bacardi.

He said: 'You know, Stephanie, there is an old proverb: "Nothing succeeds like success." It's right. It doesn't matter a damn how you do it as long as you succeed – a process that justifies the motto of Callaghan Investigations.'

Stephanie said: 'So you've got a motto? That's interesting. What is it?' Her eyes were caressing.

Callaghan said: 'We've got two mottoes – one official, the other unofficial.'

Stephanie asked: 'The official one?'

Callaghan said: ' "The customer is always right." That's the official motto. The unofficial one is: "We get there somehow and who the hell cares how." '

Stephanie nodded.

'Two very good mottoes,' she said. 'And it looks to me as if you have got somewhere. I suppose you'd say I was curious if I asked why you're so pleased?'

Callaghan leaned over the table. He hiccupped.

He said: 'I wouldn't tell anybody but you, but I've been working on this Gardell case. You've probably seen something about it.'

'Oh, yes,' said Stephanie. 'I've seen it in the newspapers. Has it been exciting?'

Callaghan nodded.

'We've been working for the Insurance Company,' he said. 'And, believe me, it's going to be a very nice case.'

She said: 'What happened? They found an old Admiral dead in a wood some place, didn't they? He was murdered.'

Callaghan said: 'The joke is I don't think he was. I think he committed suicide.'

Stephanie said: 'No! Scotland Yard thinks he was murdered. It said in the papers that the inquest was adjourned for a fortnight. It said that the police were working on a clue.'

Callaghan grinned.

'Didn't you know, honey, that the police are always working on a clue?' he said. 'And even if they're not the newspapers always say they are.'

She said: 'I think it's *exciting*. This is the first time I've ever had inside information on a murder case.' She pouted prettily. 'And now it's not even a murder case.'

Callaghan said: 'That's right, it's not even a murder case.'

She said: 'But it's funny though. It said in the papers that no pistol had been found. If he'd killed himself,' she went on, 'they'd have found a pistol, wouldn't they?'

Callaghan put a cigarette in his mouth. He struck a match. He had a little difficulty in contacting the end of the cigarette with the flame. He said:

'That's the joke, sweetie-pie. There was a gun – but my client moved it. What do you know about that?'

Stephanie thought: My God – and I thought he was *clever*. He's just the same as the rest of 'em. He has a few drinks and talks too much. She said:

'This *is* exciting. But I thought you were working for the Insurance Company?'

Callaghan said thickly: 'So I am. Why?'

'Oh, nothing,' said Stephanie. 'But you just said that your client had moved the gun.'

'Oh, that . . .' said Callaghan. 'I'm doing a bit of work for Desirée Gardell – the daughter – too.' He leaned over the table, sank his voice a little. He said: 'The old boy shot himself all right. She heard the shot and ran out to see what the trouble was about. When she got there she found the Admiral had ironed himself out, see?'

'I see,' said Stephanie. 'But what did she want to move the gun for?'

Callaghan said: 'Well, the Admiral had taken out a big insurance on his life and Desirée wasn't certain whether the two years mentioned in the suicide clause in the policy were up or not. So she took the gun away and chucked it in the lake to make it look like murder.'

Stephanie looked amazed.

'She's got a nerve, I must say,' she said. 'I say, what do you know about *that*? So that's why the police think it was murder?'

Callaghan nodded sagely.

'What the hell does it matter what they think?' he said.

'Quite,' said Stephanie. She smiled at him prettily. 'The only thing that does matter is what Mr. Callaghan gets out of it.'

Callaghan winked.

'How right you are, Stephanie,' he said.

She looked at him with admiration.

'You've got brains all right, haven't you?' she said with a smile. 'If I know anything of you, Slim, you're going to collect from both sides. You'll draw your fees from the Insurance Company, and I suppose the lady will be very glad to pay too.'

'Like hell she will,' said Callaghan. 'She'll pay and she'll like it!'

'She'll *have* to pay, won't she?' said Stephanie.

Callaghan said: 'How do you mean?'

'Well,' said Stephanie, 'you've got her where you want her, haven't you? If she didn't pay and you were to tell the police that story, they might think all sorts of unkind things about her. They might even think she killed the Admiral.'

Callaghan said: 'They couldn't think a thing like that. Oh, no . . . she's not the sort of girl who'd go around killing people.'

'Isn't she?' asked Stephanie innocently. 'I didn't know the police worried a lot about what sort of girl you were.'

Callaghan said: 'Anyway, that point won't arise.' He finished the bacardi. He said: 'Where's Starata, Stephanie?'

Stephanie said: 'He's going to ring me to-morrow and arrange for me to meet him.' She put her hand on Callaghan's. 'Don't worry,' she said. 'Give me ten minutes with Nicky, and I'll find out just where he is and anything else that's going.'

Callaghan said: 'Well, all right. Can I be sure of that information the day after to-morrow? I might want to see Nicky.'

Stephanie said: 'Yes, you can rely on that – the day after to-morrow.'

Callaghan leaned back in the chair. He was keeping his eyes open with difficulty.

Stephanie said: 'I think you're a trifle cock-eyed. I think you ought to get some sleep, Slim. I'm a little tired myself. Shall we break it up?'

Callaghan nodded.

'It's a hell of an idea, Steve,' he said. 'Let's get out of here. When you've seen Nicky, ring me up and give me the works.' He fumbled in his waistcoat pocket, produced a small leather case. 'I've got something for you,' he said. 'How d'you like it?'

She opened the case. Inside was a diamond anchor brooch.

She said: 'This is wonderful, Slim.' She squeezed his hand. 'I'll always wear this,' she said. 'I think it's terrific.'

Callaghan said: 'I'm glad you like it, but I wouldn't wear it when you're going to meet Nicky. *He* might not like it.'

She put the case in her handbag.

She said: 'You should worry about Nicky.'

II

Callaghan walked slowly back across Berkeley Square. He was wondering whether Stephanie would react in the way she ought to react. He thought she would.

He took the lift straight up to his apartment. Inside, he threw his hat on the settee, went into the bathroom, drank some cold water. He thought he would not be feeling so good to-morrow morning.

He came out of the bathroom, went to the sitting-room telephone. He dialed 'o.' He asked to be connected with the supervisor at Chipley telephone exchange. The operator said he would call him. Callaghan helped himself to a cigarette; sat in the armchair waiting.

Five minutes afterwards the call came through.

Callaghan said: 'Is that the supervisor, Chipley Exchange?'

The voice said it was. Callaghan said:

'I want to report one of your operators. She was very rude to me three of four nights ago. I was ringing through from here to a Chipley number somewhere in the region of four in the morning. I gave her the number and she told me to hold on, but nothing happened. Then minutes after I rang again. When I asked her what she was doing about the number, she said – '

The supervisor interrupted: 'Excuse me, sir, but did you say "She" . . . ?'

'That's right, I said "she." '

The supervisor said: 'I'm afraid you're making a mistake. There wouldn't be any women operators on this exchange at that time in the morning. After twelve midnight all our operators are men.'

Callaghan said: 'You don't say. Now what do you know about that? It looks as if somebody's been pulling my leg.'

The supervisor said it looked like that.

Callaghan said: 'Thanks a lot.'

He hung up.

In spite of his mouth, which was feeling like an arid desert after the whisky, brandy and bacardi, he went to the sideboard. He poured himself out three fingers of rye, drank it at a gulp, shuddered a little.

So that was that.

He began to walk up and down the sitting-room. Callaghan sighed. It seemed to him that something must be done, and the sooner the better.

He went into his bedroom, stripped, put on a swimming suit. He dressed quickly, found a silver flask, filled it with bourbon from the bottle on the sideboard. He went into the bathroom, rolled up a towel. He put on his hat and overcoat, went down to the office on the floor below. He cut an eight-foot length from a ball of string on the shelf above Effie Thompson's desk; put it in his pocket.

Then he went out; walked across Berkeley Square towards the garage.

III

Callaghan stopped the car on the dirt that curved round the right flank of Chipley Grange; drove it into the cover of the bushes. He got out and began to search for the lane that ran through the coppice.

He walked down it. It led past the hedgerow that bounded the right-hand side of The Grange flower-gardens, through a little wood into a clearing, then through the coppice. Callaghan walked for fifteen yards and stopped. Here was another smaller clearing, and thirty or forty yards away to the left Callaghan could see the ornamental footbridge that spanned the narrow end of the little lake.

The moon was going in. He thought it would be quite dark fairly soon. He walked back to the coppice, sat down on a convenient tree stump, lit a cigarette and waited. Half an hour afterwards he began to undress. A breeze had sprung up; it was cold. Callaghan, who was feeling the reaction after the large quantity of spirits he had consumed with Stephanie, felt chilly. He began to curse fluently. He cursed every one connected – directly or indirectly – with the Gardell Insurance claim. As he approached nearer to the footbridge his language became worse.

He searched about till he found a large stone which he tied on one end of the string which he had taken from his overcoat pocket; dropped the stone into the lake. The whole length of string was submerged before the stone touched bottom. Callaghan sighed – so the water was more than eight feet deep.

He stood for a few minutes looking at the placid and chilly-looking water. With a final curse he dived in.

IV

Callaghan woke up. He lay for some minutes, his hands behind his head, looking at the ceiling. Then he reached out for the house telephone. He said to the house porter:

'Send me up some strong tea . . . And put me through to my office, will you?'

When Effie came on the line he said: 'Good-morning, Effie. Is Nikolls there?'

She said he was.

'Tell him to come up here,' said Callaghan.

He got out of bed. He sat on the edge of the bed, examined the large piece of sticking-plaster which covered a cut on his big toe, the result of a sharp flint on the bed of the Chipley ornamental lake. He muttered some rude things about ornamental lakes.

He got into his dressing-gown, lit a cigarette. The tea arrived simultaneously with Nikolls.

Callaghan said: 'I have a job for you, Windy.'

Nikolls said: 'I'm roarin' to go. I'm feelin' full of energy this mornin'. I feel that nothin' could stop me.'

Callaghan said: 'I'm glad about that. But you won't have to use a great deal of energy.' He poured out a cup of tea; sat on the arm of the big leather arm-chair, sipping it.

He said: 'I've got an idea that Maynes is going to start dragging operations on the ornamental lake at Chipley.'

Nikolls said: 'Yeah? What's he doin' that for?'

Callaghan said: 'I think he hopes to find a gun there.'

Nikolls asked: 'Where is this lake?'

'It's about forty yards from the coppice where they found the Admiral,' said Callaghan.

Nikolls grunted.

'This Maynes guy must be nuts,' he said. 'An' he must think that the killer was as nutty as he was if he was goin' to crease a guy an' then chuck the gun in a lake forty yards away. It's stickin' outa foot that the cops would look there for it.'

Callaghan said: 'You mean there wouldn't be a gun there anyway.'

Nikolls nodded.

'That's what I mean,' he said.

Callaghan said: 'You'd be right. There's not a gun there.'

Nikolls said: 'I don't get this. I – '

Callaghan said: 'You don't have to. There was a gun there, but I've got it. I spent a good twenty minutes crawling around the bed of that lake, disentangling myself from weeds, last night. But I found the damn' thing.'

Nikolls whistled.

'So it was there! Well . . . well . . . well . . . ! He shrugged his shoulders. 'Still,' he went on, 'that don't make Maynes any more sensible.'

Callaghan said: 'Maynes will probably have a better reason than you think for dragging that lake. What I want you to do is to get down to Chipley and park yourself somewhere near the lake where you can't be seen. If you see anybody start dragging operations on that lake, just ring through here and let me know immediately.'

Nikolls said: 'What do I do then?'

'You come back here,' said Callaghan.

'O.K.,' said Nikolls. 'I'll be seein' you.'

He went out.

Callaghan picked up the office telephone. He said to Effie:

'Effie, is there anything important?'

'Nothing very much, Mr. Callaghan,' she said. 'A few letters – none of them important. Oh, there's a letter marked personal. I'm not sure of the handwriting.'

'What do you mean – you're not sure of the handwriting?'

Her voice was a trifle acid. She said:

'Well, it might be Miss Vendayne. Then again it might be Mrs. Riverton. Then again it might be Miss Wilbery. I never can tell which is which.'

Callaghan said: 'Well, even if you could, you wouldn't be very interested, would you?'

She said: 'Not at all, Mr. Callaghan.'

'You can send that letter up,' said Callaghan. 'I'm going to bed. If any one wants to see me to-day I'm out.'

'Very well, Mr. Callaghan,' said Effie. 'Will you take any telephone calls?'

'Only from Nikolls,' said Callaghan. 'If he comes on the line put him through – no one else. You got that?'

Effie said she'd got it.

Callaghan went back to bed.

V

It was eight o'clock when the telephone in Callaghan's bedroom began to ring. He awoke, stared at the ceiling, stretched. Eventually, cursing, he put out his hand and took off the receiver.

It was Nikolls. He said:

'That you, Slim. I'm speakin' from the Chipley Arms in the village. Your guess was right. Maynes got down about an hour ago an' started draggin' the lake at The Grange. He was still at it when I left there.'

Callaghan said: 'I hope it keeps fine for him.'

Nikolls asked: 'Am I through down here?'

'Yes,' said Callaghan. 'You can come back as soon as you like.'

'D'you want me sorta urgent?' asked Nikolls.

Callaghan said: 'What is it? Some woman, I suppose?'

Nikolls said: 'In a way . . . yeah. There's a smart little number in the Chipley Arms here – '

Callaghan said: 'Well . . . you can come back to-morrow if you want to. But make it early.'

'O.K.,' said Nikolls. 'But I was tellin' you about this little number. This dame is the very spit of a baby I knew way back a long time ago in Coronado.'

'I know,' said Callaghan. He yawned. 'She was crazy about you, wasn't she?'

'That's right,' said Nikolls. 'Now how the heck did you know that? Well, anyway, this baby in Coronado was a very sweet-lookin' bundle of woman. An' one evenin' . . .'

Callaghan replaced the receiver. He dressed quickly, drank four fingers of rye, took the lift downstairs. Wilkie, the night porter, was on duty in the hall office.

Callaghan said: 'I'm going to the Ardayne Lounge in Dover Street. If any one wants me call me there. You've got the number.'

He went out, crossed the Square, walked up Berkeley towards Piccadilly. It was a fine evening. He turned into Dover Street, went into the Ardayne Grill. He sat at his usual table in the corner, ordered his dinner, read *The Evening News*. He was half-way through his meal when the page-boy from upstairs came over to his table.

'You're wanted on the phone, Mr. Callaghan,' he said. 'Berkeley Square's on the line.'

Callaghan went upstairs, into the ground-floor telephone booth. It was Wilkie.

He said: 'Miss Gardell's here, Mr. Callaghan. She's in the hall waiting-room. She wants to speak to you. I told her I *might* be able to get you on the telephone.'

Callaghan said: 'Which Miss Gardell is it? D'you know?'

Wilkie said: 'No, I don't. Shall I ask her?'

'Don't bother,' said Callaghan. 'Is she a brunette or a blonde?'

'She's a brunette,' said Wilkie promptly. 'She's terrific. I've never seen any one like her.'

Callaghan grinned.

'That's Miss Desirée Gardell,' he said. 'You might remember that for future reference. Go and tell her I'm coming over; that I'll be with her in five minutes. Then take her up to my apartment and give her a cigarette.'

'Right, Mr. Callaghan,' said Wilkie.

Callaghan went downstairs to the Grill Room, paid his bill. He got his hat and began to walk slowly back towards Berkeley Square.

Wilkie was waiting just inside the hallway. He said:

'I've taken Miss Gardell up to your apartment. I don't think she's awfully pleased about something.'

Callaghan nodded. He got into the lift, went up to his apartment.

Desirée Gardell was sitting on the settee. She turned her head as the door opened and Callaghan came in. She looked at him for a long time. She said nothing.

Callaghan dropped his hat on to a chair, produced his cigarette-case, lit a cigarette. His attitude was casual. He said:

'Welcome to London, Miss Gardell. It's nice to see you. What can I do for you?'

'I'm not concerned with what you *can* do, Mr. Callaghan. I've come to see you with reference to some things that I insist you stop doing!'

Callaghan raised one eyebrow. He looked at her. He thought: She's a hell of a woman. She knows all about clothes and how to wear them. I think I'm sorry for her.

He said: 'Would you like a cigarette?'

She shook her head. Callaghan noted with approval the neat coiffure, and the very smart tailor-made black hat trimmed with an ocelot buckle. She wore a black coat and skirt. The revers of the coat were faced with ocelot matching the buckle in her hat. Her stockings were of sheer beige silk and her small feet were shod in neat black kid court shoes. Definitely a woman with a sense of clothes, thought Callaghan. And she's in a hell of a temper. This *ought* to be good.

He said amiably: 'So you've come to see me about some things that I'm to *stop* doing. Such as . . . ?'

'Such as sending your assistants to snoop down at Chipley; to cross-examine my servants. I would like to know by whose authority you do these things. I insist that they stop. If they don't I propose to put the matter in the hands of the police!'

Callaghan walked slowly towards the sideboard. He said to her, over his shoulder, as he passed the settee:

'You know, you ought to relax. You're worked up about something, aren't you? Would you like a drink?'

She said: 'No, I would not. And it's perfectly true that I'm worked up as you call it, Mr. Callaghan. I've come here to tell you that I propose to stand no more of your impertinent interference.'

Callaghan said: 'All right.' He poured himself out a generous whisky and soda. 'And how do you propose to stop it?' he asked.

She said: 'I've told you. If necessary, I shall most certainly go to the police.'

Callaghan walked over to the fireplace and switched on the electric fire. He sat down in the arm-chair, facing her. He said:

'That's all right. But exactly what do you propose to tell the police?'

She was white with rage. Callaghan thought she looked wonderful. He concluded now quite definitely that her eyes *were* violet.

She said: 'I shall ask them to prevent you from carrying on with your so-called investigations. I shall tell them that you are deliberately doing everything in your power to annoy me, and I shall tell them the reason.'

'That ought to be interesting,' said Callaghan. 'And what would the reason be?'

She said: 'The reason should be obvious, even to your limited intelligence.' Callaghan could see that her fingers were trembling. He grinned at her provokingly.

'Well, we live and learn. It's the first time that I've heard that my intelligence is limited.'

She said bitterly: 'Very obviously your intelligence is limited.'

He drew on his cigarette. He said:

'Never mind my behaviour and my limited intelligence. Supposing you go to the police, Miss Gardell, and tell them that I'm doing everything in my power to interfere with and annoy you. Well, what's my reason?'

'Your reason is obvious,' she said. 'You wanted to be employed by me. But I didn't need your services, so naturally you're going to make yourself as troublesome as possible.'

Callaghan said: 'This business about your not wanting to use my services . . . I don't think I asked you to ring my office in the first place, which you did; or for your cousin to get through, which she did. But there's another and more important point,' Callaghan went on. 'If you remember, your father came up to see me on the night that he met his death. I am naturally very interested to know what he wanted to see me about. I might even make some guesses, but I expect, as my intelligence is limited, that any guess I might make would be wrong, wouldn't it?'

She said curtly: 'I don't know. How can I know? I don't know what your guess is.'

Callaghan said: 'Maybe I'll tell you.' He threw his cigarette stub away; lit another one. 'The trouble is,' he went on, 'you'll think that I'm trying to stop the Insurance Company paying this claim.'

'What else are you doing?' she asked.

Callaghan said: 'All right. Let's take the point of view that I am. Why shouldn't I? I'm an investigator employed by the Insurance Company. It's my business to find out if a claim is in order. If I believe that this claim isn't in order, I shouldn't be doing my duty if I advised the Insurance Company that it was all right for them to pass the claim.'

She said: 'You know perfectly well that this claim *is* in order.'

'I know nothing of the sort,' said Callaghan. He got up. He began to walk up and down the room. 'Do you know, Miss Gardell,' he went on, 'if the police thought that I was passing this claim for payment at the present moment they'd believe I was mad? They're not at all satisfied, are they?'

She asked: 'What do you mean by that?'

'A little bird tells me that they've started dragging operations on the lake at Chipley.'

She said coldly: 'A little bird tells you? More snooping, I suppose, Mr. Callaghan?'

He said: 'Never mind the snooping. What do you think the police are dragging that lake for?'

She said: 'I haven't the remotest idea.'

'That's a silly, childish lie,' said Callaghan.

She got up. She was trembling with rage. She said:

'Mr. Callaghan, I don't intend to stay here to be insulted. I don't intend – '

Callaghan said: 'I don't intend to stay here and listen to damned rubbish either. Supposing you sit down. I want to talk to you, and if you've got any sense in that pretty head of yours you'll listen.'

Desirée gasped a little. But she sat down.

Callaghan said: 'Don't put on any acts with me. I don't like 'em and it isn't necessary. Most of my life people have been putting on acts for my benefit. Usually the people I deal with have to put on acts – they've got plenty to hide. I don't expect people like you to behave in the same way.'

She said acidly: 'A lecture on morals from Mr. Callaghan should be very interesting – '

'You're telling me,' said Callaghan. 'And *how* I could lecture.' He paused; drew tobacco smoke down into his lungs. He said: 'Now let you and me talk a little hard sense. You're in a rather tough spot, don't you think?'

She said: 'I don't know what you mean, and if you think I'm afraid of you, Mr. Callaghan – if you think I should be affected by any threats – '

Callaghan said: 'I don't *have* to threaten. People only use threats when they haven't got facts to support an argument. I've got all the facts I want.'

'Really!' she said. 'How interesting!'

'The trouble with you is,' said Callaghan, 'that you want that insurance paid. You want it paid quickly. You've got a reason for wanting it paid quickly. But if I were you I wouldn't be impatient.'

She said: 'I'm waiting to hear those facts of which you spoke, Mr. Callaghan. I don't know that I'm interested in anything else you have to say.'

Callaghan said: 'All right. Let's stick to the facts. I know the Admiral came to see me and discovered that I was out. After he'd left the note telling me he was going to commit suicide next morning, he went off, expecting to come back. He knocked up Vane, asked to see the Insurance policy. He looked at the date of the insurance policy and became aware of something – something that should interest you.' He smiled at her.

'Well, what was it?' she asked.

'He looked at the date on the policy,' said Callaghan, 'and realised that as the two years were up, even if he did commit suicide, the Insurance Company would still pay. So he decided *not* to commit suicide. Apparently the Admiral wasn't so keen on dying as everybody thought. He decided to go on living. Not only did he decide that, but he also made up his mind that he was coming to see me again so that, presumably with my assistance, he might see something through to the bitter end.'

'All this is very interesting,' she said. 'But it is merely surmise.'

'Oh no, it isn't,' said Callaghan. 'When the Admiral was round at Vane's place, he rang through to Chipley Grange. He rang through after he'd examined the policy. He spoke to someone at Chipley Grange. He told that somebody that he'd changed his mind about things, meaning that he'd changed his mind about committing suicide, which the person at the other end of the line would understand very well. He also said that he'd made up his mind to see this business through to the bitter end. You ought to know all that.'

She asked a little hoarsely: 'Why should I know?'

'Because he was talking to you,' said Callaghan. 'That's why you should know.'

She said: 'That is a lie. My father did not ring up. He did not speak to me.'

Callaghan raised his eyebrows.

'No?' he said. 'Well, Vane's got a different story. Vane will, if necessary, go into the box and prove that the Admiral rang Chipley Grange. I know what he said on the telephone because Vane told me, and it's too late for Vane to duck. There was only one person that the Admiral would speak to at Chipley Grange about this matter. That person was you.'

She repeated: 'That is a lie.'

'All right,' said Callaghan. 'It's a lie. But what do I care? It's supported by fact. You know,' he went on, 'if you think I'm making this up, go and see Vane. He'll support it all right.'

She said: 'I don't trust you. There's some trickery in this. You've some scheme afoot.'

Callaghan said: 'You're dead right. I've got several schemes afoot. But none of them exactly what you think. If you think that what I've told you sounds nonsense, let's try and find some supporting facts for it, shall we?'

'Do,' she said sarcastically.

Callaghan said: 'All right. The Admiral went back to Chipley. Somebody heard his car arrive. Somebody was rather keen to speak to him quickly; to know exactly what had happened; possibly to know why he'd changed his mind. So that somebody threw on some clothes, went out to meet him. Whoever it was knew perfectly well that it was his habit to drive round to the back lane and walk through the coppice so as not to drive up to the house and disturb everybody. That somebody met the Admiral. And then the Admiral died.' Callaghan blew a smoke ring. 'Anybody who reads any detective story knows,' he went on, 'that when you've killed a man with a pistol it's a very good thing to get rid of the gun. So somebody dropped the gun in the lake. That somebody was you.'

She said nothing.

Callaghan said: 'Well, does the second part of the story make the first part look true or doesn't it?'

She said: 'Supposing your second part of the story were true. Supposing for the sake of argument that I did drop the pistol in the lake, what difference does that make? Do you think that proves I killed my father?'

'No!' said Callaghan. 'It doesn't exactly prove it, but it doesn't look too good, does it? Quite obviously,' he went on, 'when the police find that gun they're going to discover two facts about it. The first fact might be that it was a revolver owned by the Admiral. If that gun had been found in his hand the police would probably conclude he'd committed suicide. As it wasn't, they'll know it was moved by someone. When people move pistols and throw 'em in lakes after other people have just died, the police are quite entitled to regard that as suspicious behaviour. That suspicious behaviour, taken in conjunction with the fact that the Admiral held a definite conversation with you earlier, makes things look pretty bad for you. You know, you'd feel a lot better if you told the truth about this business.'

She said: 'But surely the brilliant Mr. Callaghan knows everything that's in my mind. Don't tell me there's *anything* you don't know?'

'Once again I could make a good guess,' said Callaghan. 'I know something else about the Admiral. The Admiral wanted to stop payment on that insurance claim. If the two years hadn't been up he would have shot himself so as to stop payment of the claim. But he still intended to be revenged on the person he disliked – the person who he did not wish to receive that insurance money.' He grinned at her. 'You know to whom you were going to pay that money – or some of it – don't you?'

She said weakly: 'Do I?'

'Of course you do,' he said. The Admiral told you all about that note that Vane certified – the note that entitled the bearer to be paid twenty thousand pounds on demand from that Insurance policy. You must know the name of the person, and probably you know why the Admiral wanted to stop that payment.' He paused. 'And yet you're still impatient for that money to be paid. Well, if I was a policeman I know what I'd think.'

She asked: 'What would you think?'

'I'd think you were playing hand in glove with whoever it is is going to receive that twenty thousand pounds. Maybe he's a boy friend of yours.'

She said coldly: 'You're a fearfully common person, aren't you? I don't have boy friends.'

'Too bad,' said Callaghan. 'Well, you may not have boy friends, but that's no reason why the police, who are also fearfully common at times, shouldn't think so.'

She said: 'I don't care what they believe. I have nothing to be afraid of.'

Callaghan said: 'Oh yes, you have. That's why I'm glad you're here so that we can do a deal.'

She laughed.

She asked caustically: 'Mr. Callaghan, do you think I'd do a deal with you?'

'You'll do a deal all right,' said Callaghan. 'Listen to this: Everything you think about this business is wrong. Everything you think about me is wrong.' He leaned up against the sideboard. He looked at her quizzically. 'You'd be awfully surprised if I told you I was a friend of yours, wouldn't you?'

She raised her eyebrows in astonishment. A cynical smile appeared on her lips.

Callaghan said: 'Nevertheless it's true. I rather like you. I like your type. I like the way you wear your clothes. I like most things about you.' He smiled. 'The fact that you *don't* like me doesn't affect my opinion a bit. Believe it or not, I've turned myself into a sort of guardian for you – a guardian angel. I like that idea.'

She said: 'My God! Imagine Mr. Callaghan of Callaghan Investigations a guardian angel!'

'That's right,' said Callaghan. 'If you wait long enough you'll see some wings sprouting.' He continued: 'You know, whether you like it or not, I've always looked on the Admiral as being a client of Callaghan Investigations. He intended to be. He thought enough of me to come and ask for help. Well, in spite of the feet that he's dead, he's going to get it.'

She said sarcastically: 'What an altruist you are, Mr. Callaghan.'

'Not often,' said Callaghan. 'But in this case there are redeeming features.'

'Such as?' she asked.

'Such as you,' said Callaghan. 'If you were an old lady of ninety, Callaghan Investigations wouldn't be interested very much. But you're not.'

She said: 'I suppose I should be very grateful to you for your interest. You're amusing me a great deal, Mr. Callaghan. But I still haven't heard about this deal.'

'The deal is this,' said Callaghan. 'You tell me something that I want to know and I'll get the Insurance Company to pass that claim. The very fact that I pass that claim is an important factor as far as *you're* concerned. The police will know that as far as *I'm* concerned – and remember I've had ample opportunities to find things out – everything is in order; that I at least have found nothing that looks suspicious. Also they'll be inclined to take the point of view that I want 'em to take eventually.'

'And what is that, Mr. Callaghan?' she asked.

'That,' said Callaghan, 'is my business.' He went on: 'That is the deal. You tell me the name of the person to whom that twenty thousand pounds was to be paid and I'll advise the Company to pass that claim for payment. Moreover, I think I can promise you that the business of dropping the gun in the lake won't trouble the police too much.'

She said: 'You must have great influence with the police, Mr. Callaghan.'

He shook his head. He was grinning. He said:

'No, I haven't any influence with the police, but I've something very much more important. I've got the gun.'

She looked at him; her eyes were wide with astonishment.

'The things I do for you,' said Callaghan. 'Crawling about on my belly on the bottom of your very cold ornamental lake finding pistols which you're foolish enough to throw in.' He opened the sideboard drawer.

He took out the pistol. 'I expect you recognise it,' he said. 'Well, do we do a deal?'

She said: 'Haven't you rather delivered yourself into my hands, Mr. Callaghan? Even supposing that your idea about my throwing the gun in the lake was correct, it couldn't be proved.'

'That wouldn't matter,' said Callaghan. 'If I told the police I'd removed it, they wouldn't be surprised. I've done things like that before for clients.'

She said: 'I see.'

Callaghan said: 'The other point is I could still prove if necessary that you did throw that gun in the lake.'

'How?' she asked.

'Somebody saw you drop it in,' said Callaghan.

'Somebody saw me drop it in,' she repeated. 'But who – ?'

Callaghan interrupted.

'That again is my business. Well, do we do a deal?'

She got up. She said:

'I must be going. It's getting late. I didn't intend to stay here so long.'

'Quite,' said Callaghan. 'You merely came here to give me a little lecture. Isn't that so?'

She said: 'What I came here for doesn't matter.' She turned and faced him. She said: 'Do I take it that if I were to tell you the name of the person to whom my father wished that twenty thousand pounds paid you would get the Insurance Company to pass the claim?'

'That's right,' said Callaghan. 'Once I have the information you can take it from me that a cheque from the Insurance Company will be in Vane's hands as soon as the necessary formalities are completed.'

'Very well, I'll tell you. It was a Mr. Mendes – a Mr. Raoul Mendes.'

Callaghan said: 'Thank you. You don't know where this Mendes lives by any chance, do you?'

She said: 'I don't. And if I did I shouldn't tell you, Mr. Callaghan. You asked for the name. I've given it to you. You made a deal. I expect you to keep it.'

'I'll keep it all right,' said Callaghan. 'I'll get in touch with the Insurance Company to-morrow.'

She said: 'Very well . . . good-night . . .'

'Good-night,' said Callaghan. He was watching her. He thought that she seemed hesitant, undecided. He opened the door for her.

She said in a low voice: 'Don't worry to see me out. I know how to work the lift.'

'Right,' said Callaghan. He added, inconsequently: 'You've got a pretty good nerve, haven't you? All the same it's nearly at breaking-point. You'd better watch out.'

She was already through the doorway and in the corridor. She stopped dead, turned, faced him. Callaghan saw that her eyes were filled with tears. He smiled at her.

'Why don't you let your hair down and relax?' he asked. 'You're not feeling so good . . . hey? You're in such a state of mind that you won't even be helped? And you need help. Plenty of it.'

She said in a trembling voice: 'I don't know *who* to trust. I wish I could trust you. I – '

Callaghan said: 'The Admiral was prepared to trust me, wasn't he?'

She burst into tears. She leaned against the wall of the corridor and covered her face with her hands. Her shoulders shook.

Callaghan put his hands in his coat pockets. He leaned against the doorpost watching her. He was thinking that she was one of the few women he had met in his life who could cry gracefully.

He said: 'If you had any sense instead of being such a little fool you'd have one damned good reason for knowing you could trust me.'

She took her hands away from her face. She said: 'What do you mean?' She could hardly speak.

Callaghan took his hands out of his pockets. He put them behind her shoulders. He drew her towards him.

'I mean this,' he said. He kissed her on the lips. Then he released her, leaned back against the doorpost, grinned at her. She put her hands back over her face.

Callaghan said: 'You're going to have a drink – a whisky and soda. Then you're going back to Chipley. You're not going to worry your head about anything. You're going to do what you're told. See?'

She nodded weakly. She followed Callaghan back into his sitting-room. She said:

'I wish I could *understand* you. You're an odd person. In spite of the fact that I think I dislike you . . . I believe . . . I believe . . .'

She sat down in the arm-chair in front of the electric fire. She began to cry.

Callaghan, busy at the sideboard said: 'You should worry. With us, the customer is always right!'

CHAPTER TEN
CONVERSATION PIECES

I

CALLAGHAN had finished shaving when Nikolls came into the sitting-room. He called out from the bathroom:

'You're back early, aren't you? What about the girl at The Chipley Arms – did she give you the air?'

Nikolls said: 'Oh, that . . . I sorta didn't waste very much time with that baby. There's a guy who's a military policeman around there who's interested in her – a tough *hombre*. So I thought I wouldn't bother a lot.'

Callaghan came into the sitting-room. He said:

'Did you hear anything?'

'Yeah,' said Nikolls. 'I heard a lot of stuff last night. Everybody's talkin' about the Admiral bein' creased.'

Callaghan helped himself to a cigarette. As he lit it, he said:

'What do they think down there?'

Nikolls sat in the arm-chair. He stretched himself luxuriously.

'They all think the old boy committed suicide.'

Callaghan asked: 'Anything else?'

'Not much,' said Nikolls. 'There's a lotta talk about Desiray an' Manon.'

'What talk?' asked Callaghan.

'Well, it looks as if some big county guy wanted to marry Manon last year,' Nikolls went on. 'This fella had everythin' – looks an' money an' what have you got.'

Callaghan said: 'And then what happened?' He looked out of the window. 'Manon turned him down, I suppose?'

Nikolls said: 'How did you know?'

Callaghan grinned.

'I was just guessing,' he said. 'What about Desirée?'

'They're sorta curious about her,' said Nikolls. 'She coulda got married a helluva lot. That baby had about a dozen proposals, but she let 'em slide because she wanted to look after the old boy. She was kinda fond of the Admiral.'

Callaghan asked: 'Was the Admiral fond of her?'

'Yeah,' said Nikolls. 'I suppose so, but Manon was his favourite. Manon was his favourite because she was sorta bright an' cheerful an' laughin' the whole time. As far as I can hear, she was the only one around those parts could get a grin outa the old boyo.'

Callaghan said: 'That's understandable too, isn't it?'

'Yeah, I suppose so,' said Nikolls. 'What do I do to-day?'

Callaghan said: 'Stay around the office, Windy. This *might* be a busy day.'

Nikolls yawned.

'I'll be glad when somethin' happens,' he said. 'Me – I'm a little bit bored.'

Callaghan said: 'You'll get over that.'

II

The Scotland Yard corridor was cool after the noon sun in White-hall. Callaghan walked slowly in the footsteps of the Detective-Constable who preceded him.

Gringall was at work at his desk when Callaghan came in. He said:

'We're seeing a lot of you these days, Slim.' He smiled. 'Something on your mind?' he asked.

Callaghan said: 'No . . . I just looked in to ask a question.'

'Every time you come into this place,' said Gringall, 'you come in to ask a question. Only sometimes you don't tell us. We have to find it out afterwards. What's the question?'

Callaghan said: 'I've got my report ready for the Globe & Associated. I've advised them to pass that claim for payment. Before the report went in I thought I'd like to ask you if anything else had turned up.'

Gringall said: 'Having regard to what you told me last time you were here, it ought not to make any difference to you whether anything's turned up or not.'

Callaghan sat down. He leaned forward, put his black soft hat on the edge of Gringall's desk. He said:

'That's true enough. But there's nothing like being certain, is there?'

Gringall said humorously: 'I've never known you bother a lot about being certain. But perhaps you've given up taking chances?'

'Yes,' said Callaghan, 'that's it. I've given up taking chances.' He grinned wickedly at Gringall. 'I must be getting old,' he said.

Gringall fumbled about in the desk drawer. He produced a charcoal crayon. He began to sketch a mango in the top left-hand corner of his blotter.

Gringall said: 'Maynes has been getting a bit excited.'

'You don't say,' said Callaghan. 'I didn't know Maynes had it in him.'

Gringall went on: 'He got excited because somebody rang through here and tipped off the Information Room that it might be a good thing to drag the lake at Chipley.'

'No?' said Callaghan. 'What do you know about that? Who was it rang up?'

Gringall shrugged his shoulders.

'Nobody knows,' he said. 'They got straight through to the Information Room, said their piece and hung up.'

Callaghan said: 'I had an idea that most of the Exchanges check on calls that come through to the Information Room.'

'Had you?' said Gringall innocently. 'Well, even if it was right, it wouldn't help this time. The call came from a paybox.'

Callaghan nodded.

'What did Maynes do about it?' he asked.

Gringall finished work on the mango. He said:

'He did the obvious thing. He dragged the lake.'

Callaghan asked: 'Did he find anything?'

'No,' said Gringall, 'he didn't find anything.'

Callaghan said: 'Well, he didn't expect to, did he? If somebody had shot the Admiral they'd have been crazy to throw the gun there.'

Gringall said: 'What do you mean – if somebody *had* shot him? You're not still thinking that there's even a chance that Gardell committed suicide?'

Callaghan said: 'It's funny, but I can't get that idea out of my head.'

Gringall looked at him. He said:

'Why worry about it? It doesn't matter to you, does it?'

Callaghan said: 'No!'

'Or does it?' said Gringall. He looked at Callaghan in a way that is usually described as old-fashioned.

Callaghan lit a cigarette. He asked:

'What are you trying to get at?'

Gringall said: 'There's a possibility of course that somebody – some person who's interested in this question of suicide – might have come on the Admiral's body and been foolish enough to move the gun.'

Callaghan asked: 'Is that Maynes's idea?'

'No,' said Gringall. 'That my idea.'

A look of astonishment came over Callaghan's face.

He said: 'Well, why should somebody want to do that?'

Gringall began to draw a passion fruit. He said: 'Somebody who was interested in that Insurance policy might have been uncertain that the two years' suicide clause were up. They might have wanted to make it appear that the Admiral had been murdered. They might have moved the gun for that reason.'

Callaghan said: 'I think that's a ridiculous idea.'

Gringall said: 'Perhaps it is. It's not an idea that I'm inflicting on anybody. For instance, I haven't suggested it to Maynes.'

No?' said Callaghan. 'Why not?'

Gringall said: 'Well, I'd like Maynes to look at this from the point of view of murder. I don't want to muddle him with any extraneous ideas.'

Callaghan grinned.

'The idea being,' he said, 'that if Maynes thinks it was murder, he'll go on till he finds a murderer?'

Gringall asked: 'What's the matter with that? Unfortunately,' he went on, 'Maynes hasn't very much chance to go on. He hasn't got much information to work on.'

Callaghan said: 'No, I suppose he hasn't.'

Gringall laid down the crayon. He opened a desk drawer and fumbled for his pipe. He said:

'Well, I take it that you won't be making any more inquiries of any sort on this case – not now that you're putting that report in?'

Callaghan said: 'No, I'm finished.' He got up, picked up his hat. He said: 'Well, so long, Gringall.'

He was at the doorway when he stopped. He said:

'Oh, by the way, I knew there was something I wanted to see you about. That warehouse case – that fraudulent claim on the Sphere & International – would you know who'd be handling that?'

Gringall grinned.

'I would,' he said. 'I always know who's handling any case here that's in any way connected with Messrs. Callaghan Investigations.'

Callaghan said: 'That's just too nice of you. Always trying to co-operate, aren't you?' He added under his breath: 'Like hell!'

Gringall said: 'Somebody's got to keep an eye on you. Besides I'm always trying to make up my mind about you.'

Callaghan asked: 'As to what?'

Gringall said: 'As to whether you're a good bad detective or a bad good detective.'

'It's damned funny your saying that,' said Callaghan. 'It's a question that worries me sometimes.'

Gringall said: 'It oughtn't to worry you. Anyhow, what do you care?'

Callaghan nodded.

He said: 'Quite . . . I should worry!' He lit a cigarette. 'What about this Sphere & International thing?' he asked.

Gringall said: 'Ardway – a Detective-Inspector – is handling that. You got something for him?'

'Yes,' said Callaghan. 'I've got Starata for him on a plate. Does he want him?'

Gringall raised his eyebrows.

'Nice work,' he said. 'Ardway'll be pleased.'

Callaghan said: 'Thank God I've done something right.' The door closed behind him.

Gringall smoked placidly for a few minutes. Then he picked up his crayon and began to draw a pomegranate. Then he laid down the pencil, picked up the telephone receiver. He asked for Ardway.

He said: 'Ardway, about that warehouse thing of yours – that phoney claim on the Sphere & International – Starata. Callaghan's just been in. He says he's got Starata on a plate.'

Ardway asked: 'Did he say where we could pick up Starata?'

'No,' said Gringall.

Ardway said: 'I wonder why not.'

'For an obvious reason,' said Gringall. 'He didn't want to tell us now, but he will. I expect you'll get a telephone call. You're pretty certain to get it to-day, I should say.'

Ardway asked: 'Why to-day, sir?'

Gringall said: 'That's what he came in to see me about.' He grinned into the transmitter. 'I know my Callaghan,' he said. 'Hang up, will you, Ardway?' he went on.

When the receiver at the other end clicked, he asked to be transferred to Maynes's office. When Maynes came on the line, Gringall said:

'Are you doing anything about Gardell?'

'Not very much, sir. We're trying to check up possible connections of the Admiral's gaming activities. I thought that might lead us somewhere.'

Gringall said: 'Leave it alone for a day or two, Maynes. I've got an idea that something is going to happen.'

'May I ask why?' said Maynes.

'Certainly,' said Gringall. 'Callaghan's been in. He says he's putting that report in to the Globe & Associated. He's advising them to pass that claim.'

Maynes asked: 'Does that mean anything?'

Gringall said: 'Callaghan takes about three to five thousand a year from Insurance Companies. I've known him to do a lot of funny things, but I've never known him to do anything to the people who pay him. I've got an idea that claim's going to be in order.'

Maynes said: 'I see, sir. You mean if we hang on Callaghan will finish the job?'

Gringall said: 'That's what I mean.' He hung up.

He came to the conclusion he was tired of eastern fruits. He went back to one of his original loves. He began to draw a banana.

III

Vane stood at his office window, watching the afternoon sunlight brightening the green of the gardens in Lincoln's Inn Fields. When Callaghan came in he said:

'Good-afternoon, Mr. Callaghan. I hope you're very well.'

Callaghan said: 'I'm fine. There are one or two things I want to talk to you about, Vane. Have you heard that Maynes – the police officer in charge of the Gardell case – has been dragging the lake at Chipley?'

Vane said: 'No, I hadn't heard that. What would the idea be in doing that?'

Callaghan said: 'I don't know. The idea might be that it was a very stupid murderer who killed the Admiral; that he was stupid enough to throw the gun in as obvious a place as the lake after he'd used it. A silly thing – the sort of thing a hysterical woman might do.'

Vane said: 'Quite!'

Callaghan said: 'About that conversation that the Admiral had with Chipley, you say you're not at all certain about that conversation?'

Vane said: 'I did say that.' He looked quizzically at Callaghan. 'On the other hand, you informed me that you were perfectly certain as to what I told you when you first discussed the matter with me.'

'I've got a damned bad memory sometimes,' said Callaghan. 'I can't remember what you told me. In point of fact,' he went on, 'I've a definite idea that you said the Admiral's conversation was a very jumbled affair – that you really couldn't make head or tail of what he was saying.'

Vane looked relieved. He said:

'In point of fact you're perfectly right, Mr. Callaghan. The Admiral was very vague. Perhaps "jumbled" is the word.'

'That's the word all right,' said Callaghan. 'Candidly, between you and me, I think the Admiral was very worked up, don't you? I think he wasn't quite certain of what he was saying himself.'

Vane nodded. He said:

'I'm inclined to agree with you. The Admiral certainly was not himself.'

'Of course he wasn't,' said Callaghan. 'People who go rushing about in the small hours of the morning, trying to see private detectives, leaving notes saying they're going to commit suicide, then rushing round and knocking up their lawyers – those sort of people *have* to be upset about something. The Admiral wasn't very young and he wasn't very fit. I think his mind must have been in a very confused state.'

Vane said: 'I'm certain of that.'

Callaghan produced his cigarette-case. He lit a cigarette, began to cough.

He said: 'There's another thing I want to talk to you about. I'm surprised you didn't think of telling me about that note you certified for the Admiral – the note authorising the bearer to receive twenty thousand pounds.'

Vane said: 'Quite candidly, it was such a long time ago that I'd forgotten all about it. It was only when Inspector Maynes came here and went into a lot of details about people who *might* possibly benefit under the insurance that I remembered it.'

Callaghan asked: 'What happened?'

Vane said: 'The Admiral came here and asked me to draw up and certify a note which would enable any individual who presented it to the Admiral's executors to be paid the sum of twenty thousand pounds on demand.'

Callaghan said: 'What did you think about that?'

'Naturally,' said Vane, 'I thought it was a gaming debt. You know the Admiral was a gambler – the worst sort of gambler.'

Callaghan nodded.

'I told him,' said Vane, 'that if it was a gaming debt he wasn't legally bound to pay it, but he became fearfully annoyed about that suggestion. He said that a debt of honour must be paid before any other sort of debt. In order to calm him down I told him that he could obviate any such position by inserting in the note the words "In consideration of services rendered." So we did it like that.'

Callaghan said: 'I see. Tell me, Vane, have you ever during the time you've known the Admiral had an inkling of the name of the person who might draw that twenty thousand pounds?'

Vane shook his head.

'No,' he said. 'Nobody knows that name.'

Callaghan raised one eyebrow.

'Are you certain of that?' he said.

'Positive,' said Vane. 'The Admiral told me specifically that *nobody* knew who that individual was. He said that whoever presented that note after his death was to be paid.'

'I see,' said Callaghan. 'Thank you.' He picked up his hat, said good-bye to Vane, and went out.

IV

It was four o'clock when Callaghan stopped the cab at the end of Chapel Street. He got out, paid the driver, walked to No. 22. He took a bunch of keys from his pocket. Eventually he found one that worked. He pushed the door open, went in, closed it quietly behind him. He walked very softly up the stairs.

When he reached the third-floor landing he could hear Stephanie Duval singing. Callaghan opened the door on the right of the landing. Stephanie was lying on the bed in an attractive negligée; an open box of chocolates lay beside her. She was in the act of putting a record on the gramophone on the small table beside the bed.

Callaghan said: 'Hallo, Stephanie.'

She looked at him. She said:

'Well, I'll be damned!'

'Probably,' said Callaghan. 'This is an old racket, of course, pretending to move out of a place and keeping a couple of rooms furnished. Whose idea was that – yours or Nicky's?'

She looked sullen. She said:

'I don't know what the hell you're talking about.'

Callaghan leaned up against the doorpost. He drew on his cigarette. He said:

'Yes, you do. You're as phoney as that anchor brooch I gave you the other night.' He grinned. 'It was sort of retribution my giving you that brooch. Do you remember about five years ago Nicky opened a jeweller's shop – indirectly; stocked it with a lot of good stuff; insured it and then replaced the good stuff with fakes. Do you remember that? That brooch was one of the fakes – bread cast upon the waters.'

Stephanie said: 'I don't understand you. You've got something on. What is it?' Her eyes were angry.

Callaghan said: 'I've got plenty on. The first thing I've got on is to tell you you've been making a damned fool of yourself. What d'you think I am?'

Stephanie said: 'I've never been quite certain.' She helped herself to a chocolate.

'My advice to you,' said Callaghan, 'is to pack up, get out and get going, and keep going. I'd get as far away from Nicky Starata as you can. Any more nonsense from you and you'll go in with him.'

She said: 'What the devil do you mean – nonsense from me? I've done everything I could to help – '

'Like hell you have,' said Callaghan. 'You've been working for Nicky the whole time, trying to stooge on me, trying to find out what's been going on. It's no soap, my dear. I've known where Nicky's been from the start.' He lit a cigarette. 'You ought to know,' he went on, 'that I'm not the sort of man who likes to be pushed around by a cheap fish like Nicky Starata – not without doing something about it anyway.'

She said: 'You're bluffing. I'll bet you don't know where Nicky is.'

Callaghan said: 'I don't have to bluff. How did I know you were still here?' He grinned. 'The weak spot in your chain is Leon,' he said. 'I was waiting for him the night he came round here to see you. I was a little rough with Leon. He came to the conclusion he'd be on the winning end of the stick. So he sold Nicky out.'

Stephanie said: 'The dirty so-an'-so . . . !' But she didn't say 'so-an'-so.'

Callaghan said: 'I've had a bet with myself that Nicky's going to do seven years. You take a tip from me, sweetheart. You get out of my way and stay out. Otherwise you'll share it with him. Understand?'

Stephanie said nothing.

'There's just one other point,' said Callaghan. 'It's one that you must decide. Don't try and get through to Nicky and warn him. Don't get through and tell him to start running somewhere else. If you do you'll make things a little worse for him. He'll have something else to face beside that fraudulent warehouse claim.'

Stephanie said in a sullen voice: 'Meaning what?'

'Meaning accessory after the fact in a murder job,' said Callaghan. 'That's what I mean. I should think that, with the other job, would put him inside for twenty years. So if you're really fond of him, you duck and stay put.'

'Nuts,' said Stephanie. She sat up on the bed. She said: 'You know what you are?'

'No,' said Callaghan. 'It ought to be interesting. You tell me.'

She told him. Callaghan listened attentively.

He said: 'Well, even *that* wasn't original. So long, Steve. Whenever you wear that anchor brooch think of me, won't you?'

He slammed the door.

As it closed he heard the gramophone record smash against it.

V

Nikolls came into the bar at the Back Lounge Club. He looked self-satisfied – happy. Henna-hair, whose name, believe it or not, was Roberta, regarded the large form of Nikolls with admiration, tinged slightly with suspicion.

He said: 'Hallo, sweetie-pie. What's cookin' around here?'

She yawned delicately.

'Nothing very much,' she said. 'You're in early this evening, aren't you? It's only just eight o'clock.'

Nikolls said: 'Yeah, that's right, but I've got a busy day comin'.'

Roberta said: 'You must have a hell of a time. Being a detective must be a great job. I expect you have a lot of adventures, don't you?'

Nikolls said: 'Yeah. Plenty.'

She said: 'I read about Callaghan Investigations once in that Vendayne case. That Callaghan is pretty clever. He's a funny sort of person though. He looks at you and says things and you never quite know what he means. I suppose you're a sort of assistant?'

Nikolls leaned up against the bar. He said:

'Well, you might call it that. Really, I hold the whole bag of tricks together. My speciality is brains.'

She said: 'Is it? I didn't think so the other night.'

'That's where you got me wrong, honey,' said Nikolls. 'I'm adaptable. When in Rome do as the Romans do.'

She said: 'I'm not a Roman. And does that mean I haven't got any brains?'

Nikolls said: 'How come! What do you want with brains with a figure like you got.' He looked at it appreciatively.

Roberta got as near to a blush as was possible. She said:

'You're a one, aren't you? I bet you get around a bit.'

'I used to,' said Nikolls. 'Of course this war's queered things a bit, but when I was a private dick in the States . . .'

She said: 'Go on, tell me. I bet things was exciting out there, wasn't they? I bet you had some narrow shaves.'

'Hundreds of them,' said Nikolls cheerfully.

He ordered a large rye. When she brought it, she said:

'What do you think's the narrowest squeak you've ever had, Windy?'

Nikolls said: 'Well, I suppose really most of my narrow escapes have been concerned with jealous dames.'

She pushed a straying curl back into place. She said:

'That's what I thought.'

Nikolls went on: 'I was working on a case once. A client of the firm I was working for was being blackmailed. She was a Spanish countess and had she got something! I'm telling you that baby had so much allure that every time she walked across a room it made a *rumba* look like a sailor learning to get his sea legs.' Nikolls sighed. 'The guy who invented swing music musta been thinkin' of her,' he said.

Roberta said: 'Skip that part. Get on with the story.'

Nikolls finished his whisky in one gulp. She poured another one. He said:

'Well, this dame fell for me in a big way.' He shrugged his shoulders modestly. 'I don't know why,' he said, 'but she did. She was crazy about me.'

'What did you do?' asked Roberta.

Nikolls said: 'I didn't do a thing. Well, not much. I never believe in mixing business with pleasure.' He leaned across the bar confidentially. 'There was a guy bughouse about this countess,' he said. 'He was a Cuban playboy. One night I was going to take her to the movies, but I had to stand her up. I had a date with another dame, see? Just when I was on my way to meet this second baby, I met the Cuban guy. I'm sorta feelin' big-hearted, see? So I tell this guy that the countess is expectin' to go out; that if he goes around to her place maybe he'll be lucky. So he went.'

He began to drink his second whisky.

Henna-hair said: 'So what?'

'So she shot him,' said Nikolls. 'She was so goddam steamed up about my standin' her up she just sorta shot this guy outa sheer bad temper.'

Henna-hair began to polish the top of the bar with a duster. She said:

'The fact of the matter is you're a bad man, Windy.'

'Maybe,' said Nikolls placidly. 'But what's the good of bein' anythin' else? All the good guys go nutty in their old age thinkin' about the good times they mighta had if they hadn't been so good.'

She said: 'There's not much chance of your going nutty in your old age.' There was a pause. Then: 'What are you doing to-night, Windy?'

Nikolls said: 'Nothin' doin', baby. I got business – big business.' He looked over his shoulder. 'Scram, honey,' he said.

She went to the other end of the bar as Callaghan came in. He went over to Nikolls. He said:

'Well?'

Nikolls said: 'Maresfield was the dump all right. A nice little dump. Nicky's livin' in a place called Lancelot Lodge. He just sticks around there an' don't go out much.'

Callaghan asked: 'Is there a telephone on?'

'No,' said Nikolls. 'Nicky tried to get a phone put on, but that's not easy these days. He's still waitin' for it.' He took out a packet of Lucky Strikes, lit one. 'You don't think Stephanie'll get out there and give him the works?' he asked.

Callaghan said: 'No. Stephanie'd walk out on anybody if things looked bad. She's just like the rest of 'em – a good-looking rat.' He looked at his watch. 'We'll go,' he said.

He went out. Nikolls followed slowly behind him.

VI

The wheezy clock on the sitting-room mantelpiece struck ten. Starata looked at it through the smoke of his cigar. He was thinking that the rural life didn't appeal to him very much. He dropped the evening paper on the floor beside him. He was reaching out for the whisky bottle when the door opened.

Callaghan, with Nikolls at his heels, came in. Starata grinned.

'Hallo,' he said. 'Fancy seeing you here, Slim. How did you get in?'

Callaghan said: 'We've got lots of keys to open locks with, Nicky.'

Starata said: 'That's what I thought. What exactly is this?' He relaxed in the chair. The fingers that unscrewed the stopper of the whisky bottle were quite steady. He poured out the whisky, drank it neat.

Callaghan said: 'This is what is commonly known as the pay-off.'

Nikolls removed the cigarette from his mouth. He said:

'Yeah, baby, this is where you get yours.'

Starata said: 'I wouldn't be too fast if I were you, Callaghan. It'd be a pity if you were in too much of a hurry. You might spoil something for yourself.'

Callaghan said: 'That's too bad. I'm going to chance that. Where's Mendes?'

'I don't know what you mean – ' said Starata.

'And if you did you wouldn't tell us,' mimicked Nikolls. He said to Callaghan: 'You know, Slim, I think he's gonna be difficult.'

Callaghan repeated: 'Where's Mendes?'

'You're being silly,' said Starata. 'I've told you I don't know what you're talking about.'

Callaghan said: 'This is the end of the story so far as you're concerned, Nicky. You remember that little conversation we had the evening you kicked me in the guts; we decided you'd get seven years. I think it's time you started. But I want that information about Mendes first of all.'

Starata got up. He said:

'Listen here. All I can tell you is this. I don't even have to tell you,' he said, moving towards the table. 'I got a letter here – ' He put his hand out towards the table drawer.

Nikolls, whose hand had moved towards a vase on the sideboard at his elbow when Starata got up, threw it. It hit Starata on the shoulder, knocked him off balance.

Nikolls said: 'Just keep away from that drawer, baby. We didn't think you'd come easy.' He went over to the drawer, opened it. Inside was an automatic pistol. Nikolls put it in his pocket.

Callaghan said: 'Take your weight off your feet, Windy.'

Nikolls said: 'O.K. I always did like a ringside seat.'

He went over to the far corner. He sat down.

'You know, Nicky,' said Callaghan, 'you can save yourself a lot of trouble.'

Starata said: 'I don't know that I've ever missed any.'

Callaghan smiled at him. He said:

'Well, you're not going to miss any now. It's a pity about Leon being such a songbird, isn't it?'

Starata shrugged. He said:

'So it was that dirty so-and-so who tipped you off where I was?'

'Correct,' said Callaghan. 'But that wasn't the worst thing he did to you.'

Starata raised his eyebrows.

'No?' he queried. 'What was the worst thing?'

Callaghan said: 'The night he went over my office, picking up that statement that Willie Lagos made, he opened my desk drawer, where the statement was filed, with a skeleton key. After he'd done that he went around the office smashing things up to make out that he'd searched through the whole office before he found the statement in the drawer. He knew just where that statement was all the time.'

Starata smiled a little.

'And that told you something?' he asked.

'That told me a hell of a lot,' said Callaghan. 'Well . . . where's Mendes?'

'You go to hell,' said Starata, not unpleasantly.

Callaghan hit him. His fist caught Starata fairly between the eyes. Starata went over, but was up almost before he touched the ground. He went into Callaghan like a tiger. Callaghan caught his first punch on his left hand, brought his elbow up. It contacted with the point of Starata's jaw. He brought his left hand over with a half hook on to Starata's nose.'

Nikolls said: 'If you could see what he's doin' to that beauty of yours, Nicky.'

Starata retreated. He put his hand behind him, picked up the whisky bottle. He threw it. Callaghan ducked in time. It hit the wall. A jagged piece of glass ricocheted down Callaghan's cheek.

'Score one to Nicky,' said Nikolls. 'Boy, is this goin' to be good?'

Callaghan stood where he was. Starata, cunning by this time, came in slowly. He was nicely poised on his feet and he knew how to fight. He came in, feinted for an opening, suddenly shot his left foot forward. Callaghan bowed his body, jerked himself backwards. He caught Starata's heel as it came up. He yanked it upwards. Starata went flat on his back with a crash. Callaghan put his hand in the front of Nicky's shirt, pulled him up, hit him again. The noise of his fist hitting Starata's face made a dull thud.

Nikolls said placidly: 'Boy . . . oh boy!'

Callaghan hit Starata again on the jaw. Starata got unsteadily to his feet, stood there waving. Callaghan hit him again.

Nikolls said: 'One more and he goes out, Slim.'

Callaghan straightened up. He said:

'We wouldn't like that, would we, Windy?'

On the sideboard was a soda-water siphon. Callaghan walked over, picked it up. He squirted half the siphon over Starata's disfigured face. He picked him up, pushed him back into the arm-chair.

He put his left thumb on Starata's nose and pressed hard. He removed the pressure suddenly, slapped Starata across the face with his right hand. He alternately pressed with his left thumb, slapped with his right hand. He said:

'Indicate when you've had enough, Nicky, won't you?' He stopped to enable Starata to reply.

Starata said thickly: 'One of these fine days I'm going to get at you, and when I do – '

Callaghan recommenced operations. Ten minutes afterwards Nicky indicated that he would like to talk. Callaghan sat down. He waited for Starata to get his breath.

VII

It was half-past ten. Callaghan went into the telephone-box that stands on the end of Maresfield Green. He dialled Whitehall 1212. Whilst he waited for the connection he lit a cigarette. A voice said:

'Scotland Yard – Information Room.'

Callaghan said: 'My name's Callaghan. I believe your Mr. Ardway is trying to find Nicky Starata. You probably remember him. He's the boy who put in that claim for a quarter of a million on the phoney warehouse fire.'

The voice said: 'Yes, Mr. Callaghan.'

Callaghan said: 'I've got Starata here at his cottage – Lancelot Lodge – in Maresfield, Sussex. I'm talking from the local call-box. I think possibly you might like to get in touch with the Sussex police and pick him up.'

The voice said: 'I'll have a word with Inspector Ardway, Mr. Callaghan. Will Starata stay there?'

Callaghan grinned.

'You'd be surprised,' he said. 'At the present moment I don't think he could walk if somebody paid him.'

The voice said: 'Oh, it's like that, is it?'

Callaghan said: 'Yes, it's like that.'

The voice said: 'We could probably arrange to have somebody there in twenty minutes, Mr. Callaghan. Will that be all right?'

'That'll be fine,' said Callaghan. 'I'll leave my assistant, Nikolls, with Starata until your people get here.' He went on. 'Oh, by the way, you might tell Mr. Ardway that I'd be glad if he'd get the Press Department to release the story of Starata's arrest as soon as possible.'

The voice said: 'I'll mention it to him, Mr. Callaghan.'

Callaghan said: 'Thanks a lot.' He hung up.

He went out of the call-box, began to walk back to Lancelot Lodge.

CHAPTER ELEVEN
DARK AND HANDSOME

I

THE little house was attractive. It had white walls and a red roof. It stood back fifty yards off the roadway in the middle of well-kept lawns.

Callaghan stopped the car and got out. He walked along the well-kept motor-drive, rang the bell. He waited a while. Nothing happened. He pressed the bell-push again, kept his finger on it. He removed it when he heard footsteps in the hall.

The door opened a few inches. A grey-haired woman with sallow, acid features, wrapped in a dressing-gown said:

'Well, what is it? It's terrible disturbing people at this time of night.'

Callaghan said amiably: 'I'm sorry about that, but I want to see Mr. Mendes. In fact I've got to see him.'

She opened the door a few inches wider.

'You can't see Mr. Mendes. He's not at all well. He's not to be disturbed.'

Callaghan said: 'That's too bad.' He put his hand against the door and pushed. He went into the hallway. He said: 'I'm sorry about Mr. Mendes, but he'll have to get up.'

The door on the other side of the hall opened. Callaghan closed the front door softly behind him. He stood with his back to it. Mendes came through the door opposite.

He was tall, slender, debonair. Callaghan thought that but for the fact that one eye was bruised and discoloured, one corner of the mouth was badly swollen, Mendes would have been a remarkably handsome man. The smile on the good side of his mouth was twisted – saturnine but oddly attractive. Callaghan noticed that his eyes were large and of that deep soft brown which women fall for so easily. His hair, black and glossy, lay on his head in a series of almost perfect natural waves. The side of his face that was not bruised showed a clear-cut jaw line, ending in a chin that was a trifle too pointed, with a cleft in it.

The woman said: 'I don't know who he is, but he says he's got to see you.'

Mendes nodded. He said:

'All right, Mrs. Soames. You go back to bed.' His voice was soft. It had a deep resonant note.

Callaghan thought that most things about Mendes were too charming. He said:

'I'm sorry to disturb you at this hour. My name's Callaghan. I'm Investigator for the Globe & Associated Insurance. I expect you've heard my name.'

Mendes said; 'No. Why should I have heard your name, Mr. Callaghan?'

Callaghan grinned. He said:

'If *you* don't know, *I* don't.' He took out his cigarette-case, selected a cigarette, lit it. He was still leaning against the front door. He said: 'It looks as if Starata gave you a first-class going over. It's a habit of his. I'm surprised you can walk.'

Mendes said: 'Mr. Callaghan, what is all this leading to?'

Callaghan said: 'All this is leading to a little talk between you and me.' He exhaled cigarette smoke.

'What have we got to talk about?' asked Mendes.

He did not move. He was quite relaxed. Callaghan thought Mendes might be tougher than he looked. He said:

'Well, I want to talk about Admiral Gardell for one thing.' He grinned again. 'Mind you,' he went on, 'Even *I* think I'm a bit of an optimist coming here to see you about him.'

Mendes said: 'Really? Well . . . since you're here I'd like to know why you're an optimist.'

Callaghan said: 'Only an optimist would think that he could come to your house at this time of night and get a confession of murder.'

Mendes nodded. He said:

'So I have to confess to a murder, do I? Mr. Callaghan, you amaze me.'

Callaghan said: 'Before I'm through, I'm going to amaze you some more. Let me tell you what happened on the night that Admiral Gardell died. Somebody took a telephone message from the old boy. That message said that the Admiral had changed his mind about committing suicide. It said that he'd made up his mind to see two or three things through to the bitter end. One of the things that he was going to see through to the bitter end was *you*. Somebody phoned through and told you about that message.'

Mendes regarded the glowing end of his cigarette. He said:

'How fearfully interesting!'

'You knew that the Admiral was going back to Chipley,' Callaghan went on. 'So you went over there. You waited for him. I should think you waited for him in the little piece of woodland that's near the coppice. I should think you were standing just inside, covered by the bracken, only a few feet from the path along which he had to walk. You probably gave it to him as he went past.'

'Did I?'

'Yes,' said Callaghan. 'Well, what about that?'

Mendes shook his head.

'It's not bad guessing really,' he said. 'But I'm afraid it won't wash. You see, I didn't kill the Admiral.'

Callaghan said: 'No. Well if you didn't, it ought to be pretty easy for you to prove it. Is there anybody else in the house besides that bad-tempered old hag who opened the door?'

Mendes said: 'There's no one else. There was nobody else on that night. But that doesn't matter. I wasn't here.'

'I see,' said Callaghan. There was a silence for a moment. Callaghan changed the subject. He said: 'Nicky Starata was pretty tough with you, wasn't he? The trouble is he was wasting his time in beating you up.' He smiled pleasantly. 'My own opinion is that even if he hadn't you'd have continued to keep your mouth shut. You'd have been glad to keep quiet and hope that you might get *something* out of it.'

Mendes said evenly: 'Mr. Callaghan, you're beginning to bore me.'

Callaghan said: 'All right. You said just now that you could prove that you didn't kill Gardell. Well, you don't *have* to tell me why, but it might be a good thing for you to do it, because if I'm not satisfied with your explanation I'm going to tell the Yard that you killed Gardell. There was plenty of motive.'

'Really! That interests me. What was the motive?' asked Mendes.

Callaghan said: 'After that telephone call you received, you realised that you had as much chance of getting your hands on that twenty thousand pounds as a snowflake on a hot stove. Perhaps you didn't mind losing the twenty thousand pounds. But you didn't want the other stuff to become public – the business that the Admiral was going to talk to me about *if* he'd been able to see me.'

'What business?' asked Mendes.

'Your phoney card games,' said Callaghan. 'There's no doubt about it that when the Admiral found that he'd been twisted out of his money, he discovered that a lot of other people had been twisted too. I should think there'd have been a whole flock of them after you if the Admiral hadn't died.' He smiled again.

'How's that for a motive, Mendes?' he asked.

Mendes put a hand to his swollen face. The right eye, discoloured into two beautiful art shades of purple and orange, looked almost artistic.

He said coolly: 'As a motive it's not bad. But I still have to disappoint you. Miss Manon Gardell is in a position to tell you that it would have been impossible for me to have killed the Admiral. I was at her cottage. I was there until she left to go over and see her cousin Desirée. She took her car. I hadn't one.' He smiled. 'I can't fly,' he said, 'and I certainly couldn't have walked from Valeston to Chipley in time.'

'That's a nice story if it's true,' said Callaghan. 'What were you doing there anyway?'

Mendes said: 'I'd walked over from here. *I* couldn't sleep.'

Callaghan grinned.

'I bet you couldn't,' he said. 'I bet you haven't slept well since Nicky attended to you either. But that's one thing that needn't bother you any more. I suppose you wouldn't know about Nicky?'

Mendes shook his head.

'No,' he said.

Callaghan said: 'If you'd read the papers to-day you'd have learned that he's been pulled in on a fraudulent insurance claim. You don't have to worry about Nicky for quite a long time. He ought to be away from us for about seven years.'

Mendes said: 'I'm glad to hear that. That *is* interesting.'

Callaghan said thoughtfully: 'Well, I can make mistakes like any one else. If Manon Gardell confirms your story you'll be all right, won't you? You'll be able to get that face of yours right again and start off on the old racket of blackmailing women, running snide card games, and all the rest of your stuff.'

Mendes said quietly: 'If you think that you can make me lose my temper you're quite wrong.'

Callaghan grinned. He said:

'I don't think anybody could make you lose *anything*. You've got nothing to lose. Goodnight, Mendes.'

He opened the door, stepped out, closed it behind him.

II

Except for Callaghan, Nikolls and Roberta, the barmaid, the Back Lounge Club was deserted.

Nikolls said: 'Me – I have a lotta trouble with the beer problem around this man's town. I like Pilsener an' you can't get it. I can remember an outsize in dames up in Albany who used to drink twenty-six bottles of Pilsener every day. It had the most extraordinary effect on this baby . . .'

Callaghan stubbed out his cigarette. He said:

'I'm not really interested, Windy.'

Nikolls said: 'No, that's what I thought. You got this Gardell business on the brain.'

Callaghan said: 'Have I?'

'Yeah,' said Nikolls. 'For me – I think it's simple.' He finished off his beer at a gulp, called to Roberta: 'Honey, let's have some rye, an' don't tell me you haven't got any. An' you can leave the bottle.'

When she had gone back to her letter, Nikolls went on:

'My bet is this guy Mendes. Mendes is the guy who creased the Admiral. It's stickin' out a foot.'

Callaghan asked: 'Why? Why does Mendes want to kill anybody. What Mendes wants is twenty thousand pounds.'

Nikolls said: 'Maybe! But the Admiral's got somethin' on him. That's what he's comin' back to see you about. That's why he decides he's goin' to see this thing through. Because he don't like Mendes.'

Callaghan said: 'So because the Admiral doesn't like Mendes – because he's going to get me to investigate something about Mendes – Mendes has to kill him. You may be right,' he said, 'But I don't think so.'

Nikolls poured out the rye. He said:

'Why not?'

Callaghan said: 'If the Admiral had got something on Mendes – something that really mattered – he wouldn't have to go to a private detective, would he? He could go to the police.'

Nikolls said; 'That's as may be. But this Admiral guy is a guy who don't like publicity. If he goes to the police there has to be a stink about it. Well, the Admiral don't want a stink, see?'

Something clicked in Callaghan's brain. He said:

'You know, Windy, you might be right.' He smiled. 'Improbable, but quite possible,' he added.

Nikolls said: 'Why you always have to play my big ideas down I don't know.' He drank half his rye at a gulp, looked at the glass with affection. He said: 'There's another thing troubles me too – an' that's Gringall.'

Callaghan said: 'What about Gringall?'

'Well, look . . .' said Nikolls. 'Gringall believes this is a murder job, so he puts this guy Maynes on to it. Well, what have they done? They haven't done a goddam thing. Anybody would think they were sorta waitin' around for you to pick some thin' up.'

Callaghan said: 'Maynes has dragged the lake at Chipley.'

'That's right,' said Nikolls. 'But he only done that after somebody had phoned through to Scotland Yard. Goddam it he *had* to drag that lake. Usually on a job like this they have plainclothes dicks around the neighbourhood makin' inquiries about everybody and everythin'. Well, I can smell those boyos a mile off an' there wasn't any of them around Chipley.' He finished the rye and poured out another one.

Callaghan said: 'There's something in that too. But there is an explanation for Gringall's attitude.'

'Yeah?' said Nikolls. 'You tell me the explanation.'

Callaghan said: 'The worst thing the police can do is to bring a murder charge and fall down on it. Nothing makes the police look such boneheads as accusing somebody of murder and then falling down on the job.'

Nikolls said: 'I still don't get it. This is too deep for me.'

Callaghan said: 'We don't know what Gringall knows. We only *think* he *doesn't* know as much as we do.'

Nikolls raised his eyebrows.

'Maybe you got somethin' there,' he said. 'It would be goddam funny if he did know.'

Callaghan said: 'All we know is what people have told us. Take Vane, for instance. Supposing, for the sake of argument, that Vane had let it slip out when he was talking to Maynes that there was a phone call to Chipley Grange the night the Admiral died. Or supposing, for the sake of argument, that Gringall's been able to check such a call through the telephone exchange. You see what I mean?'

Nikolls said: 'Yeah! I think I do. What you mean is that Gringall is on to Desiray all right, but he can't make it stick?'

'Right,' said Callaghan. 'Supposing he knows what we know, then he knows this: He naturally concludes that the person he would be telephoning to would be Desirée. That's the first point. The second point is that some anonymous person calls through to Maynes, and suggests that the lake at Chipley is dragged. Well, what would that suggest?'

Nikolls said: 'I got it. It would suggest that if the gun was in that lake it was thrown there by somebody who wasn't leavin' Chipley. They gotta stay at Chipley so they can't get rid of the gun very easily, an' the easiest place for them to get rid of it is the lake. That looks like Desiray again.'

'Correct,' said Callaghan. 'Well, supposing Gringall is thinking along those lines, then he's got to suspect Desirée, but he can't make anything stick because he's got to prove his case. In a murder charge the prosecution has got to prove beyond any reasonable shadow of doubt that the accused actually did commit the murder. The fact that they *might* have committed it is no good. Murderers,' continued Callaghan, 'have been hanged on circumstantial evidence, but when a murderer in this country gets hanged on circumstantial evidence, that evidence is so tight that it's practically as good as any factual evidence.'

He lit a cigarette.

'Gringall's trouble would be this,' he went on: 'Supposing he were foolish enough to make a charge on such evidence, he'd be in a bad jam, because the accused would have a good story.'

'I got it,' said Nikolls. 'The story being that the Admiral was all odd an' funny on the telephone; that he was in a state of mind in which it looked like he was goin' to commit suicide. So when she hears the shot she goes rushin' out an' finds him. Then the next thing hits her. She thinks that if he's committed suicide the Insurance Company aren't goin' to pay.

She's very fond of the old boy. She knew he was one of those old guys who was always burblin' about payin' debts of honour before anything else. Well, she's all steamed up. She hasn't got time to be logical. All she wants to do is to get that insurance claim paid. So he thinks if she makes it look like murder it'll be O.K. and she'll be able to carry out the old boy's wishes. So she dumps the gun in the lake.' Nikolls concluded: 'It looks to me like it's a damned good story.'

'A very good story,' agreed Callaghan, 'and one that the prosecution couldn't easily break down.'

Nikolls said: 'You know. I've been thinkin' maybe you oughta have left that gun in that lake.'

Callaghan said: 'Maybe.'

Nikolls poured some more rye into Callaghan's glass.

'I wonder what this guy Mendes is goin' to do,' he said.

Callaghan shrugged his shoulders.

'He'll have cleared out by now,' he said. 'Mendes isn't the type that sticks around and faces the music. Mendes has got an idea that he's safe. Mendes is too clever to tell lies at the moment. He knows that anything he says will be checked on. He knows that his alibi is all right.'

Nikolls said: 'What's this alibi? I never heard that one.'

Callaghan said: 'No, you don't have to.' He finished his drink. He said: 'I'm going to bed. I shan't be in the office a lot to-morrow. You'd better be around in case anything breaks,'

'O.K.,' said Nikolls. 'I'll be there. I think I'll stay on a bit an' have a drink,' he said. 'I wanna talk to the dame here.' He looked towards Roberta. 'I used to know a cousin of hers up in Leeds.'

Callaghan said: 'Like hell you did. Any cousin of hers in Leeds that you knew you wouldn't tell *her* about.' He looked at Roberta. 'I'm sorry for that girl,' he said.

He walked towards the door.

Nikolls said: 'Hey, what d'ya mean by that?'

Callaghan looked over his shoulder. He was grinning.

He said: 'I give you two guesses.'

III

Callaghan awoke with a jerk. He felt as if something in his brain had twitched suddenly, arousing him from a deep sleep. He lay in the darkness looking straight in front of him. He felt wide awake – rested. His mouth was dry. He came to the conclusion that he did not particularly like the whisky at the Back Lounge Club. Maybe they doctored it a little. For some unexpected reason a picture of Nikolls and Roberta, the barmaid, came to his mind. Callaghan grinned. Nikolls was an odd bird sometimes. He put his finger on a point – usually by accident. Sometimes he said something that really mattered, but, thought Callaghan with a yawn, Windy seldom realised the importance of what he was saying.

He switched on the bedside light, got up, went into the sitting-room. As he entered the room the Chinese clock on the mantelpiece struck three. Callaghan went to the sideboard. He poured himself out a long whisky and soda. He drank it, lit a cigarette.

There wasn't anything to be done, he thought, except to tie off the ends of this business.

He went into the bathroom. He poured eau-de-cologne on to his hair, began to rub it into his scalp. It tingled. It was a pleasant sharp feeling.

He went back into the sitting-room, picked up the house telephone. He spoke to Wilkie. He said:

'Get through to exchange and find the number of The Cottage, Valeston. It belongs to Miss Manon Gardell. When you've got the number keep on ringing until you get an answer.'

Wilkie said he would. Callaghan switched the telephone through to his bedroom extension. He went into the bedroom and began to dress.

It was ten minutes before the telephone jangled. Callaghan picked up the receiver. Manon's voice said:

'Hallo, Slim, I'm glad you telephoned.'

He said: 'Are you? Why?'

She said: 'I don't know. I've been restless. I couldn't sleep. I think I've been worrying about Desirée.'

Callaghan said: 'So have I. What do you say to some coffee?'

She said: 'Why not? Do I come to you, or do you come to me?'

He said: 'I'll be with you in an hour.'

She said: 'Really! You'll have to be quick, won't you.'

Callaghan said: 'It's a fine night and the roads are clear. I'll be seeing you, Manon.'

CHAPTER TWELVE
SECONDARY LOVE SCENE

MANON stood with her back to the sideboard. She looked unutterably ravishing. She wore a long violet silk Chinese house-coat, embroidered with large dragons in gold and emerald green. Her blonde hair was caught over one shoulder with a violet ribbon. Her eyes were bright. There was an attractive flush on her cheekbones that heightened the deepness of her eyes.

She said: 'This visit is quite delightful, Slim, even if it is unconventional. Would you like a drink while the coffee's heating?'

Callaghan was sitting in the chintz-covered arm-chair by the electric fire. He drew on his cigarette. He looked at her.

He said: 'No thanks.' There was a pause. Then he said: 'What happened about Mendes? Did he just get out quietly or did he come and see you first?'

Manon did not move. He saw her fingers grip at the edges of the sideboard.

She sighed. There was an air of finality in that sigh as if she had come to the conclusion that denial, expostulation or argument were useless. She said:

'I haven't seen him or heard of him. Who told you about him?'

Callaghan said: 'I got his name from Desirée. Quite obviously there was only one person who could have told Desirée about Raoul Mendes.'

She nodded.

'The Admiral?' she queried.

'No,' said Callaghan. 'Having regard to the fact that the Admiral took all that trouble in order to keep Mendes's name out of the note that Vane certified – the note that was going to get Mendes that twenty thousand pounds – it would be ridiculous to suppose that your uncle would tell Desirée about Mendes.'

'Very well,' said Manon. 'Then who told her?'

'You did,' said Callaghan. 'Your friend Starata did the rest.'

Manon looked at the ground in front of her. Her shoulders drooped a little. Then she drew them back, raised her head as if she was marshalling her forces. She said:

'Starata . . . ?'

Callaghan said: 'Unfortunately for both of you, Starata employed a fellow called Leon. Leon was stupid. When he burgled my office in order to find the statement that Willie Lagos had made he knew just where to look for it. That told me something.'

She said softly: 'Yes, it told you something. What did it tell you?'

Callaghan said: 'Only one person outside my secretary, Effie Thompson knew where that statement was. You were that person. *You* knew where it was. Quite by accident,' Callaghan went on, 'I told you at The Blue Cloud, after Starata appeared and you'd noticed him, after you'd mentioned the fact that he was a good-looking man, that I had something in my desk drawer that would blow him sky-high. Then you got your big idea, didn't you – the idea of doing a deal with Starata?'

He inhaled, blew the cigarette smoke out slowly.

He continued: 'Starata was the boyo you needed at that moment. When you drove away from The Blue Cloud you waited down the road, and after Starata had finished with me and left, you had a talk with him. You made a deal. You told Starata you could tell him exactly where he could lay his hands on that Lagos statement, and in return he was to look after Mendes, because Mendes was getting a little troublesome, wasn't he?'

Callaghan drew on his cigarette.

'That job must have appealed to Starata,' he said. 'He's very fond of women. I don't suppose that he has a chance very often of making friends, shall we say, with one like you.'

She said: 'You're damned clever, aren't you, Mr. Callaghan? I wonder are you clever enough.'

Callaghan said: 'I don't know. I'm not *trying* to be clever, but I've got a certain amount of common sense and I watch points. The trouble is,' he went on, 'that people come to conclusions based on false premises. Those conclusions are difficult to get away from. That was my trouble all along. I believed that the Admiral had telephoned through to Chipley and spoken to Desirée. At least I believed that until I rang the Chipley Exchange and found that there were *male* operators on after midnight.'

Manon made a little hissing noise. She said:

'You think of everything, don't you, Slim?'

Callaghan said: 'Not always, but I thought of that. Then I got it. The story you told me about your movements on the night of the Admiral's death had just enough truth in it to make it look reasonable. In fact,' he went on, 'the first part of your story was true. You couldn't sleep. You were restless. You knew the Admiral had gone up to town. You knew he was going to see me – that there was some trouble brewing. You drove over to Chipley. You stopped your car at the back of The Grange because you didn't want to disturb any one by going in the front way through the drive. I imagine you were walking across the back lawn when you heard the telephone ringing.'

Callaghan smiled at her.

'Your heart must have missed a beat then, Manon, because you guessed that call would be from the Admiral. You were wondering whether you could get to the telephone in the hall in time to take the call. I bet you ran. Well, you got there. You got there through the french window of the dining-room at the back. And you got to the telephone in the hall the second after the bell stopped ringing. You picked up the receiver just in time to hear Grant, the butler, speaking from the extension line in the library, saying: 'Hallo, Exchange . . . do you want me?'

'Then,' said Callaghan, 'you had a very bright idea. You said: *I don't want you . . . Sorry you've been troubled.'* Poor old Grant put the receiver down in the library just as the Admiral came on the line.'

Manon said: 'You know, really you're rather wonderful. I wish I'd met you years ago, Slim.'

Callaghan said: 'I don't.' He went on: 'Naturally, the Admiral thought he was speaking to Desirée. He was excited and angry. He told you that he'd changed his mind about what he was going to do; that he wasn't going to commit suicide, but that he was coming up to town to see me again; that he was going to see things through to the bitter end. He told you he was returning to Chipley right away. Then he hung up. I imagine you hardly spoke at all.'

Manon said; 'That's right. I didn't have to speak. Uncle hung up directly he'd finished.'

Callaghan said: 'I can imagine you standing in that dark hall, realising that the game was up, realising that the Admiral was wise to you and Mendes. Unfortunately for himself, he hadn't realised he'd given himself away to *you*.

'Something had to be done, hadn't it, Manon?'

She said: 'Yes, obviously, Slim. Something had to be done.' Her voice was odd. She was trembling.

Callaghan went on: 'You were pretty close to the Admiral. If anything, I imagine he preferred you to Desirée. You were much more amusing. more light-hearted than she was. I don't wonder at it. She spent most of her time worrying about him, whereas you didn't give a damn. You knew where the old boy kept that pistol of his. You went and got it. Then you left the house and waited for him in the coppice. You shot him as he passed within a foot or two of you, and that was that!

'But having done so, a doubt assailed you – a terrible doubt. The Admiral didn't mention on the telephone that the two years stated in the Insurance policy clause were up. You didn't know that. *If you put the gun in the Admiral's hand and made it appear suicide and the two years weren't up, there wouldn't be any insurance money and there wouldn't be any twenty thousand for you and Mendes. So you had to do something about that.*

'I imagine,' said Callaghan, 'you were pretty scared by this time. You didn't want to leave the gun with him. You wanted to get rid of it. You dropped it in the lake. As you were moving away from the footbridge, You saw Desirée coming across the lawn. You told her what had happened. You told her that your uncle had committed suicide; that you'd heard the shot just as you were arriving; that as he'd committed suicide there wouldn't be any money to pay off Mendes; that you'd dropped the gun in the lake. Naturally,' said Callaghan, 'she believed you. In any event, she didn't think you were a murderess.'

Callaghan lit a fresh cigarette.

'Well, that was that,' he said. 'Ten minutes afterwards Desirée "discovered" the body. Well . . . how wrong am I?'

Manon said: 'It's not too bad, Slim. You're doing very well.' She turned, poured a little brandy into a tumbler, drank it neat. The flush of her cheek-bones deepened a little.

Callaghan said: 'Then you were so far in that you had to get a little farther in. I imagine it was your idea that you should ring up my office, meet me, try and discover whether the Admiral had seen me, how much I knew. You must have been very relieved to discover that I knew practically nothing.'

Manon said: 'You'd be surprised. I was fearfully relieved. I thought everything would be all right then.'

'Precisely,' said Callaghan. 'Now you had to take care of something else. You had to take care of Mendes. Mendes, with his twenty thousand pounds in sight, was likely to become more obnoxious than ever, and you didn't want anybody to start anything. So you got your other boy friend – Starata – to take care of Mendes. I like the idea of Starata going for Raoul. But it worked out all right. Mendes agreed to play ball and say his piece as you wanted him to. He agreed to the story which would, in fact, provide you with a very good alibi.

'The next thing was to tell me that it was Desirée who dropped the gun in the lake. Slowly and relentlessly you were working along the lines of the story that it was Desirée who had discovered the Admiral's body; that it was *she* who had wanted the insurance paid so badly that it was she who had dropped the gun in the lake in order to make certain. If it came to a showdown, it was her word against yours. But you had Mendes to support you. He, if necessary, would supply you with your *alibi*.'

Callaghan stubbed out his cigarette.

'Now some more trouble started,' he went on. 'The police produced the idea that the Admiral had been murdered. But by now you've discovered that the two years' time limit was already up. Now you're a little bit afraid of this murder idea, so the thing to do is to play up the suicide angle. The thing to do is to prove to the police that the gun was dropped in the lake by somebody – and of course that somebody must be Desirée because she discovered the body.'

Manon said: 'You're really rather amazing. How did you know that?'

Callaghan said: 'It was easy. I told Stephanie Duval – Starata's girl friend – the story. She thought I was tight. I said Desirée had dropped that gun in the lake. Well, you know what happened. Stephanie told Starata. Starata told you. I wanted to see if someone would telephone Scotland Yard and tell them.' He grinned. 'I was so sure they would,' said Callaghan, 'that I sent an assistant down to see if police started dragging operations. They started the day after they received that telephone call. I imagine it was Mendes who made that call.' He smiled again. 'But the joke was on you,' he said. 'They didn't find the gun.'

Manon said: 'Why not? It was there.'

'No,' said Callaghan. 'It wasn't. I'd got it. I came to the conclusion that I'd like to spoil your story. I came to the conclusion that it was quite on the cards that if the police began to make inquiries that came too close to you for your liking you'd tell that story. Well, if the gun wasn't there you'd be a liar, wouldn't you? Your story wouldn't be believed. Do you see, Manon?'

'I see,' said Manon amiably. 'So now . . . ?'

'So now,' said Callaghan, 'the murder theory is still wide open – a dead Admiral and no gun. All we want is a murderess.'

Manon said: 'All this is very good. But it's what they call circumstantial evidence, isn't it? Very circumstantial evidence . . .'

Callaghan said evenly: 'That's how it is. All we want is a murderess.'

Manon began to laugh. It was a low, odd sort of laugh. It began somewhere in the throat, finished on a higher note.

'It's awfully funny,' she said softly. 'It's *fearfully* funny to realise that we're talking about *me*. "All we want is a murderess" . . . ! *All* we want is a murderess . . . All we want is a *murderess*! Doesn't that sound lovely and tragic and thrilling. It's like the end of the first scene in a play.'

Callaghan nodded.

'A hell of a play,' he said. 'I wish it was a play . . .'

Manon poured out some more brandy. She said:

'Why don't you have some brandy? Don't you like drinking with me, Slim? Is that it? Does it make you feel creepy to be here with me? Don't you feel that I might slink up to you and cut your throat, or that Raoul

– the wicked Raoul – might come suddenly through the door and spring on you and throttle you . . . ?'

Callaghan said: 'Raoul couldn't throttle any one. I'd like to kick his teeth down his throat. But he couldn't kill any one . . . not a mouse . . . You ought to know that.'

She smiled. Her face was almost vivacious.

'You're quite right,' she murmured. 'But then you're usually right, aren't you, Mr. Callaghan? Clever Mr. Callaghan. Yes . . . Raoul couldn't do any physical hurt. He went in for more cruel things.'

She began to sip the brandy. After a while she said:

'But you can't prove anything, Slim. You and the police can think what you like. You can *suggest* what you like. But you can't prove anything. Any evidence is circumstantial . . . and flimsy at that, if I stick to my story. All I have to do is to stick to my story. I can *prove* my story is true and you *can't* prove it isn't.'

Callaghan said: 'Maybe you're right. Your story is that you went over and arrived some time after the Admiral shot himself. You arrived just in time to see Desirée drop the gun in the lake and then you came straight back to the cottage. Not a bad story. But it isn't very good for Desirée, is it?'

'Damn Desirée,' said Manon. She laughed. Callaghan thought he did not like the sound of the laugh very much. She said: 'Let me tell you that I loathe Desirée. I always have. She's the very opposite to me in every-thing. She pities me. She always pitied me. She's more beautiful than I and she doesn't get into troubles and scrapes like I do. She's beautiful and remote and *good*. And she loved her father and tried to keep him in order whilst I . . .'

She came over to Callaghan. She dropped down on her knees in front of him. She said:

'My greatest joke is about Uncle Gardell. It's a lovely joke. I'll tell you . . . or perhaps I won't. But Uncle Gardell thought I was wonderful. I made him laugh. I commiserated with him when he lost. I never tried to reform him. I never tried to make him give up gambling. I was always the bright little thing. You see . . . ? I won't tell you the other thing. It might be dangerous. I'll keep that to myself.'

Callaghan said: 'I should worry about that. I could make a pretty good guess about that too.'

'Aren't you clever,' said Manon. 'Do tell me.'

Callaghan said: 'It's pretty obvious, isn't it. You encouraged the Admiral to gamble, and a dyed-in-the-wool gambler like he was doesn't need much encouragement. You got the Admiral to play at the places that Raoul was running. I bet the games were as crooked as hell. The pair of you must have rooked the old boy for thousands. And then, only just recently, for some reason he began to suspect. He found something out or he heard something. Then he came to the conclusion that he'd rather commit suicide – if the time was right – than Raoul should get that twenty thousand pounds after he was dead.

'That was when he made up his mind to come to town and see me. He came straight to Berkeley Square. When he found I wasn't there he went round, saw Vane, read the policy. Then, and only then, the old boy realised that the two years were up. Now he was going to get his own back on you two – now he was *not* going to commit suicide. He was coming up to see me and he was going to put the whole thing in my hands, which would have meant, my dear, that we should have found out all about Mr. Mendes and all about you.'

Callaghan stopped talking. He lit a fresh cigarette. He looked at her through the smoke. He said:

'I should like to know what the Admiral said to you on the telephone, thinking that you were Desirée. He probably told you that he had discovered something about you. That put you into a devil of a state, didn't it? I can understand you hating Desirée because she's pitied you. I suppose in her time Desirée has guessed one or two things about you, even if she's never realised that you're quite as black as you are. The idea of Desirée hearing all this stuff about you and Mendes wasn't too good, was it? More especially as you'd pulled some story on her – a story which is responsible for her impatience to get that insurance claim paid.'

'Yes,' said Manon. 'So you've got a suggestion about that?'

Callaghan said: 'Yes, I've got a suggestion about that. I should think you told Desirée that you were being blackmailed. I expect you told her that you'd got to have some money somehow: or you might have told her that you owed a lot of money somewhere. That was one of the reasons why she wanted the insurance money paid quickly. She wanted to keep you out of any more trouble. She probably knows you've been in enough. And you didn't mind that. You didn't mind her knowing that.'

'Didn't I?' said Manon. 'Why not?'

Callaghan said: 'I'll tell you why. Because her attitude ever since the beginning of this affair has been that she wanted the insurance money paid, and quickly. That attitude is going to match up with the rest of the story you want believed – the story that she dropped the gun in the lake to make certain of getting that insurance money for *herself*.'

Manon picked up the glass of brandy. She sipped it delicately. Callaghan inhaled slowly, watching her. He said:

'It's an awful pity about Raoul.'

Manon asked: 'What do you mean by that?'

Callaghan said: 'Right the way through you've been banking on one thing. You've been banking on this – that if it came to a showdown as to exactly what happened at Chipley at the time the Admiral was killed, in the ordinary course of events it would boil down to your word against Desirée's. But, with Nicky Starata's help, you were able to improve that situation, weren't you?'

Callaghan grinned.

'Nicky is dark and handsome, and Raoul is dark and handsome. It looks as if dark and handsome men are going to be your undoing. They're going to be your undoing in this job.'

'Ha!' said Manon. 'So I'm to be undone by dark and handsome men. How romantic and how thrilling!'

'*Not* so romantic and *not* so thrilling,' said Callaghan. 'You thought Nicky Starata would take care of Raoul. You thought, after Raoul had had a good hiding – and Raoul doesn't like physical force, does he – you thought he'd do and say just what you wanted him to do and say. You thought he'd provide the additional evidence so that you two could break down what Desirée had to say. It wasn't going to be her word against yours. It was to be her word against yours and Mendes's.'

She said: 'If Desirée wants to argue about it – and I don't think she will – that will be the position. It will be her word against mine and Raoul's. Raoul will support everything I have to say. After all *he was there.*'

Callaghan said: 'That's the joke. He wasn't.' He grinned at her maddeningly.

Manon said in an odd voice: 'What do you mean?'

Callaghan said: 'It was quite obvious to me that if Starata had got at Mendes it would be for the purpose of making him tell the story you wanted. It's easy to guess what that story would be. The story would be this: That you couldn't sleep – you were restless. So you telephoned through to Raoul. You asked him to come over and see you. He walked over here. That you were worrying about the Admiral; asked him to go over with you to Chipley. He agreed. You drove over. As you were approaching the coppice lane you heard the shot. You left the car. You hurried through the coppice in time to see Desirée dropping the gun in the lake. That was going to be your story. It's an awful pity that Raoul's thrown it down.'

Manon said in a brittle voice: 'I don't believe it . . . I don't believe it.'

Callaghan said: 'You'd be surprised. And if I were you I wouldn't drink any more brandy, Manon. You'll need all your brains in a minute. In fact you might as well start to use them now. That beauty that you've lived on for such a long time is not going to be very much use to you now. Judges and juries aren't affected by beauty in murder trials.'

She put her glass down. She said:

'You're trying to bluff me. You're trying to bluff me about Raoul. Desirée said you were a bluffer.'

Callaghan said: 'That's true enough, but I'm very careful to pick the right times to bluff. This isn't one of 'em. Why don't you get in touch with your friend Mendes and find out. *I* went to see him yesterday.'

Manon moved a little. The long slit in the side of her Chinese coat opened. Callaghan could see that the silk-clad knee beneath was trembling.

She said: 'So you went to see Raoul. Well . . .' Her voice was impatient. 'Tell me . . .'

Callaghan said casually: 'If I'd gone to see Mendes and *asked* him what happened on that night, he'd have told me the story that you and Starata had arranged for him to tell. But, you see, I didn't ask him. I thought of something better than that.'

She said in a slow voice: 'You think of everything, don't you, Mr. Callaghan? What did you think of?'

Callaghan said: 'I thought of a good one. I accused him of the murder. I pointed out to him that there was ample motive for him killing the Admiral. He knew that the Admiral was after him. He knew that the Admiral had discovered that his games were crooked. He knew that on the night that he won that thirty thousand pounds the game was crooked from the start. That's ample motive, isn't it?'

Manon said: 'But how would he know that? The Admiral never had a chance to tell him. How would he know that . . . ?'

'You told him on the telephone,' said Callaghan. 'You told him when you rang him up. That's how he knew.' He went on: 'I let him know something else too. I let him know that he'd nothing to fear from Starata. I told him that Nicky wouldn't trouble us for a long time.'

She said: 'What's happened to Starata?'

Callaghan said: 'I've wanted Nicky for some time. You see, my dear, the fact that with your help Leon was able to steal that Lagos statement from my office doesn't help Nicky a great deal. There'll be lots of other evidence against him. He'll still do his seven years. I've known where

Starata's been all along. I waited till *I* wanted him. Well I've got him. He's been arrested.

'So, you see' – Callaghan flipped his cigarette into the ashtray – 'Raoul was in a tough position. On the one hand, I accuse him of murder. On the other hand, I tell him he has nothing now to fear from Starata. Raoul is no fool – you know that – he realised he was in a bad spot, so he told the truth in order to get out of it. He let you down, my dear. He smashed that nice piece of evidence that you and Starata had taught him. He admitted to me that he came over to The Cottage; that he waited there till you came back. It's going to be quite obvious,' said Callaghan, 'that when you did come back you were able to give him the good news that the Admiral was no more; that he couldn't talk; that if this thing were played carefully you'd have your money. There'd be no scandal, and if any one fell in the cart it was going to be Desirée.'

She said: 'Even so, Mr. bloody-clever-dick, even so . . . it's all circumstantial.'

Callaghan shook his head.

'No,' he said, 'it's not circumstantial. Not all of it.' He got up. He stood with his back to the fire, his hands clasped behind his back. 'The joke is – it's the Admiral who's going to hang you. It's the Admiral who supplies conclusive evidence against you. Would you like to know what it is?'

She said hoarsely: 'Yes.'

Callaghan said: 'When the Admiral telephoned through to Chipley, naturally he would only discuss this business with Desirée. We know Desirée didn't take that telephone call. If Desirée didn't take that telephone call, there's only one other person with whom the Admiral would have discussed the matter. That person was you. The fact that we can prove that the Admiral did make that telephone call – and remember,' said Callaghan, 'that Vane heard him doing it – proves conclusively, as Desirée was not there, that he was talking to you. It proves, in other words, that you were at Chipley at the time the call was made – a long time before the Admiral arrived back there.'

She said quickly: 'How can you prove Desirée didn't take that telephone call. If you can prove that, I admit what you say is true. But you can't prove it, can you?'

Callaghan lied. He said easily:

'The joke is we can. You forget someone else who was on the telephone – Grant, the butler.'

She said: 'Well, what about Grant?'

Callaghan continued to lie glibly: 'When he heard the telephone bell ringing he came down from his room on the third floor to the extension line in the library on the second floor. He passed Desirée at her bedroom door. She'd thought that possibly he hadn't heard the telephone. He told her he would take it. So she couldn't have answered that telephone call. That being so,' said Callaghan, 'it looks as if you're licked, Manon.'

She came over to him. She stood in front of him. She looked at him. Callaghan thought that he had never seen beauty look so evil in his life.

She said: 'So I'm licked, am I?' Her voice was soft and low – almost caressing. 'We'll see, Mr. Callaghan.' She drew a deep breath, sent it out hissing between her teeth. She said: 'You've gone to an awful lot of trouble about all this, haven't you? Why? There hasn't been any money in it for you. I suppose you're keen on Desirée. I suppose you admire that beautiful *good* creature.'

Callaghan said: 'How right you are. I think she's marvellous. I'd do anything for her.'

She said: 'All right. So I'm licked. Well, possibly I am, but perhaps I'm not – not quite. Possibly I've a trump card, Mr. Callaghan.'

Callaghan grinned. He said:

'People who cheat at card games very often have a card left up their sleeves, but it's not always a trump card. Don't worry, my sweet, they'll hang you yet.'

She said: 'Damn you.' She hit him across the face. Callaghan felt one her rings cut his cheek. He laughed at her. He repeated:

'They'll hang you yet, Manon. They'll stretch that pretty neck of yours.'

She said: 'You get out of here. Get out . . .' Her voice was almost a shriek. 'You – '

He said: 'I always knew that you had something in common with Nicky's late girl friend, Stephanie. You use the same oaths.' He yawned. 'By and large you're very alike,' he said. 'She's good-looking too – possibly a little more common, but that's all.' He grinned. 'Sisters under the skin.'

Manon said: 'I've told you to get out. If you don't – '

Callaghan said soothingly: 'Don't say you'll kill me too, Manon. That would be the last straw. You can't go in for *wholesale* murder.'

He took out his cigarette-case, selected and lit a cigarette. She was still in front of him. She was trembling from head to foot. She looked the picture of incarnate rage. Callaghan put out his hand. He swept her aside. He picked up his hat from the armchair. He said:

'Well, honey pot, go and play your trump card. I'll still beat you to it.'

He went over to the door. As he opened it, he said:

'So long, Manon. See you on the gallows!'

He went out.

CHAPTER THIRTEEN
TRUMP CARD

I

The Chinese clock on the mantelpiece of Callaghan's sitting-room struck eight. The early sun illuminated the pattern on the carpet, gilded the toe of Callaghan's left shoe. He sat, an unlit cigarette dangling from one corner of his mouth, thinking. He was thinking about Manon. More especially he was thinking about the trump card which Manon still had, and which she would doubtless play. So far as she was concerned, thought Callaghan, the game was obviously up.

Knowing that most of the things that he had said were true, she was prepared to accept the one lie he had told. The lie about Grant, the butler, having spoken to Desirée on his way to answer the telephone. Accepting that, Manon must know that the case against her was cut and dried. Yet she was not concerned with that. She had shown none of the disappointment, the depression that comes to the evildoer who has been discovered, about whom the meshes of the net are slowly tightening. Manon had merely been angry – very angry – at her failure, but already deciding to put her failure behind her and to play her trump card.

Callaghan leaned back in the arm-chair and relaxed. He put his hands behind his head, gazed at the ceiling. He concluded he was tired. He concluded also that he was a little bored with the Gardell case, which had offered none of those charming interludes which had distinguished other cases in which beautiful women were concerned.

But through those thoughts, and before the pictures that came before Callaghan's mind, the thought of Manon's trump card persisted. With a sigh Callaghan concluded that Manon was no bluffer. Why should she bluff? What had she to bluff about? In front of her was the certainty of the gallows and a four-foot drop; or maybe, thought Callaghan, as she was a tall fine woman, the executioner might even make it five feet. Callaghan realised with another sigh that in any event inaction was impossible – for half a dozen reasons.

He went over to the telephone. He said to Wilkie:

'Wilkie, I'll be down in five minutes. Make a cup of coffee and keep it down there in your office. I'll drink it on my way out. He went into the bathroom, washed, rubbed some eau-de-cologne into his hair. He put on his hat, went out of the flat towards the lift. As he got in he said to himself: 'I've been one jump ahead of the market with you so long, my lady, maybe my luck will hold. I wonder!'

Downstairs he drank the coffee, got into his car parked outside. He let in the clutch wearily. He began to drive towards Mendes.

II

It was ten-thirty when Callaghan stopped the car outside the gates of the pretty red and white house. He walked up the drive, rang the bell. While he waited he lit a cigarette. The door opened. Mendes, in a blue and white foulard dressing-gown, freshly shaven, looked at him with inquiring eyes. He gave a little sigh. He said:

'Mr. Callaghan again!' He smiled a trifle wearily.

Callaghan put his hand on Mendes's chest. He pushed him back into the hallway. Mendes hardly resisted. He merely raised his eyebrows. He looked surprised – a trifle pained.

Callaghan said: 'You're a man who doesn't go in much for hurting people physically, Mendes. I've got that on good authority. I got that from that side-kicker of yours – Manon. My experience has always shown me that people who are mentally cruel don't like being hurt physically. Let's see . . .'

He smacked Mendes across the face hard, making certain of hitting the still bruised and discoloured eye. Almost before Mendes had overcome the shock of the first blow, Callaghan struck him again. He said:

'That's just to show you that I'm not going to waste any time on you. Understand?'

Mendes leaned against the side wall of the hall. Two large tears were rolling down his cheeks. He said in an almost shrill voice:

'You damned beast! What is it you want?'

Callaghan said: 'I'm interested to find that you're still here. That tells me something. That tells me that probably the story you told me the other night was true; that you've even got enough nerve to hang around and hope that, in spite of everything, you might get away with that twenty thousand pounds, or some of it. In that lousy heart of yours there's still a sneaking hope that Desirée Gardell might be decent enough, in spite of everything that I might say to her, to want to pay you that money. Well, if you've enough nerve to stick around here, it's because your story of the other night was true. But it's not going to help you.'

Mendes asked: 'What does that mean?'

'It means that the case against Manon is finished – closed. It only wants "settled" written across it. She killed Gardell. That surprises you, doesn't it, my friend? Nevertheless it's true. She admits it. She'll hang.' Callaghan drew on his cigarette with pleasure. 'The joke is,' he said, 'there's a damned good chance that you'll hang with her. The cream of the jest being that if you do hang you'll really be innocent. They'll hang you for something you didn't even do.' Callaghan began to laugh. 'What a supreme joke,' he said.

Mendes said: 'What the devil do you mean?' The words almost tumbled out of his mouth. When he had said them, he ran his tongue over his dry lips. His tongue was pink and pointed like a cat's, Callaghan thought.

Callaghan said: 'It's always been understood under English law that if two people are associated together in a criminal action, and that action ends in murder, they are both responsible – each as an accessory to the other. Do you get that, pal?'

Mendes said: 'Is this true or is this some more of your bluff?'

'I should worry about bluffing with you,' said Callaghan. 'If you're not damned careful, my friend, you're going to hang. Be advised by me. You've a chance, but only if you do what I want you to do.'

Mendes said: 'What is it you want?' He was still leaning against the wall. The fingers of his right hand were beating a nervous tattoo on the wallpaper.

Callaghan said: 'Just answer this question truthfully. You're not the sort of person who gets up at this hour and shaves and bathes. You're the type that's usually in bed at midday. What are you up for? What have you heard from Manon?'

Mendes said: 'I'll tell you. Why shouldn't I tell you? I've nothing to hide – nothing at all.' He spoke in jerky sentences. He found difficulty in speaking. He went on: 'Manon came through at eight o'clock this morning. She told me some things.'

'I don't want to know about the things she told you. I want to know what she *said* word for word as far as you can remember, and I'll bet you do remember.'

Mendes gulped. He swallowed hard. He pulled himself together. He said:

'Manon said: "That swine Callaghan is too good. Unless we move quickly there's no hope. I shall be with you at eleven-thirty. Be ready for me to pick you up then. If we act quickly all may yet be well." That's what she said,' said Raoul Mendes. 'Just that – or as near to those words as I can remember. Then she hung up.'

Callaghan said: 'All right. Well, you be ready for her. Maybe I'll be seeing you again – perhaps sooner than you think. Maybe we'll be having another talk. Maybe . . . !'

He opened the door. Over his shoulder he took a final glance at Mendes. Callaghan knew it was a final glance. He knew he would not see Mendes again.

He went out into the sunshine.

III

Desirée was standing by the french windows, looking out over the lawn, when Callaghan was shown in. She was wearing a green linen frock with white lawn collars and cuffs. She looked fresh and delightful, but her eyes were tired.

Callaghan said: 'There's a lot of things I've got to say to you. Before I start you'd better make up your mind that you're going to trust me implicitly.' He grinned at her. 'No matter what you *think*,' said Callaghan, 'my advice to you is to trust me for the moment. Events will prove that I'm right.'

She said: 'I think I do trust you. You're an extraordinary person. I don't profess to understand you, and in any event the police seem to have a very good opinion of your intelligence.'

Callaghan said: 'Well, they ought to know.'

'Would you like a cigarette, or some coffee?' she asked. 'You look tired.'

Callaghan said: 'I am tired. I've been up all night, and I've spent the greater part of the last few days – day and night – worrying about you.' He grinned at her again. 'Why, I don't know,' he said.

She said: 'I'm sure *I* don't.'

'That's not the truth,' said Callaghan. 'You can make a pretty good guess, can't you?'

She looked out of the window. She said demurely:

'I'm not very good at guessing.'

Callaghan said: 'All right. You're not very good at guessing. We can come back to that point later. Sometimes you're a little bit stupid, aren't you, Desirée?'

'I expect I'm often stupid. What is in your mind particularly?'

Callaghan said: 'Why didn't you tell me it was Manon who dropped that gun in the lake?'

She said: 'I've been asking myself the same question. But if you'll consider the circumstances – when you realise that the only time I've really talked to you – that night in your flat – I didn't feel like explaining anything then, and I was afraid. I began to be afraid for Manon. I began to wonder . . .'

Callaghan said: 'You began to wonder! You ought to know Manon well enough to know that one doesn't wonder at anything *she* does.'

She said miserably: 'I know. But one is always sorry for Manon.'

Callaghan grinned.

'I'm not,' he said. 'She's one of those smart people who make people sorry for her. She's one of those clever people who go through life getting the best of everything, leaving everybody else with the dregs – as she intended to leave you with them.'

Desirée said quickly: 'What do you mean?'

'Her story is that you discovered the Admiral's body; that you dropped the gun in the lake, see? Then the police can have it which way they like. They can either be nice and think that you were afraid about the time-limit in the insurance suicide clause and dropped the gun in the lake to make it appear murder; or they can think that you were not so nice and killed your father in order to get the insurance money. Much Manon cares.'

She said slowly: 'I see! So that's why you took the gun out of the lake.'

Callaghan smiled at her. He said:

'Yes! I told you I was a friend of yours, didn't I? The simple act of removing that gun from the lake kicked the bottom out of Manon's story, and as she built everything round that story, I very much doubt if she'll be able to get a new one.'

Desirée hesitated for a moment. Then she said:

'I'm awfully worried about Manon. I'm beginning to think – '

Callaghan interrupted.

'If I were you I shouldn't think about Manon,' he said. 'She's perfectly capable of looking after herself.'

She said: 'I've always worried about Manon. All my life I've been worrying about her and my father.'

Callaghan said: 'Worry killed the cat. It never got anybody anywhere. If you hadn't been so worried you'd have been a little more amiable that night I came here to dinner. That would have made things easier.'

Desirée raised her eyebrows. She said:

'I like that. *I* might have been more amiable. Do you remember your own attitude?'

Callaghan smiled. He said:

'Not very well. What was it like?'

She said: 'You were rude and impossible. I thought I disliked you.'

Callaghan said: 'That's a failing of mine. Whenever I'm really stuck on a woman, my first reaction is to be a little tough. That's more or less normal, I suppose.'

Desirée smiled for the first time. She said:

'It's a pity I didn't know that, isn't it? If I'd known you were stuck on me, as you call it, my attitude might have been different.'

Callaghan said: 'Might being the operative word.'

'Yes,' said Desirée. 'Might being the operative word.'

Callaghan said: 'We can come back to that too. There are lots of things I want to talk to you about. But in the meantime I think we'll concentrate on the business in hand for every one's sake . . .'

From the hallway came the sound of the telephone jangling. It was almost a harsh note, thought Callaghan. He stopped speaking for a moment. Then: 'Excuse me . . . I'll be back in a minute.'

He went out of the room, down the passage into the hallway. Grant, the butler, was at the telephone. He was leaning against the wall. Callaghan could see that the hand that held the receiver was shaking. He said:

'Mr. Callaghan, something terrible's happened! There's been an accident – Miss Manon and a friend were driving over here. The car skidded over the quarry . . .'

Callaghan said: 'Where's the quarry?'

'On the other side of the wood,' said Grant. 'The side-road that leads past the coppice runs to it. It's the left-hand fork between here and Valeston.'

Callaghan said: 'Thanks a lot. What are you going to do now?'

Grant said: 'They've asked me to ring for an ambulance. They're ringing for the police.'

Callaghan said: 'All right. But go and tell Miss Gardell first. And take your time about it. Break it gently. Ring for the ambulance afterwards.'

Grant began to walk towards the drawing-room. Callaghan darted through the doorway into his car. He let in the clutch. He was accelerating before he was out of the drive.

IV

Callaghan, covered with clay and dust, managed to slide the last fifteen feet down the almost perpendicular face of the quarry. He picked himself up. He went towards the car. It lay on its right-hand side. The engine and frame were buckled. It was two minutes before he managed to get the off-side rear door open.

Manon was at the wheel. She was not a nice sight. Mendes, in the passenger seat, lay back in a position that was almost natural except that his head lolled sideways from a broken neck.

Callaghan stood away from the car. He looked at the top of the quarry and round him. There was no one in sight. The ambulance or the police-car, he thought, even if it were here, would come round by the longer way. They would not climb down as he had done.

He went back to the car. It was necessary to move Mendes in order to get at Manon. It was no easy job. Callaghan thought it characteristic of Raoul to be difficult even in death. Eventually he got him over the back of the passenger seat into the rear of the car.

Manon's handbag was where he expected to find it – placed carefully under the driving seat so that that should be safe. Callaghan reached for it, brought it out. He opened it. In the top of the handbag was an envelope. It was addressed to the Sussex Coroner. Callaghan smiled a little. He put the envelope in his pocket, closed the bag, replaced it under the seat.

He put Mendes back as nearly as possible in his original position. He closed the door of the car.

He stood looking at it for a moment. This, he thought, was an apt ending of the story of Manon Gardell and Raoul Mendes. Standing there, cupping the flame of his lighter in his hands, lighting a cigarette, he wondered just who had been the leader in their joint enterprises.

He thought it was six to four on Manon.

He looked through the one unbroken window of the car at what had once been a very beautiful woman. He said:

'Not a bad trump card, Manon. Not bad . . . but it was our trump – not yours, my dear.'

He drew tobacco smoke down into his lungs; began to walk towards the pathway at the far end of the quarry.

V

Gringall finished drinking his cup of tea, replaced the saucer carefully on the corner of his desk as Callaghan came into the room. He said.

'Hallo, Slim. Have you heard about Manon Gardell and Mr. Mendes? A pretty bad business.' He raised his eyebrows, looked astonished. He said: 'Why, what's the matter?'

Callaghan's face bore an expression of contrite humility. He looked like a schoolboy who is sent to the headmaster for a caning. Everything about him betokened an unspoken apology.

He said: 'Everything's the matter. I know about the accident. That's what I've come to see you about. That goddam accident would happen just at a time like this – just when Manon Gardell and Mendes were on their way up to town to see you.' He shrugged his shoulders. 'What a bit of luck,' he said, 'the only two people who *could* have put me right with you – dead.'

Gringall produced his pipe. He began to fill it. He said to Callaghan:

'I thought you'd been up to some of your tricks again. Well, you'd better get it off your chest. What have you done this time?' He smiled. 'It looks as if we've really caught you out for once,' said Gringall.

Callaghan said: 'You've caught me out all right. But it wouldn't have mattered so much if Manon had been able to say her piece.' He walked over to the window, looked out. He said: 'The next time I do something for a woman I hope somebody'll take a running kick at me.'

Callaghan faced Gringall.

'Well, I might as well admit it. Yes, I fell for Manon. Are you surprised? Have you seen her?'

Gringall said: 'No, but I've heard about her. They tell me she was pretty good.' He lit his pipe. 'Well, Slim,' he said, 'get it off your chest. What were Manon Gardell and Mendes coming to see me about?'

Callaghan said: 'You probably wondered why I reported to the Insurance Company that that claim was O.K for payment. Well, I knew I was safe. You see, *I knew that the Admiral committed suicide.*'

Gringall looked out of the window. He said: 'I see. So you've allowed somebody to make fools out of us.' His voice was sterner than Callaghan had ever heard it.

Callaghan said: 'I realised I'd made a mistake, so I did the obvious thing. I arranged for Manon and Mendes to come up and see you and tell you the whole thing. It's quite obvious.'

Gringall said: 'Well, what was it they were going to tell me?'

Callaghan said: 'Manon Gardell and Mendes – who wasn't a bad sort of a chap – wanted to get married. The Admiral wasn't too keen on Mendes for an obvious reason. He owed Mendes twenty thousand pounds. That note that Vane certified for the Admiral – the note that authorised the bearer to receive twenty thousand pounds – was for Mendes. Not because Mendes had won the money off the Admiral, but because Mendes had paid it for him.'

Callaghan lit a cigarette. He inhaled, blew a smoke ring.

He said: 'They couldn't get married without the twenty thousand pounds. Mendes is pretty hard up. The Admiral, who was a cantankerous old cuss, made things as difficult as possible for them. But the one thing he wanted to do was to stop the marriage.' Callaghan flipped the ash off his cigarette. 'You see,' he went on, 'the old boy had always been awfully keen on Manon. She used to cheer him up. They were good friends. He didn't like the idea of her marrying somebody and going off. I suppose there was some sort of vague possessive instinct somewhere in the old boy's being.

'Well, Mendes wanted the money, or at least some of it. He had talked with the old boy, and the Admiral – in one of his fits of cussedness – conceived the idea that by killing himself he'd stop Mendes getting the money. He thought, you see, that the two years mentioned in the Insurance policy weren't up.'

Gringall said: 'I see.'

Callaghan went on: 'Then the Admiral came up to see me about something – I don't know what, because I never saw him. I don't suppose it was very important, because I think the old boy was almost out of his mind when he arrived. He'd made up his mind to kill himself then. We know that because of the note he left for me saying he was going to commit suicide. You'd better see that note,' said Callaghan. 'It's in the Admiral's own handwriting.

'Then he went round to see Vane, the lawyer. Vane says that the Admiral was in a very odd frame of mind. He rang up Chipley from Vane's house and spoke to somebody there. Vane thought he was speaking to Desirée. He wasn't. He was speaking to Manon. She had been fearfully worried about the Admiral. She'd gone over to find out what was happening. She arrived just in time to take the Admiral's telephone message.

'Vane at his end wasn't certain of what the Admiral said. His conversation was "jumbled" Vane says. But Manon got it all right. She told me that the Admiral told her he was fed up with the whole bag of tricks, that he didn't like Mendes, but that as he couldn't stop her marrying him, he'd take damned good care that Mendes wasn't able to marry her. He'd kill himself and that would nullify the Insurance policy. Before she had a chance to say anything, the old boy hung up.

'Manon didn't know what to do. She thought she'd better hang around and try and head him off. She did. But the Admiral short-circuited her. Instead of driving up to the front of the house along the carriage drive – a process she expected – the old devil drove round the back of the house, went into the coppice and shot himself. The fact that he intended to commit suicide was premeditated because he had the gun with him in his pocket.

'Manon heard the shot. She dashed out, found the Admiral dead. She was terribly frightened, terribly upset. But she was fearfully angry with him. She'd been a good friend to the Admiral. She'd got Mendes to pay that twenty thousand pounds gambling debt for him, and this was the thanks that both of them got.

'The predominant thought in her mind was to get that money paid somehow to Mendes, because she knew that Mendes wouldn't marry her whilst he was broke. So she picked up the gun and dropped it in the lake. She thought that would make it look like murder; that the Insurance Company would pay. A ridiculous idea,' said Callaghan, 'but remember *her* state of mind at the time.'

Gringall said: 'That's understandable. You remember *I* had an idea that something like that might have happened. But why didn't Maynes find the gun?' He looked at Callaghan quizzically.

'That's the point,' said Callaghan. 'I fished that damned gun out of the lake.' He shrugged his shoulders. 'I didn't like your attitude,' he said. 'I knew Manon was speaking the truth. I knew you thought this was murder – at least you pretended to. I was damned worried about it. After all, she discovered the Admiral's body. Desirée only came on the scene afterwards. I thought you might possibly have a case against Manon. So I fished the gun out.'

Gringall said: 'What a damn' fool you are, Slim. One of these days one of your good-looking women clients is going to get you in a jam. You might have known that if you'd produced that note from the Admiral, saying that he was going to commit suicide, we could never have made a murder charge stick.'

Callaghan said: 'I know. I'm damned annoyed with myself.'

Gringall said: 'Go on.'

'Last night,' continued Callaghan, 'I realised I'd played this thing badly from the start. I went down and saw Manon. We had a long talk. She made up her mind there and then that she was going to bring Mendes along to see you to-day. They were going to tell you the whole story.'

Callaghan heaved a sigh.

'It's a damned shame,' he said. 'She didn't get much sleep last night. She was worrying. I suppose her nerves weren't too good this morning and she was in a hurry to get up here. So she took the short-cut from Valeston by the quarry. It's a dangerous road. Well, they went over the edge, and that's that.' He grinned ruefully. 'You can imagine how *I* felt when I heard the news,' he concluded.

Gringall put down his pipe. He picked up a pencil. He began to draw a tomato. He said:

'You know, Slim, one of these fine days you're going to get in bad with us. Possibly this will teach you a lesson. I thought something like that had happened, but you've played this badly. You might have made things look very serious for Manon Gardell.'

Callaghan said: 'I know. You don't have to tell me. I've been kicking myself ever since I heard the news of that smash.'

Gringall said: 'Well, you'll have to take your punishment.' He grinned almost happily. 'I wouldn't like to be you in five minutes' time,' he said.

Callaghan asked: 'What's the big idea?'

Gringall said: 'I'm going to send you down to Maynes to tell him. You're going to have a *good* time.' His grin became broader. He put down the pencil, picked up the telephone. He asked to be put through to Maynes's room. He said:

'Is that you, Maynes? About this Gardell case, I thought Callaghan had been up to something. There *was* a gun in the lake. He fished it out. I'm sending you over a note written by the late Admiral a few hours before he committed suicide, saying he intended to do so. You can have that inquest now as soon as you like. I'll send Callaghan down. I thought perhaps you'd like to give him a piece of your mind.'

He hung up. He said to Callaghan:

'You'll have to add another motto to that collection of yours.'

Callaghan said: 'Such as what?'

'Such as "We can take it," ' said Gringall, 'because if I know Maynes you're going to.' He picked up his pipe. 'And I wish,' he concluded, 'I had some reasonable excuse to be there. I'd get a big laugh.'

CHAPTER FOURTEEN
SWEET FAREWELL

DESIRÉE was standing at the end of the flower-garden, looking over the low wall. She turned as Callaghan came along the pathway.

He said: 'I've tied the ends up. Your father committed suicide. Everything is all right.'

She said: 'It's Manon I'm worrying about. Poor – poor Manon. She was an odd girl, but really underneath she was all right. Life just wasn't very kind to her.'

Callaghan said: 'Don't you believe it. She killed your father. You might as well know it. He told her over the telephone just what he was going to do to her and Mendes. He'd found them out. They were partners. Well, she wasn't going to have that. You know Manon was a girl who liked to be wicked under cover. She didn't like people to know.'

Desirée leaned up against the wall. She said:

'My God! How terrible!'

Callaghan said: 'You'd be surprised. Manon was a nasty piece of work.'

Desirée said: 'But you said . . .'

Callaghan said: 'I said the Admiral committed suicide. The police accept that story. That will be the verdict at the inquest.'

Desirée said: 'I suppose you're responsible for that. Why?'

Callaghan said: 'Because Manon had a trump card to play. I knew she was going to kill herself. I knew she'd kill Mendes too. I had a showdown with Manon last night. She knew she was for it, so she took the easy way out. But she was still going to be nasty. She told me she had a trump card.' Callaghan lit a cigarette. 'It wasn't a bad trump card.' he said. 'All she wanted was revenge, on me and therefore on you.'

Desirée's eyes were wide.

'Why?' she asked.

Callaghan said: 'Manon had always hated you. She hated you because you were as beautiful as she was, and you had one or two attributes she hadn't got. Mainly she disliked you because you were good. She disliked me first of all because I'd found her out, and secondly because she knew I was keen on you. So she arranged to put us both in bad.'

Desirée said: 'How was she going to do that?'

Callaghan felt in his pocket. He said:

'I got to that quarry pretty quickly after that accident. I knew she'd leave a letter. Here it is. It's addressed to the Sussex Coroner,' said Callaghan. 'I'll read it to you.'

He read:

Dear Mr. Coroner,

I am taking – with my fiancé, Raoul Mendes – the easiest way out of a difficult situation. My uncle – Admiral Gardell – recently died. I'm not certain how. Either he committed suicide or he was murdered. I am not in a position to say.

But I do know that Mr. Callaghan, the Investigator employed by the Globe & Associated Insurance Company, who seems to have been working very fervently on my cousin Desirée's behalf, has launched a series of the falsest accusations against me. I am so hurt and distressed that I can hardly think, but I have decided to end everything, and I shall take my fiancé with me. I have thought of a plan by which we may be at least united in death.

I make no accusation against my cousin Desirée. The fact that I saw her drop the pistol with which my uncle was shot in the lake soon after the shot was fired does not prove that she killed him. The fact that Callaghan has admitted to me that he removed that pistol, in order to remove any evidence against her, does not prove it either. I state these things because they are facts.

At this moment I am in no frame of mind to bring accusations against any one. All I want is peace.

Manon Gardell.

Callaghan said: 'She was a nice little thing, wasn't she? You can see what the letter would have done.'

Desirée nodded miserably.

'Nobody would have been able to prove you killed the Admiral,' said Callaghan, 'but everybody would have *thought* you did. Life would have been pretty terrible for you.'

Callaghan took out his lighter. He watched the letter burn. He said: 'Well, that's that.'

She looked towards the Valeston crest. She said:

'You're the strangest person, aren't you?'

Callaghan said: 'I wouldn't know. Perhaps you'll be able to tell me about that.'

She said: 'I ought to tell you something . . . At the moment I can only say that I'm very grateful to you . . . although that is an understatement. You've done an awful lot for me.'

Callaghan said: 'Do you think I have?'

She nodded.

'Yes, I do,' she said.

He said: 'I suggest repayment. Ask me to stay to dinner.'

She smiled.

'You shall stay to dinner. I'll give you the best dinner I can. Do you consider that adequate repayment?'

Callaghan shook his head. He grinned. He said:

'That'll do for a start . . .'

THE END